CW01083817

Sherlock Holmes and

The Folk Tale Mysteries

Volume 1

Gayle Lange Puhl

Paperback ISBN 9781780928036
ePub ISBN 978-1-78092-804-3
PDF ISBN 978-1-78092-805-0

Published in the UK by MX Publishing
335 Princess Park Manor, Royal Drive,
London, N11 3GX
www.mxpublishing.co.uk
Cover design by www.staunch.com

To my daughter Gayla
and all my family,
both near and far, far away.

Table of Contents

"The Case of the Curious Culprit", "The Case of the Mystified Major", and "The Case of the Wobbly Watcher" in altered forms have been previously published in The Serpentine Muse, the magazine of the Adventuresses of Sherlock Holmes.

Into the Woods with Sherlock Holmes

Teenagers are liable to run off in pursuit of all sorts of interests, many of them of transitory appeal. Every now and then, the right combination of teenager and topic will produce lasting results. One example is Gayle Lange Puhl and Sherlock Holmes.

Gayle was hooked by the appeal of the character of Sherlock Holmes more decades ago than she and the writer of this introduction might care to remember. In those days, before the existence of the Internet and when the telegram was still a legitimate means for communication, individuals at a distance who shared an interest had to resort to an institution called the United State Postal Service. Communications did not tend to fly back and forth with the speed of today's electrons, but perhaps they could be composed with a trifle more deliberateness.

The decade of the 1960's was a fine time for Sherlockians. The wealth of publications devoted to the doings of Holmes and Watson continued to pour out from scion societies from coast to coast. There were even national (and international) junior groups, like the Baker Street Pageboys and the Three Students Plus. As a reflection of the times, the latter had exclusively male membership but had a female auxiliary called the Watsonians. One member of the Watsonians was Gayle Lange Puhl, and her contributions to the Sherlockian literature were available in the publication *Shades of Sherlock*.

Copies of those issues can still be found in collections in libraries, and they have also been made available electronically.

Fortunately, Sherlock Holmes remained an important part of Gayle's reading and writing through the decades. She has produced articles and activities, art work and archival material. She is a speaker sought after by audiences both Sherlockian and general. She is also the writer of the stories that you have before you.

There is a wealth of wisdom and hidden history in the folk tales that have come down to us. Little children appreciate them as stories, as J.R.R. Tolkien reminds us in his essay on the subject, even while scholars try to unpack the origins of the characters and the plots. Gayle has done a different sort of unpacking here. She has introduced the character of Sherlock Holmes and some aspects of his methods of deduction into thirteen frameworks recognizable as arising from different folk tales. When we read the original Sherlock Holmes stories, as they appeared in the *Strand* and elsewhere, we enjoy the excitement of the hunt as we accompany Holmes to the site of the crime and then try to anticipate the path that will take him to a solution. In these stories, we combine that same excitement with the effort to recognize the folk tale on which the Holmesian adventure is based. While there is no matching the style of the original narratives, these tales pay homage to them without being suffocating imitative.

In today's era of the wide appeal of everything connected with Sherlock Holmes, it is easy to get caught up with spectacular special effects. That is scarcely the spirit in which the original stories were written, which may explain how remote the plots of current films are from those that appeared under the name of Sir Arthur Conan Doyle. Since we are not likely to be receiving any further stories from that source, even if one is willing to follow him into the realm of the Spiritualism that occupied so much of his later life, we can be grateful for those who keep the memory of Sherlock Holmes alive in a fashion that respects the language and the personalities of the originals. Gayle Lange Puhl thrives in Wisconsin. She offers her Sherlockian scholarship and views to friends as far removed from home as New York City and as close as nearby Janesville, WI, where she is one of the mainstays of the Original Tree-Worshippers of Rock County. If your experience with pastiches of Sherlockian stories has not included anything from Gayle, prepare to be carried away, not just to the world of Baker Street, but into the realm of folk tales, where a distinctive figure in a deerstalker works to defend Truth, Justice and the Sherlockian Way.

Thomas Drucker

Whitewater, WI.

Once Upon a Time in Baker Street, in a Kingdom Far, Far Away......

None of the stories in this collection of folk tales start with those words, but any of them could have. Bedtime stories like "The Three Little Pigs" and "Little Red Riding Hood" often start with variations of those immortal words. They are the first examples of timeless literature Western children hear. The tales are so pervasive in our culture that they become part of our lives, so familiar that the words become a sort of shorthand for the everyday experiences we all go through as we grow and mature.

The purpose of telling the story of "The Three Little Pigs" is to entertain, but it also impresses upon our offspring the lesson that security is found in the strong and well-thought-out plan, not the make-shift and hasty idea of the moment. Life is not all fun and games. Rather, it demands sober planning and labor in order to survive the "big, bad wolves" who roam our environments, seeking to take advantage of the thoughtless and the unprepared.

"Little Red Riding Hood" tells the story of a young girl who talks to a stranger, a lass who listens to his suggestion to pick flowers for her grandmother instead of heeding her mother's wise instructions not to dally. By influencing her, the wolf bends her actions to his plan in order that he may devour Granny and lie in wait for his true victim, the helpless child. Only a passing hunter saves her, a chance encounter she could not have foreseen.

Folk tales usually contain a lot of violence. Hundreds of years ago, when real danger did lurk in the dark thickets of the forests, and strangers could snatch up an unwary child and spirit him or her away from home and familiar things forever, children needed to be warned in order to get a chance to just grow up. The most effective way to do that was to emphasize that a terrible thing could happen when you did not listen to your parents' warnings.

Yet there is something in the inner spirit of humans that thrills, even at an early age, to the bizarre and the horrible in cautionary tales. Safe within the family circle, perhaps tucked warmly in their own little beds, children can allow themselves to enjoy the macabre and terrible stories of ogres and giants, of twisted old witches and gangs of robbers found in tumbledown huts in the forest, uttering terrible oaths and pawing over piles of ill-gained treasure. The presence of their parents and the sense of their love protect them.

Violence is present in many tales. Granny is eaten by the wolf and Humpty Dumpty is smashed beyond repair. The ugly stepsisters, desperate to marry Prince Charming, try in turn to force their feet into the glass slipper. One even cuts off her big toe in order to gain her goal, but in vain. When Cinderella produces the matching slipper, the resulting humiliation brings all their evil designs against her to a point that overwhelms their vain and haughty hearts. By the end of the story, they are grateful to marry palace servants, the baker and the cook, and bow to their stepsister the Queen.

In "Rumplestiltskin" a father's incautious bragging about his daughter's accomplishments sends her into danger when the king commands that she spins straw into gold or give up her life. When her only salvation lies in the promises of an odd little man, she agrees to an unholy bargain in order to survive. Only when disaster becomes immediate does she use her brains and her resources to gain knowledge that will banish the threat forever.

Economics drives the story of "Hansel and Gretel". The father loves his children, but he is persuaded that by sending his offspring out into the dark forest that act may leave enough food to save his life and the life of his new and seductive wife. During the Dark Ages when these stories developed, many poor families had many children that they couldn't support, and sending them out early in life to fend for their selves in order to ease the family's burden was not uncommon. In those uncertain times of famine and pestilence not every child survived to adulthood.

The element of magic is a basic property in fairy tales. The fairy godmother in "Cinderella", the evil witch in "Hansel and Gretel", the magic beans that grow the giant beanstalk in "Jack and the Beanstalk" are integral parts of the stories that add to their allure, but at the same time their excesses reassure children that these tales are not reality. They eagerly listen to the tales, but they know in their hearts that there is no giant up in the clouds planning to "grind their bones to make his bread". No fairy godmother will magically appear by means of a wish to take them out of poverty or boredom to a better, richer life. But wouldn't it be wonderful if there was such a being? Wouldn't it be great to ride through life on a cloud of magic, to have all your dreams come true? Alas, the story warns that midnight always comes and all the dreams will dissolve, leaving behind nothing but broken bits of pumpkin and scampering mice. It does not pay to depend upon wishes and dreaming to fulfill your life's goals. In hardscrabble reality, there is no profit on counting upon fairy godmothers or hidden pirate treasure to solve one's problems.

Sherlock Holmes is not a child. His world is logical and solid. Faced with the possibility of a Sussex vampire, he rejects the idea. "This agency stands flatfooted upon the ground. No ghosts need apply!" The mysterious Hound of the Baskervilles may frighten Dr. Watson as he wanders over the moors at midnight, but Holmes chooses to live there alone in an ancient stone hut. Watson has spent days absorbing the spooky atmosphere of Baskerville Hall, but Holmes has spent the same time checking with London pet shops for sales of large dogs.

What place can Sherlock Holmes have in the world of folk tales? He would run a criminal background check on Cinderella's fairy godmother and classify in Latin the genus of Little Red Riding Hood's wolf. Yet he admits that "without imagination there is no horror". Holmes' success depends upon the "observation of trifles" but he admits that sometimes an exercise in imagination helps him to the correct answer. Even the super-scientific sleuth admits he has heard the same stories most children grow up with, when he tells Dr. Mortimer that the legend of Hugo Baskerville may be interesting "to a collector of fairy tales".

There is a possibility that folk tales developed out of real-life situations. To protect their children, hundreds of years ago parents may have spun a cautionary story out of an actual tragedy. A child disappears and the adults murmur of a stranger seen near the last known location of the victim. Imagination constructs a story that evolves into "Hansel and Gretel". Wolves are heard howling in the forest and "Little Red Riding Hood" is born.

In such a world Sherlock Holmes can function as the Great Detective. The Big Bad Wolf kills and eats one of the Three Little Pigs. What is that but murder? Rumplestiltskin terrorizes the Queen by demanding her first-born child. What is that but blackmail? Prince Charming searches the kingdom for his Cinderella. What is that but a missing person case? The stories on these pages do not claim to be faithful reconstructions of the classic tales, but endeavor to demonstrate how in a Sherlockian setting the original situations may have set up the circumstances that evolved into the familiar stories we know today.

Of course in these stories there is no evidence of magic. Magic isn't logical. Yet hints of the original guiding force seem to lurk just under the surface of most of these tales.

Inspector Sarpent leads Holmes and Watson into a room hung with the broken and scorched remains of dragon-hunting medieval weapons. The Giltglider brothers contend with destruction of their supplies of straw and wood along with threats to their lives. Children go missing in these stories, lost in real woods or in the metaphysical wilderness of London. Sherlock Holmes, the archetypical mythic hero, does his best, not always successfully, to solve his clients' problems and restore balance to the folk tale universe.

Personally, I have a theory that Sherlock Holmes can be linked to anything. I stated that aloud one day and my younger granddaughter tried to flummox me by tossing out the word "trampoline". A moment's thought brought out Watson's quote, "Brag and bounce!" from the first Sherlock Holmes story, "A Study in Scarlet". If the legendary Great Detective can be fitted into the modern world, why could he not fit into the world of folk tales? He can, and the adventures within this book demonstrate that.

Gayle Lange Puhl

Evansville, WI

The Case of the Curious Culprit

A white envelope gleamed in the pool of light cast by the shaded lamp sitting on the table before me. The remains of a sketchy late supper lay beside it. The sitting room of 221B Baker Street was silent save for the subdued crackle of a sea coal fire on the hearth behind me.

It was late and I was alone. Many hours before I had answered an emergency call: a traveling woman collapsed in a local shop. I had her conveyed, at her insistence, back to her hotel, and notified her own physician. I tended both the patient and her frightened companion until he could arrive from a distant town. The case handed over to her doctor, I returned home after midnight, hungry and fatigued, through the streets of a dark and deserted London in mid-May.

I had misplaced my key. Mrs. Hudson, our landlady, responded to my repeated rings wrapped in a flannel robe. She also provided me with something to eat hours after the rest of the household, including Sherlock Holmes, had retired to bed.

The envelope was addressed to me. I finished my meal and tore it open. It contained a note in Holmes's handwriting, dated the afternoon before.

"My dear Watson," it read, "If at all possible join me at Charing Cross Station tomorrow morning for the early train to Croydon. Sherlock Holmes."

The message seemed clear enough, yet it still left questions. I had not seen the newspapers for two days and could recall nothing pertaining to Croydon before that. I must admit that the invitation bore away much of my exhaustion. My sleep that night was fitful, full of imaginative conjectures, despite Holmes's oft-repeated admonition never to theorize without all the facts.

I arose the next morning to find the house quiet. After dressing, and eating one of Mrs. Hudson's excellent breakfasts, I took a cab to Charing Cross Station. I found Sherlock Holmes ensconced in a first class carriage surrounded by all the early editions of the London papers. He indicated the seat opposite himself with a smile and a nod of his head. He wore a grey suit and the ear-flapped cloth cap he favored for out-of-town excursions.

"Welcome, Watson. I knew you would make it."

"We haven't seen each other in two days. How did you know I got your note?"

"I was up quite early this morning. The envelope was missing from the table and Mrs. Hudson removed used plates before she brought me my own breakfast."

"How simple."

"Yes. Mrs. Hudson also gave me her opinion on inconsiderate patients that keep honest, hard-working medical men away from hot meals and clean linen to all hours of the night."

I laughed. "Mrs. Hudson is a treasure."

"Quite so. Has your patient improved enough that you may leave town?"

"I left her in the care of her own physician. My time is yours."

"Excellent." Sherlock Holmes handed me an opened letter from his breast pocket. "Please do me the favor of reading this, Watson." He picked up a newspaper and spread it across his knee. The train started out of Charing Cross Station as I unfolded the piece of paper.

Within the letter was a clipping from The Evening Suburban News dated two days before. I read that first.

"Mysterious Incident at Bern Lodge."

"A break-in at Bern Lodge near Croydon has local police baffled. It was reported very early this morning that Mr. and Mrs. Raubtier Bhaer and their daughter were victims of an intruder at their isolated home. They returned from a morning walk to discover their front door ajar. Persons unknown had gained access to Bern Lodge in their absence. Muddy footprints were found in the hall. Nothing appeared to be taken but a child's chair had been smashed to pieces. Police admit that they have no suspects, but issued a warning that local residents should keep alert to the presence of any strangers in the neighborhood."

"Now the letter," murmured Holmes from behind the London Times. I smoothed out the missive, written in black ink with a broad nib on thick handmade paper. It was dated the evening of the break-in.

"Mr. Holmes," it ran, "Enclosed you will find a newspaper account of the invasion of my home this morning. As reported, the police have no idea of the identity of the vandal. I am unwilling to wait for them to get a clue. I have heard of your exploits and I strongly urge you to come to Croydon and look into this problem. This wanton act has greatly upset not only me, but my dear wife and our daughter.

"Allow me to tell you about my circumstances. I was born in the Black Forest and earned my degree at Berlin University. Shortly after that, I immigrated to England and took up the position of junior librarian for the Hibernian Institute of London. After years of service, I reached the highest position in my department. Late in life, I married Miss Ursula Stief of Norfolk Square, Paddington. We established a home outside Croydon. Four years ago saw the birth of our little daughter, Bebe. Last year I retired from the Institute.

"Our property is situated at the end of a long lane that runs from Croydon over a mile into Graffing Woods. We are able to indulge in a large garden and keep a horse and carriage. We are also fond of long walks along the many paths through the woods. My wife is an enthusiastic berry picker.

"As for servants, there is a local boy who cares for the horse and helps in the garden. My wife has a cleaning woman who comes in twice a week.

"Our lives were quiet and uneventful until this morning. I must add that the chair that was destroyed was an antique that had come down from my wife's family. It was Bebe's own particular chair.

"I am depending on you, Mr. Holmes, to discover who is responsible for this outrage. Upon receipt of your telegram I will meet the London train at Croydon Station.

"Your servant, Raubtier Bhaer."

Holmes folded up the Times. "I received that letter yesterday by the afternoon post. Any thoughts, Watson?"

"The man doesn't take no for an answer," I replied. "There is no doubt expressed in his letter that you will not take his case at once."

"Good man."

"He is impatient. The break-in occurred barely two days ago and he is not willing to give the police time to investigate the case."

"Quite sound. Anything else?"

"I see nothing else. Is there more?"

"Ah, perhaps not. We may check your theories now, Watson," said Holmes as the train pulled into Croydon Station. "This is the Bhaer family waiting for us, I believe."

Standing on the platform were the three Bhaers. After introductions all around, we stepped into a waiting carriage and started to Bern Lodge.

I studied with interest the three people seated across from us. Raubtier Bhaer was a large, hulking man, over six feet tall and broad in the chest and shoulders. He had a great grizzled beard and the backs of his hands bristled with reddish hairs. He wore a somber black suit and, surprisingly, a loden green Bavarian hat.

Ursula Bhaer was young and plump, fully a foot shorter than her husband. She was neatly groomed, wore a striped pink morning dress and a straw skimmer trimmed with artificial berries and leaves. Sitting next to her was a roly-poly mite in a pink and lavender plaid dress and matching beret with a white fur bobble.

"It's too bad there is not an earlier train from London to Croydon," growled our client. "We've had another break-in this very morning."

I was startled. "What?"

"Indeed," remarked Sherlock Holmes. "Tell me about it. Have the police been informed?"

"No, and I am not going to tell them," responded Mr. Bhaer. "What did they accomplish after the first invasion? They just trampled my tulips and poked around the fireplace. Moreover, I haven't heard a word from them since and I don't expect to."

"That's why you are here, Mr. Holmes, and your friend Dr. Watson," Mrs. Bhaer said in a pleasant low voice. "Raubtier has great confidence in you."

"More than in the local police, at any rate," muttered her husband. "I've seen their work."

"Pray tell me about this morning," said Holmes.

"I received your telegram last night so we decided to have an early breakfast and meet the train together. Ursula made my favorite dish, oatmeal porridge."

"But it was too hot," Bebe Bhaer piped up.

"Yes, it was too hot to eat at once, so we decided to take a turn around the garden in order to let it cool. We were only gone a few minutes, checking on the new plantings, but when we returned we saw at once that the culprit had struck again."

"The front door appeared untouched, but the bowls of porridge on the kitchen table had been disturbed. My bowl of porridge had been tasted and a large spoon left thrust into it, Ursula's bowl had been moved and the porridge tasted, and Bebe's porridge…."

"Had been tasted too, and someone ate it all up!" wailed the little girl. Mrs. Bhaer leaned over to comfort her as the child began to cry. "It's all right, darling. We had a nice breakfast in the café while we waited for the train, didn't we? The fur bobble nodded up and down and a tiny handkerchief appeared.

"We left the house immediately, of course," rumbled Mr. Bhaer.

I felt a wave of sympathy for Bebe Bhaer. Sherlock Holmes's cases seldom involved small children. I realized that this young child felt that she was under personal attack by some shadowy intruder. Her chair had been broken. Her breakfast had been eaten. Strangers had been introduced into her life to solve a problem her parents could not control. I set my jaw and looked at Sherlock Holmes.

His head was tilted back against the cushion and his hooded eyes were concentrated on the scenery out the carriage window. "We have arrived at Bern Lodge, I believe," was all he said.

The carriage had stopped before a wicker gate. Beyond the brick garden wall, we saw a large two-storied half-timbered cottage with a steep, freshly thatched roof. It sat in the center of a sizable formal garden elaborately designed with geometric flower plots filled with colorful May blossoms and rimmed by neatly trimmed box hedges. Blooming shrubs and fanciful topiary trees were tastefully placed to the best advantage about the property. Beds of daffodils made a brave show but the multi-colored tulips and the lavish lilac bushes promised to overtake them in another week. Graffing Woods surrounded the land on nearly all sides. Small outbuildings in back were tucked up right under the twisted limbs of the ancient trees. Behind us, the lane curved away behind an outcropping of old oaks. There was no sign of the nearest neighbor.

The three Bhaers led us through the gate and up the gravel path to the front door; Holmes bent down and examined the latch. "The door is locked. Was it so this morning?"

Raubtier Bhaer's voice rumbled as he turned his house key to open the door. "I do not lock my door while I am on my own property, sir."

The Bhaer front door opened into a hall floored in flagstones that divided the ground floor into two equal halves with a set of stairs leading up at the back. On the left was an archway giving into the sitting room. An identical arch on the opposite wall afforded a glimpse of the kitchen. Sherlock Holmes stood upon the hall mat and surveyed the floor before him.

"This corridor has been cleaned," he announced, displeased. "The newspaper account mentioned muddy footprints.

"Of course it has been swept and mopped," exclaimed Mrs. Bhaer. "I take great pride in the orderly upkeep of my home."

"Forgive me." Holmes suddenly smiled at her. "Of course you do. It would have been useful, however, if the scene could have been preserved. And this is the sitting room, also swept and dusted? Assuredly so. What an interesting room! Are some of these pieces from your native land, Mr. Bhaer? I see the remains of the chair have so far escaped the dustbin."

"I put those aside, Mr. Holmes, after I decided to engage your services," said Mr. Bhaer.

"Please, all of you remain in the archway. Watson, what do you think of this?" Holmes picked up a shattered leg from the pile of debris stacked on one side of the hearth. He held up his magnifying glass to intensify a view of the cracks and splinters that bristled from the broken stump.

"It just looks smashed to me, Holmes," said I.

"There is a pattern, Watson," murmured Holmes. "There is most certainly a pattern. " He swiftly examined each piece in the pile. From that, he turned to the rest of the room.

The sitting room was decorated with many Bavarian touches. Tables, chairs and chests were heavily hand-carved or brightly painted with rustic design. Light draperies screened windows filled with tiny panes of hand-blown glass. Two chairs faced the fireplace. One was a large brown leather armchair, obviously Raubtier Bhaer's, set next to a middle-sized rocker which was amply padded with embroidered pillows.

"That must be Mrs. Bhaer's chair," said I.

Holmes did not reply. Using his glass, he gave them both a thorough inspection, and then prodded the seats with his strong, thin fingers.

We passed the Bhaer family in the hallway and entered the kitchen. More Bavarian touches were evident there but Holmes concentrated on the kitchen table. It was constructed of thick wood hand-carved and painted in a motif of hearts and roses. Three matching chairs were pushed away from the three bowls sitting on the blue painted tablecloth.

The largest bowl had a big spoon sticking up over the rim. The medium-sized bowl was pulled to the edge of the table and the smallest bowl was tipped on one side, scraped clean. Sherlock Holmes brought out his magnifying glass again and scrutinized them. He tasted the contents of each

dish, and then held up a spoon from the table.

"Very suggestive," he remarked. "A most interesting case. Come, Watson, what do you make of this?" He turned the spoon's shaft toward the light. I looked at it closely.

"There are smudges on the handle," said I

"Do you see anything else?"

"What should I be looking for, Holmes?"

"Watson, Watson! Look at the size of the smudges."

I peered at the marks through Holmes's glass. A sharp thrill ran down my spine. "It is a complete fingerprint, but small. Holmes, a child has done these destructive things!"

A low growl came from behind us. We turned and found the three Bhaers scowling at us from the kitchen archway.

"Not my child." It was a flat statement from Raubtier Bhaer.

Holmes took the little girl's hands in his and turned them over to look at her fingertips. "No, not Miss Bebe," he agreed. "Her fingers are far too narrow." He moved to the stairs. The third step caught his attention and he crouched over it. He picked up something invisible to me and rubbed it between his fingers.

"Leaf mold. I wonder...," I heard him mutter. He turned to Mrs. Bhaer. "Were these steps swept along with the rest of the house after the police left?"

"Why, yes, of course," she answered.

"What a fool I have been!" Sherlock Holmes shouted. "Watson, follow me!" He bounded up the stairs with me at his heels. The three Bhaers followed.

The top of the stairs revealed a long corridor that ran the entire width of the house. Three doors were irregularly spaced along its length. Holmes grasped the nearest doorknob and turned it.

"That's my bedroom," boomed Raubtier Bhaer.

We stepped into a large room fitted out as a sleeping chamber. Three tall windows filled it with sunshine. The light gleamed off more carved and painted furniture. The most striking item was an enormous handcrafted sleigh bed set against one wall. A vast white fur cover lay half on, half off the mattress, one corner dragged down to the floor.

The Bhaer family walked in behind us. "This is intolerable!" rumbled Mr. Bhaer. "Someone has been sleeping in my bed!"

Sherlock Holmes gave the fur cover a swift survey with his magnifying

glass, and then opened the connecting door to the next room. It proved to be a medium-sized bedroom, decorated in the same Bavarian style but with lavish feminine touches. The prevailing color was pink. Ruffles adorned every surface, including the filmy curtains at the two windows. Frilly pillows trimmed with lace had been tossed to the floor from the four-poster bed. Holmes lingered briefly at the bed, looking at an impression on the soft coverlet where a weight had rested upon it.

"I tidied up this room before breakfast," gasped Mrs. Bhaer. "Someone has been sleeping in my bed!"

Another door led to a smaller room that was equipped as a nursery. My gaze swept over a Bavarian toy box and shelves of storybooks flanking a single window to a little camp bed in the corner. On it was heaped a tangle of blankets.

A tiny voice shrilled behind me. "I did make my bed this morning, Mummy, I did! Someone has been sleeping in my bed!"

With a dramatic flourish, Sherlock Holmes stretched out a long arm and threw back the coverlet. "And here she is!"

I stood frozen in amazement. Lying on her side under the blankets was a sleeping young girl of about seven or eight years. Long blonde curls cascaded over the pillow beneath her head. She was wearing a light green dress trimmed in dark green braid. A bracelet gleamed on her wrist. On her feet were white stockings and scuffed black shoes. Holmes gently touched her shoulder.

The little girl opened her eyes and looked up. Behind me Raubtier Bhaer snarled, "Young lady, what in blazes are you doing in my house?" The three Bhaers advanced past me toward the bed, scowling at the little culprit.

She quickly took stock of the situation. With startling agility and speed, she leaped up and dashed out the door leading to the hallway. A moment later, we heard her footsteps clatter down the stairs. The three Bhaers made a concerted move toward the hall as if to give chase, but Holmes got there first.

"I think not, Mr. Bhaer," he said smoothly but with a dangerous look in his eye. One hand was thrust deep into his coat pocket. "She is just a child. I am certain she will not return."

A loud report sounded from below as the front door slammed shut. Through the window, I caught a glimpse of her green and gold figure running into Graffing Woods.

The Bhaer family glared from Holmes to me, standing with my back to

Mrs. Bhaer's bedroom door. I witnessed many things during my time of service with the Army in Afganistan, but never during the worst battles did I ever see a more terrifying sight than that of Raubtier Bhaer and his family, as they stood before Sherlock Holmes in baffled rage. Their teeth bared in fierce grimaces, three pairs of black eyes snapped in anger and six hands raised up as if to claw the air.

But they did not move. Sherlock Holmes stood his ground before the

door. After a tense, endless minute, Raubtier, Ursula and Bebe Bhaer growled in unison, "Get out."

We did not need a second invitation. The three Bhaers followed closely as we navigated the upstairs corridor, the steps leading downstairs and the length of the flagstone hall.

They only stopped when the wicker garden gate clicked shut behind us.

We continued rapidly down the lane that led to Croydon until the curve of the road hid us from view of the Bhaers' house. There we stopped and I peered cautiously around a tree. I saw the three Bhaers march up the gravel path to their house, enter, and firmly shut the door.

I turned and looked at Holmes. He was standing on the side of the road and his eye caught mine. He threw back his head and laughed.

"That's one fee I shall never collect, Watson," he chuckled.

I took a deep breath. "I'm glad you found all that amusing," I retorted. "I was never so frightened in my life."

Sherlock Holmes was composed in an instant. "My dear Watson, I do apologize. I thought there might be trouble, but I underestimated the level of fury in that house against the intruder." He displayed an empty coat pocket. "I am very glad you were with me. I believe I would have had serious difficulty getting out of that room by myself."

I felt my face redden. Such remarks from Holmes were rare. We resumed our walk toward Croydon at a much slower pace. My head was spinning with questions. "Who was that girl, Holmes? What was she doing in the Bhaers' house? Why, after the first break-in, did she come back? I must admit, I find it all confusing."

Holmes had an actor's appreciation of an audience, even if it was just me. "We have a little walk before us, Watson, and the weather is excellent for an English May morning. Now is as good a time as any to go over the important points of this case. It does display singular features.

"I had deduced from the client's letter that he possessed a bad temper and

was of a controlling nature. His language in in the letter, using words like "outrage" and "invasion", indicated that. He didn't write of the family attending activities in Croydon, but of solitary long walks in the woods. He consulted me because he had no faith in the local constabulary and wanted quick results. Those are not the actions of a thoughtful and accommodating man.

"I knew before we left Baker Street that the break-in posed little physical threat to the Bhaers. In fact, it bore all the signs of a crime of opportunity. The family was absent only momentarily. The front door latch had not been tampered with. The breaking of the child's chair seemed purposeless unless it could be explained as being accidental.

"I was disappointed to find after we arrived that the place had been cleaned and any evidence cleared away. Mr. Bhaer did have the good sense to retain the remains of the little chair. As you saw, I went over the pieces with my glass. I determined that the stress marks of the wood showed that the chair broke because of a heavy weight applied to the seat that splintered the legs. The chair was old and the force came from above. The supports cracked and the chair collapsed.

"I determined that of the two remaining chairs, Mr. Bhaer's chair was too hard and uncomfortable for anyone but himself. Mrs. Bhaer's rocker was piled with many cushions and was too soft and offered little support for most people.

"The porridge presented a different question. Why was only Bebe Bhaer's breakfast eaten? A simple taste test answered that. The big bowl, again Mr. Bhaer's, contained salty porridge. Mrs. Bhaer's medium-sized bowl was heavily treated with sugar. There was only a trace of porridge left in Bebe Bhaer's bowl, so I deduced that her breakfast tasted best to the intruder, and so all of it was eaten."

"Amazing, Holmes!"

He smiled. "This time there were no signs of muddy footprints in the hall or even the kitchen, but I found fresh leaf mold on the stairs leading up to the first story. The three Bhaers had left the house at once after the theft of their breakfasts was discovered. The steps had been swept the day before. Therefore, I decided that it was a good possibility that the miscreant was still in the house.

"You saw, Watson, the signs of occupancy in Mr. and Mrs. Bhaer's bedrooms. For the culprit, the father's bed was too hard and the mother's was too soft even after the removal of the pillows. The parents' beds had proven too uncomfortable, but Bebe Bhaer's bed was just right and so Goldilocks fell asleep."

"Goldilocks?"

"I fear that you will lose all respect for my powers, Watson, when I tell   you that I read the name engraved on her bracelet."

"Do you think she will return?" I asked.

Gravely Sherlock Holmes shook his head. "No, as I told Mr. Bhaer, I do not. Curiosity got her into the house the first time, but the accidental destruction of the chair frightened her away. The interior of the Bhaers' house is admittedly unusual and curiosity drew her back. But now, having come face to face with her reluctant hosts, Goldilocks's curiosity has been fully satisfied. She will not return and it is better for her that she does not."

We walked up a small hill and came within sight of Croydon.

"It was a good thing that we were both there when the culprit was discovered," mused Holmes. "There was really great danger to her from the three Bhaers. Who would expect such a young child to be so fleet of foot?"

"Quite a reversal from your ordinary cases, Holmes," said I. "You solved the problem but were forced to protect the miscreant from your own client. You have lost your fee and we have been escorted from the house. Tell me, what have you gained from this adventure?"

Sherlock Holmes clapped me on the shoulder. "Experience, Watson, and a fine dose of fresh country air, a walk in the bright May sunshine and lunch with my good friend. The next train to London does not leave until mid-afternoon and I spotted a little café just a block from the station as we arrived. Let us indulge our curiosity and find out what is inside, shall we?"

The Case of the Anonymous Architect

My friend, Mr. Sherlock Holmes, when not involved in a case, could be a difficult man with whom to live. An enforced idleness frequently brought on a dark fit of depression, marked by days and nights of silent brooding, during which I had learnt not to approach him but to eye him closely for signs of that insidious need for self-medication that drew him to the cocaine bottle and the syringe. In his own manner he resisted that final step by attempting to occupy his great brain with studies on many subjects, ranging from research into the history of early prehistoric man in the caves surrounding Cheddar to the chemical composition of an obscure South American poison brought back by the latest expedition of the British Museum. The stench and clouds of vapor that resulted from such an experiment were first welcomed by me, therefore, as I stepped into the sitting room of 221b Baker Street, one Wednesday morning in June.

I was glad to see his mind occupied, even if the grey smoke reached up to cloud the gaslight lamp overhead. I threw open a window as he raised his head from the bubbling retort. Holmes stretched out a hand before his eyes and flexed his thin, strong fingers.

"Tell me, Watson," he said in his abrupt way, "Do you feel any tingling in your fingertips? Perhaps you have a buzzing in your ears or a blurring of your eyesight?"

"No! I feel only a sour taste in my throat from this infernal atmosphere!" I snatched up a newspaper from the breakfast table and fanned some smoke out the window.

Sherlock Holmes dropped his hand and shut off the tiny flame of his Bunsen burner. "I do not, either," he sighed. "I have been inhaling these fumes for over twenty minutes without any adverse physical affects at all."

I stood aghast. "Holmes! It might have killed you!"

"Ah, but it did not, Doctor, and that is the point. The fact that I am not writhing on the carpet at this very moment, in dire need of your professional services to save my life, advance my research exceedingly. Although I must confess that your labors would have been ineffectual due to the present lack of an antidote."

"My God, Holmes!"

He stood up from the stool where he had been bent over the chemical table and stretched out his arms. I could easily deduce from his tousled hair and loosened collar that he had not gone to bed the night before. His mouse-colored dressing gown hung from his narrow shoulders like a piece of sacking and his eyes gleamed from the hollows of their sockets like two lit coals in the depths of a mine. His hands dropped down and I did not miss that one landed gently on the fireplace mantel near his syringe case and his cocaine bottle.

He saw that I had noticed and for a minute we stared at each other, he defiant and me heartsick. I had just nerved myself to speak when a knock sounded on our door.

"Come in!" Holmes bellowed. Mrs. Hudson entered bearing a folded piece of paper on a salver. She came forward with a placid air and extended the tray to Holmes. "There is a gentleman waiting downstairs, Mr. Holmes. He sent up this note." He tore his eyes from mine and his hand moved to pick up the small sheet. I watched as he opened it and read the contents.

"It is a client, by Harry! Mr. Justin Service." His eyes slid sideways to me and he smiled. "We have a badly needed client, Watson. Pray show him up, Mrs. Hudson. Just give us two minutes while we straighten the room."

I heard the landlady sniff as she scooped up some debris from the floor on her way out. Holmes disappeared into his bedroom as I stacked papers on my desk and threw the pillows I found on the hearthrug back onto the sofa. He reappeared with his face washed, his hair combed; his collar ends done up, his dressing gown tugged tightly around his thin body and slipping cuff links into the sleeves of a clean shirt.

Our client proved to be a medium-sized young man of no more that four-and-twenty, dressed in the subdued garb of a clerk. His hair was sandy and he had light blue eyes that blinked at us both from a pale, anxious face. He nervously rolled a brown bowler around in his twitching fingers and looked eagerly from my face to that of my friend.

"Mr. Sherlock Holmes?"

"I am he. This is Dr. Watson, my friend and associate. Do sit here, Mr. Justin Service." Holmes dropped into his armchair and motioned the young man to the sofa. I took a seat by the table to one side.

Sherlock Holmes swept keen eyes over our visitor and held up the note he had been given. "You say here your problem is of the greatest urgency. Please, tell us about it."

"I have heard of you from friends, Mr. Holmes," Justin Service began, leaning forward from his seat to better insure Holmes' attention. "I am sure that you can tell from the color of my necktie and the scuffs upon my shoes that I am a junior architect with the firm of Lawler and Kingman, Battersea, London. I was hired just six months ago and it was within a week of my employment that my problem began.

"I was born in Warwickshire. My father was a captain in the British Army who unfortunately died when I was six and my sister Anne was four. My mother was left little money and her family arranged a small allowance for our upkeep. We lived quietly in the country. My mother's one wish was that I receive as fine an education as she could afford. My mother and my sister have made many sacrifices, Mr. Holmes, so I could succeed in life. I, in return, along with love feel a great obligation towards them."

"Of course," Holmes nodded.

"After my education ended I searched for work, applying to many firms. Finally I was hired by Lawler and Kingman on the recommendation of an old friend of my father's.

"You must understand that the Lawler of Lawler and Kingman is deceased and that old Mr. Kingman heads the business. The firm has a good name in Battersea but Mr. Kingman's age, along with his excessive drinking in the last few years, has reduced the revenues. The offices had moved into a new building just before Mr. Lawler's death four years ago and still had a few employees whom had been with the firm since its founding. I was told later that the very day I was hired the last remaining original draftsman was let go. A new beginning, it was believed, would rejuvenate the business.

"Within a day or so, I realized that Mr. Kingman was unstable. His mood would swing from optimistic to the depths of despair in a single hour. This was my first job and I determined to keep my head down and do my best for a few months before I looked for other employment. I would need a good recommendation and that became my goal.

"It was within the first few days that Mr. Kingman called me to his office. He stared at me with bleary eyes and a twisted mouth. He did not look well. The essence of our conversation was that he commanded me to devise, draw and turn in a finished plan for a large arcade to be built on a plot in Cornwall Way, on the east edge of Battersea. I was flattered to receive such an important assignment until I was told that he wanted it the next day.

"It was impossible, Mr. Holmes! There was simply not enough time. I would need to survey the lot, determine the best use of the land and complete myriad other tasks before I could even put pencil to paper. My employer was in one of his moods. He was totally unreasonable. Either I completed this assignment by the next day, with the plans on his desk, or I was fired!

"I returned to my room in despair. All I could think of was my mother and my sister Anne. I stared at their photograph that stood on my desk. How could I support them with my occupation gone? To be dismissed within a week of employment would preclude any other firm from considering me for a position. Suddenly there was the sound of footsteps on my carpet. I raised my stricken face from my hands and beheld a little old man standing before my desk. He was dressed in a suit of black and had a great shock of white hair upon his head. His face was obscured by a flowing beard of white that spread out over his chest like a blanket. He stood with his hands on his hips and looked at me sympathetically.

"Who are you?" I asked in astonishment.

"It doesn't matter who I am," the little man replied. "I know about your assignment. What will you give me if I draw up the plans?"

"It can't be done," I groaned. "There isn't enough time."

"Let me worry about that," responded the strange little figure. "If it's that important to you, what will you give me?"

"I reached into my waistcoat and pulled out a gold pen that had belonged to my father. "I could give you this," I stammered.

"He cocked his head and considered the pen. "It's not much, but I will take it," he declared. Suddenly there was a dusty bottle and two glasses on my desk. "Let's have a drink to seal the deal, Mr. Service," he chuckled.

"The mysterious appearance of the strange old man and the swift bargain he drove had totally unnerved me. I gulped down what he poured out without looking at it. A few moments later I felt my head grow heavy and I must have fallen asleep in my chair."

"Indeed, how interesting, Mr. Service," murmured Sherlock Holmes. "Did you notice the color of his eyes? Or the condition of his hands?"

"No, sir, it all happened so quickly. I awoke in the morning, still seated at my desk, in the clothes I had worn the day before. On my desk was a large bundle of papers. When I opened the package, I found surveying records and a complete set of plans, right down to plumbing and sewer designs, for a large shopping arcade, the perfect size for that lot in question in Cornwall Way.

"I looked around. The strange little man was gone, as were the two glasses and the dusty bottle and my father's gold pen."

"That is amazing!" I exclaimed from my corner. "What did you do next?"

"What could I do? I carried the plans into Mr. Kingman's office and placed them on his desk. He shuffled through them, grunted thanks, and dismissed me with a wave of his hand.

"I went back to my office and tried to tidy my appearance. I phoned my mother and told her a story about having to work so late the night before that I missed the last train. I tried to eat something at my desk, but the food turned to ashes in my mouth when I was summoned again to Mr. Kingman's office. Mr. Holmes, this interview was a repeat of the one the day before. Again he looked ill. He told me to design a row of luxury flats. If the plans were not on his desk by the next morning, he would throw me out without mercy.

"I staggered back to my office and collapsed in my chair. Was this some dreadful dream? I heard a sudden cough and I raised my head to find that strange little man before me again. With a surge of hope, yes, hope, Mr. Holmes, I waited for him to speak.

"This time he demanded my watch. I handed it over gladly. He gave me another drink from the old bottle and a few moments later I was asleep. When I woke up the morning sun was streaming in through the window and a paper-wrapped parcel was on the desk. I opened it enough to see that it contained plans for my assignment, just like the first one. I marched down the hall and deposited it on my employer's desk. I watched as he pawed it over and waved me out as before. This time my story to my mother sounded feeble even to me. I could tell she was concerned but I had no answers to her questions."

I stood up and placed a large glass of water by his hand. Holmes' eyes flickered to the sideboard but Service declined brandy and gulped at the water.

"Was that the end of the affair?" inquired Sherlock Holmes.

Justin Service blinked at my friend and shook his head. "No, Mr. Holmes. That afternoon another summons brought me to Mr. Kingman again. He looked even more ill than he had earlier. Our conversation was like a nightmare. This time he wanted plans for a small suburban bank, complete with elaborate security requirements. I was to place it on his desk the next morning.

"I was too shocked to respond. Back in my room, the little man appeared again but I had nothing of value to offer him.

"He smiled and rubbed his hands together. "We must come to an arrangement, Mr. Service, yes, we must. Here is my idea. I will supply you with the bank drawings and in return you will give your sister Anne to me in marriage."

"That is monstrous, sir!" I cried.

"Would you rather see her out on the streets?" the little man snarled. "Would you see your own mother spend her last years in poverty, dressed in rags and shivering with cold and hunger? Here is Anne's picture on your desk. She looks a fine, likely girl. Surely she would agree if it meant her mother would be spared such a pitiful fate."

"I groaned aloud. My mother's meager savings had been spent on my education and she had actually gone into debt for it. . We were living on a stipend, depending on my earnings to maintain us in a small, respectable manner. I thrust aside the glass he offered me and staggered to the door.

"Do we have a deal, Mr. Service?" the little man shouted.

"Yes!" I gasped and fled the building.

"For hours I wandered the streets. I couldn't think. I believe for a short while, Mr. Holmes, I went mad. Finally I found myself on the evening train home. My mother heard me as I entered our lodgings and, seeing the state I was in, insisting on putting me to bed. I refused to eat and slept fitfully. That next morning I crept out and made my way to Lawler and Kingman. The plans were waiting for me.

"I put the bundle on his desk. Mr. Kingman looked dreadful. He took no notice of my errand and just waved me away. I retreated to my room and sat in terror, waiting for the next summons to his office. I must have sat there for over two hours. Suddenly I heard a row in the hallway. My nerves were at the cracking point. I flung open my door just in time to see Mr. Kingman bore past me on a stretcher. He had collapsed while with a client, and died at the hospital an hour later.

"The firm was inherited by his two sons, who took an interest in their employees. Conditions in the office improved, we gained more clients, and no more unreasonable demands were made of me. The last few months have been quiet and productive. I had forgotten about the strange little man until this Monday evening, just before closing time, when he appeared on my carpet again. He smiled and chuckled as he rubbed his hands together and insisted that I invite him to my home this weekend in order that he may meet my sister. I became upset and argued, then pleaded with him. Finally we came to an agreement. If I guessed his name within a few days, he would never bother me again. Otherwise, I should regard him as my future brother-in-law.

"I immediately began listing every name I could think of in my excited state. He chuckled and laughed at each attempt and after an hour departed, saying he would be back the next evening for me to try again. I spent a miserable night and day. When he returned, I had armed myself with the London and Suburban telephone directory. It was useless. He is to return to my office tonight, at seven o'clock, to settle the details of his visit. You must help me, Mr. Holmes. The very sight of him chills my blood. Please, remove this blight from my life!" Mr. Justin Service attempted to steady his shaking hands as his eyes darted from Holmes to me and back in a pitiful fashion.

Sherlock Holmes sprang to his feet and searched along the fireplace mantle for a pipe and matches. He drew out tobacco from the toe of his Persian slipper and tamped it down in the bowl of his oily clay. He began to pace up and down the room, his long legs moving rapidly under the swirl of his dressing gown. Great clouds of tobacco smoke puffed out into a veil around his head. As he walked he clasped his hands behind his back and sank his chin upon his chest.

Both of us waited silently. After several minutes he laid aside his pipe. Sherlock Holmes turned a smiling face to our client and spoke in a confident voice.

"Mr. Service, I have rarely heard of such an unusual case. I accept it with pleasure. Pray do not worry about my fee. The pleasure of this case will be payment enough. But our time grows short. This is what we shall do. Your employers know you have left the office?"

"I told them I was inspecting a building site today."

"So you shall. Proceed to your building site, Mr. Service, and concentrate your mind upon those matters that earn you your bread and cheese. I must go out. I have several errands. We will meet this evening at six o'clock at Battersea Station."

"What will we do then, Mr. Holmes?"

Holmes paused from exchanging his dressing gown for a frock coat. "We shall find the truth, Mr. Service, and the truth shall set you free. Watson, you will be there?"

The door closed behind him and we heard his footsteps on the stairs. Justin Service looked at me and drew a ragged breath. "Dr. Watson, I don't understand any of this."

Privately I also had my doubts, but it would not do to express them to our client. "I trust in Mr. Holmes, though he can be inscrutable at times. Our best decision is to do what he says. I will see you this evening, sir."

I occupied the rest of the day in my own concerns. But first, before I left the sitting room, I spent time carefully cleaning and reloading my old service revolver

I saw no sign of Holmes or Justin Service when I boarded the Battersea train at Waterloo. There was a delay upon the line and my anxiety increased as time ticked past while I was forced to sit in a stationary coach. It was well past six-thirty as my train pulled into the station and I found Sherlock Holmes and Justin Service waiting for me on the platform. They had a four-wheeler waiting and we started off at once for the offices of Lawler and Kingman.

Holmes looked at me ruefully. "It is too bad your train was delayed, Watson. I had hoped to examine Lawler and Kingman's offices before Mr. Service's appointment. As it is, we do not enter this edifice blind. I have spent the day going to several places in London and Battersea. As a result I have learned that the building where Lawler and Kingman have their rooms was designed by Mr. Lawler as his own magnum opus. He was concerned with security and had built in several unique features. I also found out that the draftsman who helped him draw up the plan had the initials R. S."

I pondered these facts as we drew near our destination. What kind of security features could have been provided by Mr. Lawler? Who was R.S.?

The address we sought was a large handsome modern building across from a small public park. Shaped cream and white stone dazzled the eye and the sun behind us gleamed off many wide windows. Mr. Service led us up the broad steps and through a pair of tall carved doors.

A large electric chandelier illuminated a foyer that had several corridors leading away from it. The building appeared deserted. "The staff has gone home by this hour," Justin Service murmured. "The cleaning people will be done by eight. That is why the doors weren't locked."

"Pray show us your office," said Sherlock Holmes. "Watson, be very quiet. It is nearly seven and Mr. Service is supposed to be here alone."

Silently we went up a marble staircase to the first floor and down a corridor on the left. Halfway down Justin Service opened a door and ushered us into his plainly-furnished room. Sherlock Holmes lingered on the threshold.

"Mr. Kingman was carried past your door toward the main staircase. Where was his office?" he whispered.

Our client answered in a like manner. "It was at this end, Mr. Holmes, with windows facing the park. My window, as you see, looks out upon the back."

"Quite so." Holmes stepped into Justin Service's office and cast his keen eyes over its interior. There was a wooden desk and office chair, a drafting table in one corner, an empty coat rack and several cabinets containing rolled-up plans and drafting materials. The double window behind the desk was hung with a thick plain curtain. A few pictures hung on the walls and a framed photograph of two women stood on the desktop next to an electric lamp. Sherlock Holmes held an battery torch in one hand as he silently surveyed the furnishings. Then he took out a large magnifying glass from his pocket and began to examine the walls, pressing and prodding with his thin fingers at the wainscoting. It lacked but a few minutes to seven when he ceased his silent search, glanced at his watch and turned to us.

He drew our ears to his lips and spoke very softly. "Mr. Service, please step outside your door and enter the room in your customary manner. Take off your hat and sit at your desk. Turn on the light. Watson and I will stand behind these curtains. It is time for your appointment. Do not mention us to your visitor. Follow the instructions I gave you at the station. When the time is right, read this aloud."

He pressed a slip of paper into Justin Service's hand and pulled me behind the curtain. We had barely arranged ourselves so that we were invisible from the room when we heard Justin Service re-enter his office and close the door. A soft rustling and a low creak indicated that he had hung up his hat and seated himself at the desk. A light clicked on. The next few minutes crawled by in utter silence. I watched Holmes, his eyes bright and gleaming, his mouth tensed into a straight, tight line. His ear was turned to the curtain and his entire body seemed to be listening for the faintest sound. I fingered the revolver in my coat pocket as I waited.

Suddenly Justin Service spoke. "How did you get in here?"

"You haven't yet figured that out, Mr. Service? Dear me. If you spent less time with your head buried in your hands, you might find out. Have you," and here we heard a hideous chuckle, "determined my name yet?"

"Please, can't we stop this now? I've offered to pay for the work you did making up those plans. Somehow I will find the money, if you just stop tormenting me!"

"We had a bargain, Mr. Service. Or should I call you Justin, since you are to become my brother-in-law?"

"That will never be!" A chair scraped the floor.

"Stay where you are! The time has come. I give you three last guesses, sir!"

"Is it Tillotson?"

"No," the voice chuckled.

"Waxflatter!"

"No," and we heard an odious laugh.

"Could your name be...Rumpel Stiltskin?"

A dreadful scream rang through the room. "What? How did you find out?"

"You lost your job as draftsman here at Lawler and Kingman six months ago! Your last address was 42 Underhill Lane which you left last week!"

Suddenly we heard a crash and a thump. Holmes and I burst out from behind the curtain to see the desk swept bare and Justin Service on his knees scrabbling at a section of wainscoting. He looked up at Sherlock Holmes. "He went through here!"

Our client fell back as Holmes attacked the wall. Soundlessly a panel slid back. He plunged into the aperture and we followed him. He had his torch turned on and the circle of light slid over a narrow passageway lit by slits high up on the walls. At the end of the passage, Holmes dashed up a set of stairs to the next floor. Mr. Service and I ran up the steps behind him and found Holmes pulling down a collapsible ladder from an overhead hatch.

"The rope handle was still swinging, Watson! His footsteps in the dust end here! He went up!"

We climbed into a small room under the eaves. I saw a drafting table and chair, cabinets piled with architectural drawings and electric lights hanging from the rafters. A pallet on the floor and some old blankets made up a crude bed. Sherlock Holmes and I ran to an opened skylight in the angle of the roof and thrust our heads and shoulders out into the clear air. I pointed my revolver at a pair of hands which slipped out of sight over the edge of the leads.

We heard a clatter and a rush down below. "Gone down that drainpipe and out through the alley, Watson!" Holmes cried. He craned his neck. "It's no use to follow him. He's halfway to the Thames by now. By God, look at this!" He pulled in his head and flourished a large handful of white hair. He tossed it to me and turned his attention to the piles of papers heaped on the closest surface.

I stepped under a light and examined Holmes's trophy. It was a long white wig and beard, spreading out and down my arm and clinging to my coat. Justin Service gasped and said, "It is his! He must have used it as a disguise. But why?"

Holmes looked up from a sheaf of papers. "It was an added precaution in case someone from the firm saw him in the building. My researches today showed that Rumpel Stiltskin had worked for Lawler and Kingman since old Mr. Lawler hired him in the early days. In fact, he was Lawler's favorite draftsman. He assisted in the drawing up of the plans for this building. Only he and Lawler knew about these secret corridors and rooms. Lawler meant to use them to guard against industrial sabotage. After he died, I think Stiltskin used the system to spy on his fellow employees.

"Without friends or family, he spent many private hours in this room drawing up plans like those orders given to the real architects. He developed a backload of common assignments. See, here they are in this cabinet. When he decided to wreak his revenge on the people he saw as taking his job, he lurked inside the walls and chose plans from his supply."

Holmes picked up a dusty, half-filled wine bottle from a shelf and sniffed at the contents. "This has been drugged, as I thought. That was the reason for your deep slumber after each bargain, Mr. Service. Hello, what have we here?" He found a notebook amongst the litter and flipped through the pages.

"According to this journal he has left behind, Stiltskin knew the reorganization was coming even before he was fired, so he persecuted Mr. Kingman by whispering to him through the walls as Kingman sat alone in his office. That convinced Kingman that he was going mad and drove the poor man to drink even more. It was that mysterious voice that commanded Kingman to give Justin Service those impossible assignments."

Our client dropped into the one chair. "But why persecute me? I never even met the man."

Holmes regarded the young architect gently. "Pardon me, Mr. Service, but you are young and inexperienced. This was your first job. Add to that your financial situation and your devotion to your family, facts which he could have easily found out by listening from the hidden passageways, and you were fated to become the subject of Stiltskin's dark and devious plans."

"But, Holmes," I protested. "What did he hope to gain with such activities? It would not get him his job back."

"I believe his job had become his life, Doctor, and when one ended, so did the other. Pure malevolent revenge became his raison d'être. I do not think he ever intended to meet your sister, Mr. Service, much less marry her. He knew that the very thought of such a thing was enough to force you to despair. Your pain was what he was after and when he saw it he rejoiced. Mr. Kingman's death, perhaps brought on by his evil whispering campaign, must have satisfied his black soul for months."

"But he has escaped us, Mr. Holmes!"

Sherlock Holmes put down the journal and carefully closed and locked the skylight. "Yes. He was a younger man that he appeared, especially in that white wig and beard, and he swarmed up and down that drainpipe with quite a sailor's skill. You must inform your employers of this room and the hidden corridors tomorrow morning, Mr. Service, so that they may take steps to secure every last bolt hole against his return. It is possible that he may never come back now that his secret is out. Eventually such a twisted brain is bound to express itself in some manner, however. I shall just drop a word in Inspector Lestrade's ear for future reference."

Justin Service stood and wordlessly wrung Sherlock Holmes' hand in gratitude. Holmes turned to leave, pausing at the top of the ladder.

"Now it is back to my researches into that interesting South American poison, Watson. I wonder what would happen if it were injected into a subject? "

A horrible image sprang into my brain. "Holmes, I must insist that you…!"

Sherlock Holmes smiled and raised his hand. "Alright, Doctor, do calm yourself. I think Mrs. Hudson's traps caught a couple of mice in the back scullery last night. I promise to try my experiments out on them first."

I climbed down from the hidden room silently resolving to lay out some crumbs in the back scullery every night from now on.

The Case of the Secluded Stepchildren

Late one August evening Inspector George Stone unexpectedly called upon us in our sitting room at 221b Baker Street. He found a pretty domestic scene; Mrs. Hudson bearing away the remains of a late cold supper and me at my desk with my notes before me, my mind still pre-occupied with the details of the case we had concluded just that evening. Mr. Sherlock Holmes stood before the curtained window, pipe in hand. Holmes stopped attempting to light his old clay and regarded George Stone with interest.

"Hello, Inspector, do come in. Mrs. Hudson, bring back the joint. Mr. Stone looks as if he could use some of it. Sit down, man, before you fall! Watson, bring a chair and get him a drink. All work and no meals make for a very long day, sir." Holmes filled a plate from the sideboard and placed it before our visitor.

The Scotland Yard detective, whom Sherlock Holmes had previously mentioned to me as one of the young up-and-coming men of that stately institution, attacked the meal without apologies. I placed a glass of port by his plate. Holmes shook his head and gently chastised our visitor.

"Inspector, you must remember to take a moment and eat. Your body cannot take the strain of continuous work without nourishment. Have an apple."

I stared at my friend in disbelief. "Holmes, I have been telling you that for years!"

Holmes laughed at my indignant expression. "And you can see that I have been listening, Watson. Inspector Stone hasn't yet developed the bad habits that I nurture. If you had been around to drop a friendly word in my ear at a tender age, I might be a better man today."

Stone looked up at us. "Speaking of a tender age, that's why I'm here, Mr. Holmes," he said.

"It's the missing Woods children, isn't it?" Holmes lit his pipe.

"Yes. I've been looking into it all day and I came here as soon as the search broke up. It will resume early in the morning and I'm hoping you will be able to join us. I'm baffled, Mr. Holmes, I will admit it, and there is no time to spare."

"I am not aware of any missing children," I said.

"You have not been looking out the window at the news seller across the street, Watson," Holmes said. "The latest edition appeared ten minutes ago, and the placard is easily visible by the light on the corner."

"I have all the details here," said Stone, as he laid his notebook on the table.

"We have been busy all day, Inspector, and I know only of the headline I saw."

The Scotland Yard detective began flipping through his notes. "At seven o'clock yesterday morning Mr. Cutter Woods of the village of Smaller Chippings walked to his job as a forester in Bushy Park. His home, Starvelings, is on the edge of the Park, southeast of Richmond. At noon his wife sent the children, six-year old Henry and five-year old Gladys, out with a lunch for him as was the custom. The children never arrived, although they had brought him his lunch the day before at the same place. Mr. Woods wondered at this, but he was engaged in a complicated tree-felling operation and decided not to return home before the end of the day. Upon reaching home at dusk, he discovered that his wife had sent off the kiddies at the regular time, but they had not returned. She naturally thought that they had stayed with him, as they have done before. They both searched the surrounding area and inquired of the neighbors, but found no sign of them. The alarm was raised and the police began an investigation at once. Small bands of men roamed through Smaller Chippings and the nearest part of Bushy Park but found nothing before it became too dark to see.

"Smaller Chippings called in Scotland Yard, but we couldn't do much last night. This morning search parties were formed and the entire day has been spent looking for the children. I was able to interview Cutter Woods a little, but his wife was too upset for questions. Everything will begin again tomorrow morning. Could you be there, Mr. Holmes? I would count it as a particular favor. I haven't forgotten your help with that affair of the poor Knights of Windsor."

"This case has its points of interest, Inspector, and I will join you tomorrow at Smaller Chippings. How about it, Watson? We have had a long day. Would you be too fatigued to accompany me?"

"Of course not, Holmes. Those poor children must be found as soon as possible."

"Staunch old Watson! If you have finished your supper, Inspector Stone, you must excuse us to get what rest we can. You may count upon us both. Do try to get some sleep yourself. The sun rises early these August mornings."

I got a good look at the morning sunrise the next day, as our train pulled into Smaller Chippings well before my accustomed breakfast time. When we stepped off the carriage we could see a large crowd of townsmen, police and a few small boys milling about in front of a public house opposite the platform. Inspector Stone came out of the building under a large sign that read "Le Chapelure" and pushed through the crowd to us. He grasped our hands gratefully. He introduced us to the local constabulary and the mayor, but Holmes was able to disengage himself from them with ease. He led Stone down to the other end of the platform with me at their heels.

"I knew it would be too much to expect an undisturbed scene, since the crowds have tramped over everything during the search. However, I do want to examine Starvelings, as well as ask questions of Mr. and Mrs. Woods. How soon may we see them?"

"We are organizing the search parties now, Mr. Holmes, and assigning them their areas. "Le Chapelure" serves a good English breakfast. Why don't you wait for me there?"

Holmes agreed and I was able to get a hurried breakfast after all. As expected, Holmes ordered nothing, although I urged him to drink some coffee. Within an hour of arriving at Smaller Chippings, we were walking down a nearby street of identical cottages. I noticed that behind the window pane of one or two a curtain was drawn aside as if someone was following our progress. George Stone ushered us into the small but tidy home of Mr. and Mrs. Cutter Woods.

Cutter Woods sat silent and glum in the parlor which, from his manner, he was clearly unaccustomed to using. He was a strong, heavily muscled man, as befits a forester who works with axe and knife all day. He looked to be in his middle thirties, with a weather-beaten face under a thatch of brown hair. He sat on the edge of a chair, his work-roughened hands clasping and unclasping in his lap. He was dressed in the sturdy clothing of his employment and his face displayed worry and confusion.

His wife, by contrast, appeared much younger than he, her pink softness only emphasized by the golden glints in her fair hair and the delicate molding of her cheekbones. Large, lustrous brown eyes looked out from under thick lashes. Dainty lips were poised over a rounded little chin. She reclined on the sofa, dressed in a morning gown of something thin, with touches of white at the wrists and throat.

At the first sight of her brave little face and her graceful figure my heart went out to her. What horror she must have felt, to find that her little children had not found their father but were wandering lost in the vast woods, far from their home and those sworn to love and protect them.

Holmes briskly asked her of her actions the day of the disappearance.

"My husband left for work at his usual time. Henry and Gladys don't awaken until the sun shines in their window, so they seldom see their dad off in the mornings. They played quietly in their room, then after a bit of lunch I sent them off down the path to where their father was working, carrying his sandwiches. That's the last time I saw them. Oh, they were so happy!" She sobbed softly into a white handkerchief.

Cutter Woods' story was the same as the one he had given the police. His children had never appeared and when he returned his wife knew nothing of their whereabouts. They had searched around the cottage and then raised the alarm.

Holmes asked to see the children's room. It was a whitewashed little chamber off the kitchen with two little beds and two little toy chests. Clothes hung on pegs behind a curtain. Braided rugs were spread on the wooden floor and the light came from a large window on the east wall. Holmes examined everything, even taking each pathetic little toy out of the gaily-painted chests and looking at it closely with his magnifying glass. Finally he spent some time going over the window and its fastenings, closing the shutters and shaking the window in its frame.

I watched him closely and I could tell from his demeanor that he was unsatisfied.

He left Inspector Stone and me in the sitting room while he went outside. Through the window the four of us could see him bent over the flower beds and crawling on his hands and knees along the grass verge of the gravel path. Finally he stood up and motioned for us to join him. We made our excuses and met him on the pavement before the little cottage.

"Inspector, may I see maps of this region? I need to get a better idea of the area."

"Of course, Mr. Holmes, there is a complete set at the police station."

A constable, followed by several men, ran up to Inspector Stone. In his hand, he held a pruning knife. I saw that the gleam of the blade was dulled in several spots with drops of a dark substance. The policeman held it out to us.

"Inspector, this was just found in a clump of weeds off a path that wanders through Bushy Park."

Sherlock Holmes lifted the knife from the constable's hand and examined it with his magnifying glass. I leaned over his shoulder. "That looks like blood!" I exclaimed.

"It is dried blood," Holmes said. "The initials C.W. are burnt into the handle. Does this belong to Mr. Woods'?"

"I'll soon find out," Stone said grimly. He went into the cottage with the knife and emerged moments later with Cutter Woods in tow.

"I admit that knife is mine," the forester protested, "but I don't know anything about the blood. It disappeared days ago."

"I have heard that song before." Inspector Stone fastened handcuffs to Woods' wrists. "You are under arrest for the murder of your children." The small group of men began to murmur. "If you wish to examine those maps, Mr. Holmes, I will meet you at the police station."

"I will be down in an hour, Inspector," Holmes said. He looked around at the angry faces of the men around us. "Please do not release Mr. Woods until I have had an opportunity to talk to him."

"There won't be any danger of that!" said a voice from the back. I watched as the others nodded and stirred restlessly. A moment later Stone and the constable, with the prisoner between them and followed by the crowd, walked down the pavement in the direction of the High Street.

"What a sad, ugly business, Holmes. I see Inspector Stone didn't need our help after all," I remarked.

"On the contrary, he needs all the help we can give him, Watson," my friend replied. "I only let him arrest Woods because of the current state of mind of the village. Cutter Woods will be much safer in gaol than on the streets after the discovery of that knife."

"You don't believe he did it, then."

"I don't believe I have all the facts yet, Watson, and I cannot make bricks without clay. Here is what I want you to do. Mrs. Woods must be upset. I want you to offer her your services as a physician. Stay with her until I return."

"Of course I will, Holmes. What will you do?"

Sherlock Holmes cast a speculative eye over the houses around us. "I need to dig out some clay," he answered.

A few minutes later I stood in the parlor of Cutter Woods' home, taking the pulse of his wife. After admitting me she had returned to the sofa and collapsed in a half-fainting condition. Her pulse was fast and I fetched a little brandy for her. Her clear brown eyes gazed gratefully at me over the rim of the glass. I settled her more comfortably on the cushions and patted her little hand.

"Now there, you must rest, Mrs. Woods," I said. "You have had a terrible time."

"Doctor, please call me Clarisse," she said softly. "Oh, to think that Cutter has done such a horrid thing and to his own children, too! I would never have believed it possible when we married just a year ago."

I was surprised. "Then the children were not your own?"

"I loved them as my own, of course, but they were the children of Cutter's first marriage. His wife died two years ago. We were two lonely people and it just seemed right when he asked me to marry him. Now it is all destroyed!" She lifted the little handkerchief to her eyes again.

My heart ached for this brave, helpless little woman and I sought to comfort her. "You must not let this blight the rest of your life, Clarisse," I said as I patted her hand again. "You are a very attractive woman. I'm sure your future is much brighter than it seems right now."

"Do you think so, Doctor? Do you truly think so?" Her sensitive, trusting face looked up at mine with hopeful eyes. I gazed into their depths and spoke from my heart.

"Yes, I truly do. Now you must rest. Look here, I will sit quietly in this armchair and you will try to take a little nap. I will let nothing disturb you."

"You are very kind. Thank you." She snuggled down under the light afghan throw I drew over her and I took my seat near her feet. The room grew silent as I waited, watching her breathe as I relaxed in my chair.

My energies expended in the days before, coupled with the lost hours of sleep before our arrival in Smaller Chippings, must have made me drowsy. I suddenly awoke. I could tell time had passed for the angle of light in the room had changed. I stared around before I realized where I was. I looked to the sofa. Clarisse Woods was lying under the afghan, her eyes closed and her breast rising and falling in a regular pattern. She was asleep. After a minute or two I rose from my chair and silently stepped out the cottage door.

The sun felt warm on my face. I sat down on the step and lit a cigarette. I was sitting there only a few minutes when I saw Sherlock Holmes and Inspector Stone walking up from the High Street. Holmes stopped before the Woods' cottage and spoke to me sharply.

"Why are you out here, Watson?"

I felt nettled by his rudeness. "I'm only having a smoke," I retorted. "Clarisse…Mrs. Woods is taking a nap in the parlor."

"She has been with you this entire time?"

"Yes."

He came closer and looked into my eyes in a curious fashion. "You have been awake all this time?"

"How long has it been?" I asked defensively.

"It has been over two hours since we parted. You fell asleep, didn't you, Watson?"

I looked away from his gaze. "I may have dozed a little."

"Watson!" He suddenly relaxed and smiled, shaking his head. "Now that I am here I have one more task. I must examine the children's room again."

I followed the two men into the cottage again, feeling confused. Why would Holmes need to look over that bedroom again? What could the sight of little coats and dresses tell him now that he had not learned the first time? I stepped into the parlor and gently woke Clarisse Woods.

She made a pretty sight as she blinked up at me and smiled. She put her soft hand in mine as she sat up among the cushions to greet my friend and the Inspector. Holmes' request to look over the little bedroom again obviously bewildered her, but she readily gave her consent. We waited together on the sofa as he and Stone rummaged about in the back. I noticed that her slender fingers pulled a small white handkerchief about. She kept glancing down the hallway. When she saw that I noticed that she smiled at me.

Our silence was broken by Sherlock Holmes. He strode into the parlor with a dark bundle and sat down across from Clarisse Woods. His sharp eyes flashed and his body was alive with the energy only mental stimulation could bring him. I recognized the signs. He was near the end of the case! Only a few more questions and Cutter Woods would be guaranteed to swing for his crimes and the bodies of the poor victims could be recovered and given decent burial. Mrs. Woods must unknowingly hold some small bit of information that would insure justice. Protectively I inched closer to her, waiting for Holmes' first words.

The detective proceeded to undo the bundle in his hands and disclosed a long black cape. "Mrs. Woods, does this belong to you? I found it hidden under the mattress of your son's bed."

She looked at it, her face awash in confusion. "I never saw it before in my life. Henry must have found it and hidden it there."

Holmes smiled thinly. "I think not. It wasn't there when I examined the room earlier today."

"You are mistaken, sir." Her eyes flew to mine in distress.

"These bits of grass on the hem of the cape match that blade adhering to the edge of your left shoe, Mrs. Woods," said Sherlock Holmes.

"Holmes, what does this mean?" I asked.

"Watson, I am afraid that you have been taken in by a pretty face. Mrs. Woods has set up a nasty little plan to rid herself of both her husband and her stepchildren. I regret to add that we nearly helped her to succeed."

"This is intolerable! Explain yourself!"

"Calm down, Watson, and listen. I fear that you have allowed your emotions to overcome your reserves of good sense. Do you remember that once I told you that to learn everything about a village you should frequent the local public house?"

"Yes, but ...."

He held up a hand and my voice died away. "That applies best to the male inhabitants of a community. To learn about the females the best way is to engage that font of information, the local gossip. Every neighborhood has at least one. This street has two. Lonely women, they sit by their windows, keeping a sharp eye on the comings and goings of their neighbors. It takes but a kind word and a willingness to listen to tap into years of fact and speculation. Eliminate the speculation and you are left with the facts."

"You would listen to gossips?" Mrs. Woods' voice was low and bitter. I looked at her in surprise. I had not heard such a tone from her before.

"Each bit of gossip hides within itself a kernel of truth. The trick is to find that tiny kernel and discard the rest. After I sent Dr. Watson in here, I had a pleasant chat with the women whose interest in our movements had drawn my attention

earlier. From the first I gleaned the story of Cutter Woods'
first marriage, his wife's death and his remarriage to you. Did
you realize, madam, that your treatment of those two children
when their father was at work is well known in this
neighborhood?"

"Bah! They are bitter old shrews with nothing to do all
day but spy!"

"The law calls them witnesses. The second lady, whose
window overlooks your back garden, had a more recent story
to tell. I heard of a hooded and caped figure that moved back
and forth from your door to Bushy Park repeatedly in the past
few days. If this were a fairy tale the figure might be
described as a witch."

"It is a fairy tale, Mr. Holmes."

"No." He picked up the cape and turned back the
attached hood. "This proves the story's reality. You hid this
in the children's room because you thought that once searched
the room would not be searched again.

"Unsatisfied with your marriage to a poor man with two
children, you plotted their downfall. The children were to
disappear and the dark deed to be ascribed to their father.
Once he had been put into the clutches of the law, you thought
the children could be shipped off or sold. Bands of gypsies
still roam Bushy Park and you have heard those old wives'
tales all your life. Free, and with the little savings your honest
husband has saved, you could use your natural advantages to

70

contract a more salubrious marriage that would remove you from Smaller Chippings to a larger arena. Was a trusting and susceptible London doctor to be your first step, or had you other plans already in place?"

I looked at Clarisse Woods and shock flooded my body. It was all there. Everything Holmes had said was true. It showed in every line of her beautiful face, in every movement of her graceful body. A physical revulsion caused me to rise and move away from her. I got up and stood by the door that led outside. Dimly behind me I could hear Holmes continue to explain his findings.

He told Inspector Stone of the elderly woman who had seen repeated trips of a hooded figure into Bushy Park from Starvelings' back door. He related how in the garden the night before Clarisse Woods was seen, cutting up a bit of butcher's meat in order to drip drops of blood on a pruning knife. Later the mysterious figure carried the knife away down the path. Finally he related how he had watched from the old woman's window that very morning as a person wearing that cape and hood left the cottage through the back garden as I slept. He attempted to follow, but he lacked knowledge of the terrain and lost his quarry in the undergrowth of Bushy Park. When Holmes examined the maps provided at the police station after he returned, he pin-pointed the area he deduced the children were being kept. He handed a sheet of paper to Inspector Stone.

Stone brushed past me to summon constables from the street. He left the men to convey Mrs. Woods to the station while he led the rescue party. I stepped back as she was taken out. I dared not to look at her.

Sherlock Holmes stood awkwardly beside me on the pavement before Starvelings. "Watson…"

I stopped him. "Don't say it, Holmes."

"I wasn't going to, I just…"

"I'm a fool, Holmes, and I don't deserve a friend like you. I feel embarrassment more than anything else. To think that I could be taken in so easily and so quickly! I was convinced that hers was a pure and noble soul."

"Were you attracted only by the soul, Watson?"

"Holmes! I…I…"

"Do not blame yourself too harshly, Doctor. I have never met a woman so skilled in the wiles of her sex as Mrs. Clarissa Woods. Had she only gone on the stage, we might be singing her praises to everyone we meet. She surely was made for wider worlds than that one in which she found herself. Instead we assist the authorities as they punish her ambition instead of rewarding it."

By the time we boarded the next train back to London the news of the safe return of the children had swept through the village. Cutter Woods was released from custody in time to greet his returning son and daughter. Exhausted by the ordeal the three retreated from the general thanksgiving back to their cottage.

In a similar fashion I retreated to Baker Street. The familiar sight of Mrs. Hudson greeting us at the door, the furniture and books awaiting us in our sitting room, even the odor of Holmes' favorite pipe served to sooth my nerves. Yet I felt a nagging sense of having lost something I valued.

It was telling of my friendship with Mr. Sherlock Holmes that a few days later he objected to my intention to write of the case. "It will serve no purpose, Watson, and shows you in an unfortunate light."

"On the contrary, I think it was one of your finest efforts and deserves to be memorialized."

Holmes smiled sadly and reached over to close the lid of my inkwell. "Ambition has brought me to the level my modest efforts allow me to occupy. Ambition has brought your tales to readers that enjoy them. But ambition did no favors for Clarissa Woods and all who knew her. Let bad judgment, bitterness and misplaced hostility alone. Such things should never be perpetuated."

"I say let them be exposed, so that others may learn from the experience."

My friend gave me a penetrating look. "It is too soon, Watson. In her fashion, Clarisse Woods was quite a fascinating woman. One might even say bewitching. You proved susceptible to her charms. When the spell was broken the shock stripped away your faith in womankind."

"Holmes!"

"No, do not protest, the symptoms are clear. In a man such as you, the loss proved as crippling as another man's loss of a limb. The counter spell is time, Watson, to heal your own soul. Only then can you calmly judge if such a story is worthy of publication. Indeed, only then can you decide if you wish to write it at all."

My friend turned away and took up his violin. As melancholy strains of music filled the room, I closed my notebook and put it away. Perhaps Holmes was right. Perhaps it was too soon for me to put down the details of this case. But I did not forget just where in my desk I filed the notes.

The Case of the Mystified Major

"I have a puzzle for you, Mr. Holmes," said Major Thimbleton as he refreshed our glasses. "I will even wager that you fail. No one has devised a logical explanation for the contents of the Worcester Box in a hundred years."

Sherlock Holmes leaned back in the armchair he occupied before the fireplace in the Major's library. The lamps had been lit, the curtains drawn, and conversation between Holmes, Thimbleton and I had continued here from the dining room where we just enjoyed a fine meal.

Major Arthur Thimbleton, a widower and retired Army officer, was a former client of Holmes's. He lived a bachelor's existence, his daughter married and his two sons gone into the Army. He heard that we were in Worcester assisting the local police in solving a particularly unpleasant murder and invited us to stay with him in his ancient family seat after the case was solved. As a result, we had spent the previous two days under his roof. The Major proved to be an affable gentleman, knowledgeable about foreign lands and curious about the methods Sherlock Holmes used to solve his cases.

From the practiced way the Major spoke, it seemed that the Worcester Box was a regular conundrum that generations of Thimbletons had put before their guests. The Major smiled as he rummaged in a cabinet and brought forth a plain wooden box which he set on the low table before my friend. I leaned forward and examined it as Holmes lit his pipe.

About nine inches long on each side and six inches deep, the box had a fitted lid decorated with a marquetry design. Its sides were smooth and polished. There was no lock. From the way the Major handled it, the box was not heavy.

"I accept your challenge, sir. Tell me about the Box," said Holmes.

"My ancestor, General Marcus Thimbleton, decided upon some alterations in the house in 1789. The Box was found when a wall was torn down to enlarge the dining hall. It was covered in dust and obviously had been hidden there a long time. Curiously enough, the section of wall in which it was discovered concealed a hidden cavity, a priest's hole, which led from the room next to the dining hall to an exit near the stables. Both ends had been sealed and all family knowledge of this passageway had been lost. Nothing else was found with the Box. Since then, each generation of Thimbletons has puzzled over the contents. Mr. Holmes, if you can put forth a credible explanation for the collection held in this box, you will have justified your reputation a thousand times over."

I reached out and ran my hand over the lid. "Open it, Watson," murmured Holmes from behind a veil of tobacco smoke. I gently lifted the top and set it aside. Several linen-wrapped bundles lay inside. Carefully I picked up each one and laid it out on the table's surface. When the box was empty I sat back and transferred my attention to Sherlock Holmes.

He leaned forward, his elbows on his knees and his fingers steepled before his chin. A thin wisp of smoke rose lazily from the bowl of his pipe. Keen grey eyes lingered on each bundle in turn, and then shifted to include the box. Several moments passed before Holmes removed his pipe and laid it aside. He picked up a bundle, fingered the cloth, brought it to his nose, and then removed the wrapping. A crudely-shaped nail lay in the palm of his hand.

The second bundle was opened to reveal a flat leather wallet of antique design. An irregularly-shape splotch stained one corner where there was a long slit in the leather. Holmes unfolded it and carefully extracted a jagged, stiff fragment of rust-colored paper. He laid them both on the table.

The third bundle disclosed a trio of tarnished coat buttons and the last one contained a battered horseshoe. Holmes spread all those items out on the table, and then picked up the box. With his magnifying glass he minutely examined the box's interior and exterior. Then he did the same with the lid and each of the things on the table, including the wrappings.

When he leaned back and picked up his pipe again, I quietly left my chair and wandered over to the bookshelves. Major Thimbleton watched Holmes smoke for several minutes and then joined me.

"What happens now?" he inquired.

I shrugged. "He thinks. We wait. I have never been able to explain how his mind works. He could spend the entire night here, smoking, or he may jump up and decide to go somewhere else to collect more information. Or he could give us his answer in the next five minutes. With Sherlock Holmes one never knows."

Major Thimbleton gestured to the bookshelves. "If he needs more information about my family, there are several biographies here. There are also account books dating back to when the house was built in the early 1500s. Old General Edmund Thimbleton was a favorite of Good Queen Bess in her later years and got the estate by Crown grant a few years before she died. It was quite a bit farther out from Worcester then. The Royalists with Lieutenant-General David Leslie were stationed at Pitchcroft meadow to the west of us just before the battle of Worcester in 1651."

"That was the last battle of the Rebellion, wasn't it? After the rout, Charles the Second fled to France."

"That's right. There were two young Thimbleton brothers at the battle. William was killed during a sortie from Charles's position on the southeast edge of Worcester to Red Hill and Rodger actually helped the king escape and spent the next ten years of his life in France. He returned to England after the Restoration."

"Quite a family history." I turned to look at Holmes. He was stretched out in the armchair, his eyes closed and a slight smile on his face. He spoke without stirring.

"I shall remain here for some time, Watson. Major, I plan to work on this problem through the night. If I need anything, may I just help myself?"

Major Thimbleton smiled. "Of course, Mr. Holmes. My entire home is at your disposal. Perhaps, Dr. Watson, you would care for a game of billiards before we retire?"

"I would be delighted. Good night, Holmes."

"Good night, Watson, and good night, Major. May I give you a word of warning, sir? Watch out for Watson. At billiards, the man is a shark."

Major Thimbleton chuckled and we left the great detective alone in the library.

The Major greeted me rather ruefully at breakfast the next morning. "I should have listened to Holmes, Doctor. You wield an excellent cue."

I smiled modestly. "It was luck, Major. You own an excellent table."

As we sat down with our filled plates in the dining room, Sherlock Holmes appeared in the doorway. He was washed and brushed and gave no sign of having been up all night. He took up a plate and peered into the chafing dishes on the sideboard.

"Good morning, Mr. Holmes," Major Thimbleton said. "Have you had any luck with the family puzzle?"

"I am afraid I made a bit of a mess in the kitchen last night, Major. Good morning, Watson. I can see that you had as profitable an evening as I did." Holmes joined us with his filled plate and began eating.

"It's true that Watson beat me three games out of four at billiards, Mr. Holmes, but how could you know?" asked the Major in surprise.

"Watson always puts his winnings in his right waistcoat pocket and I perceive a bulge there that was not there last evening."

Major Thimbleton laughed. "Well, it may cost me more money, but I hope you have been as successful. What is this about a mess in the kitchen? Have you solved the mystery of the Worcester Box?"

"I had to use some things in the kitchen to determine the composition of that stain on the leather wallet. It was dried blood."

"Dried blood!"

"I'll explain everything after breakfast, Major. My, this ham is delicious. Is it home-cured?"

Holmes kept the conversation on food for the rest of the meal, despite the Major's efforts to question him about the Box. Only after we were all settled in the library again and Holmes had lit his pipe would he explain how he had occupied himself the night before. The Worcester Box and its contents were still spread out on the low table before his chair.

"I overheard those interesting highlights of your family's history you told Watson, Major, and after you left I took full advantage of the books on your shelves. I had already determined from the appearance of the marquetry design on the lid of the box that it was Spanish and dated from the 1620s. I saw that the nail and the horseshoe were of mid-seventeenth century manufacture. The wallet was from the same period, although it showed signs of French origin. The scrap of parchment…"

"Parchment?"

"Yes. That was what was in the wallet. It was drenched in blood, turning it that rust color and showing that it was in the wallet at the time a sword sliced through the leather and wounded whoever was carrying it. Unfortunately the fragment left carried no writing. You remember the monograph I had written on dating documents, Watson. I dated this parchment by the method of preparation used on the sheepskin. It was of the same era as the horseshoe, wallet and nail, but all were later than the box.

"The linen wrappings were difficult to date, but from the creases, the color and the weaving I believe they too were from the mid-1600s.

"The three buttons were most interesting. I had to consult several volumes on your shelves, Major, before I found one that showed plates of the uniform buttons of the Royal Army of King Charles the Second. When Charles brought his army to Worcester a few days before the definitive battle, he contracted with a local firm to clothe and outfit the few recruits that joined from the neighboring area. The three buttons are from that royal order."

Major Thimbleton sat up straight in excitement. "Amazing, Mr. Holmes! William and Rodger Thimbleton joined King Charles's troops just a few days before the September third battle. Their old father, Judge John Thimbleton, had been crippled in the Battle of Powick Bridge on the old King's side nine years before. Publicly he took no side with the son but within the family he was secretly sympathetic. He had deemed the boys too young to fight, but with the conflict so near, they had run away to Worcester and joined Charles' forces without his knowledge."

"Was there a Spanish connection to your family back then?" I asked.

"John Thimbleton had traveled in Spain as a young man. He brought back all sorts of Spanish things. That little table in the corner is one of them."

Holmes and I got up and examined the table. The mellow old surface displayed a similar pattern of marquetry as that on the box. The Major sat in his chair, wonderment on his features. "All these years and no one had connected the Worcester Box design to that one on the table. Why not?"

Sherlock Holmes sat down and took up his pipe. "People see, but they do not observe. Since the Box had been found separately from the table and even in a different part of the house, no one thought to put them together. That does furnish the final clue to confirm my reconstruction of the history of the Worcester Box and its contents, however."

"I have always said that I would pay one hundred pounds to anyone who could give a reasonable explanation of the Worcester Box. Do it, Mr. Holmes, and the money is yours." The Major gazed at my friend with an eager face.

Holmes put down his pipe and steepled his fingers. He crossed his legs and settled back. The look in his eyes grew dreamy and his whole posture seemed to soften and melt into the armchair. His high voice carried easily as he began to speak as if he saw the action of the story playing out before his inner eye.

"Long ago in the mid-seventeenth century in England Charles the Second, son of a deposed and beheaded monarch, came down with troops and cavalry from Scotland in an effort to reach London and regain his crown. Others told him to stay in Scotland, which had welcomed him as its King, but he believed the countryside would rise up in support of his claim and help him defeat Oliver Cromwell and the Parliamentarians. But that did not happen. By the time Charles reached Worcester in late August of 1651 even his Lieutenant-General David Leslie did not believe he could succeed.

"Charles entered the city and began to fortify it for the promised battle. He placed General Leslie with his cavalry in Pitchcroft meadow on the west of Worcester and the Duke of Hamilton on the east. To the south went Keith and Montgomery. Charles ordered clothes for the few locals who joined his fight and laid plans against his enemies.

"Nearby were two gallant sons, thought by their father too young to fight, who yearned to assist their king. One night, though surrounded by neighbors who supported the Parliamentarians, they rode into Worcester and joined the Royalists.

"On the third of September Cromwell and his forces attacked. Charles led a charge to capture Red Hill outside the city and quickly realized that he needed more help. He decided to send a message to Leslie in the west to bring up his cavalry and engage the enemy.

"The King chose William Thimbleton, because he was a zealous local lad who knew the area and had a fast horse, to carry the mobilization orders. His brother Rodger stayed with the King and later gave his horse so Charles could escape. But this is William's story.

"William was given a leather wallet to carry the message, written by Charles on a sheet of parchment. He mounted his horse and set out to cross the Duke of Hamilton's lines on a path that would skirt Worcester to the north and reach General Leslie in the west. He wore his new Royalist uniform. He was young and very eager.

"Half-way to Pitchcroft meadow, his horse began to limp. William stopped and dismounted and found that one of the horse's shoes had lost nails and was at the point of falling off. He caught the last nail and the shoe as they dropped and as to not leave any trace of his mission, put them in his pocket. He tried to urge his horse onward, but the animal faltered because of the missing shoe. Finally William abandoned his mount and continued on foot as fast as he could run.

"Most of Cromwell's army was in the south and the east, crossing a pontoon bridge over the Severn and fighting the King's men near Red Hill. But there were a few sympathizers between Worcester and the meadow and at least one of them found William. I am sure your ancestor gave his best, but the final result was that William was badly wounded and the message was destroyed. Young Thimbleton was left for dead."

The Major stared at Holmes as if mesmerized.

"When William was found, too much time had been lost. The battle raged in the city. The sun was setting and the cause was lost. But William was found near his own home. He managed to tell his story and die in the arms of his father.

The old man was proud of William but he knew that if his neighbors found out his sons had fought for the King, his own life and the lives of all those under his roof would be forfeited.

"William was buried secretly on the grounds. John Thimbleton couldn't bear to get rid of the evidence of his son's heroism, however, so he packed up the nail, the horseshoe, the wallet and three buttons from William's uniform in an old box he had brought from Spain years before. He hid it in the priest's hole and had both entrances sealed. He then made the household swear never to speak of the secret passage again.

"Rodger didn't return to Worcester for ten years. Everything had changed. All he knew about William was that he died during the battle. The box rested in its hiding place until 1789 when it was discovered behind a wall. For the next one hundred years it posed a riddle for every Thimbleton and for every one of their guests."

"Until today," said the Major. He stood up and vigorously shook Sherlock Holmes's hand. His face glowed and a big smile was spread across his features. "I have never been happier to lose a wager. What a wonderful story, Mr. Holmes. Do you really think it is true?"

"There is no way to check it, besides uncovering William's grave." Holmes answered. "But I can say that all the facts fit together and history supports it. General David Leslie never did receive any orders to advance his cavalry. They stayed in reserve in Pitchcroft meadow until the battle was over. As a result of the Battle of Worcester, the Parliamentarians and Oliver Cromwell prevailed and changed the course of English history. Charles fled to France and wasn't crowned King of England until 1661."

Major Thimbleton and I sat silently as Sherlock Holmes carefully rewrapped each item and returned it to the Worcester Box. Finally the Major stirred.

"If William had only made it through with that message…"

"It might have been so different," I mused. "But for want of that message the battle was lost and for want of that battle a kingdom was lost."

"And all for the want of a horseshoe nail," said Sherlock Holmes.

The Case of the Beleaguered Brothers

July had been a very quiet, hot month. A lack of paying cases had depleted Sherlock Holmes' bank account. I too, had suffered unexpected financial reverses and payments made to my turf accountant had drained my resources. I had my patients to draw me out of our rooms but a lethargy born of boredom and straited circumstances kept my friend cooped up in the heat. There was nothing in the newspapers. The criminal element of London appeared to have taken a holiday. International news was dull and even the weather was monotonous. At first Holmes spent the time sorting through his many documents and updating his extensive scrapbooks. I grew anxious about him, however, when he dropped even these mild activities and preferred to lay motionless upon the sofa for hours, staring at the ceiling. Even his violin could not engage his interest. His appetite shrank to nothing and Mrs. Hudson gave me many worried looks as she carried away yet another tray of untouched toothsome morsels prepared just for his palate. The atmosphere of the sitting room became gloomy. Each time I returned to 221b Baker Street I made a special effort to greet Holmes in a cheerful manner, but as the days stretched onward I found it more and more difficult to find positive things to say.

Therefore, as I paused outside the sitting room door one Monday afternoon to deposit my hat and cane and put down my medical bag, I was glad to hear lively voices from within.

I knocked and heard my old friend's voice vigorously bid me enter.

"Come in, Watson, come in! Let me introduce you to Mr. Trey Giltglider, of Reading. Mr. Giltglider, this is my long-suffering friend and invaluable colleague Dr. John H. Watson. Watson, pour out a brandy and take a seat. Mr. Giltglider, who is a pipe smoker, an epicure and a traveler in the American West, has favored us with a little problem even Scotland Yard cannot solve."

Seated in a chair across from our client, I looked him over as I sipped my drink. My eye traveled from the tobacco stain on Mr. Giltglider's right forefinger and a tiny spot of Béarnaise sauce on his tie to the pointed boot tips showing beneath his trouser legs. He was a stout man of about forty years, a little under the average height, dressed in an expensive suit of summer grey. His American Western boots looked to be made of snakeskin. The sunlight streaming through the windows caused his bald pate to gleam in the center of a straw-colored nest of wispy hair. Large pink ears backed black eyes that peered through a pair of silver-rimmed spectacles. A generous nose hung over a wide thin-lipped mouth and short, almost dainty fingers adjusted the thick gold watch chain that stretched across his expansive waistcoat.

"How do you do, Dr. Watson?" he said, half-rising from the sofa and extending his hand. "I have enjoyed your stories in the *Strand* immensely. They gave me the courage to put my problem before Mr. Holmes. I don't know what to do."

"So you first went to Scotland Yard?" I glanced at Sherlock Holmes, who stood upon the hearthrug before the empty fireplace with his pipe in one hand and a couple of sheets of notepaper in the other. In his eyes I saw the welcomed gleam of the hunt which had been missing for the past few weeks. He handed the notes to me.

"Mr. Giltglider has informed me that he and his two brothers are partners in one of the largest construction firms in Reading. A week ago on Saturday his youngest brother, Mr. Augustus Giltglider, disappeared. The same night one of his warehouses in Reading burned to the ground. An examination of his brother's apartment uncovered only these notes locked in his desk, and his will found spread out upon the blotter."

"That does not sound good," I murmured.

Trey Giltglider nodded. "Indeed not, Dr. Watson! I went to his flat to tell Augustus of the fire and found that no one had seen him since that morning. The story has been in the papers and I have even advertised for him these past few days, but to no avail. My brother is a light-hearted man who loves a good joke but he would never absent himself from the business without explanation. The local police investigated and at my insistence Mr. Lestrade of Scotland Yard came into it, but after all this time they can neither tell me what started the fire or where my brother is. I'm very worried, Mr. Holmes.

Silently I examined the papers in my hand. Each was roughly printed on cheap white paper torn from a tablet. The wide, crudely formed letters were large and legible. I read the messages aloud.

"You've got one chance. Use it," went the first one. The second note was more emphatic. "You've got only one more try. Miss it and what happens will be on your own head." I looked up at Holmes and Mr. Giltglider. "They are undated."

"They are also written with dirty fingers in pencil by a right-handed man with access to a rough wooden surface on which to rest the paper. Note the smudges on the notes from the handling of the paper. Yet there are no useable fingerprints," said Holmes. "The angle of the letters show he was right-handed and the messages show the grain of the underlying surface wood. But it is the pencil that shows the most interesting indications." He lit his pipe.

"They look like ordinary pencil marks to me, Holmes."

"Do they, Watson? Mr. Giltglider, where were the notes found?"

"I found them tucked into my brother's diary," said Mr. Giltglider. "The first was between the pages for Tuesday of two weeks ago and the second for that Thursday. The fire alarm was given Saturday night and the warehouse was completely destroyed in a few hours."

"Lestrade has had those notes for a week and has discovered nothing," said Holmes. "Now it is Monday and

Mr. Giltglider has come to us. Much time has been lost. Is there anything else you can tell us, Mr. Giltglider?"

"Only that Giltglider Construction is jointly owned by my brothers Augustus and Bernard and me. The warehouse was one of the assets of the business. We have been in business together for nearly twenty years."

"Are any of you married?"

"No. I never found the right woman. My brothers have escorted many ladies over the years, but they never settled down. I must confess, Mr. Holmes, that both my brothers, while doing their duty for the business, have spent their free time and money in what I consider frivolous pursuits like entertainment and pleasure."

"Where is your brother Bernard?" asked Holmes.

"He was in the United States on a lumber buying trip," replied Mr. Giltglider. "I used to do those trips, but twelve years ago he asked to do it and proved to be even better than I. I telegraphed him as soon as I found Augustus was missing after the fire. He set out immediately for home on the steamer *Pegasus*. I expect him to arrive in Reading by rail from Southampton tonight."

"We shall meet you and your brother tomorrow morning at 10 o'clock at your place of business," Sherlock Holmes declared. "Watson, can you come with me? Your assistance may be invaluable."

"Of course, Holmes."

"Excellent! Pack a bag and bring your revolver. Two final questions, Mr. Giltglider, and you must forgive me if the first is painful. You are sure that no sign of your brother's remains were found in the ashes of the warehouse?"

"So the police have assured me, Mr. Holmes."

"What were the contents of the warehouse that was destroyed by fire?"

"It was completely filled with a recent shipment of straw, Mr. Holmes. We use straw in our brick-making operation."

A few words to my helpful neighbor obtained his cooperation about my practice. The next morning, carrying a bag and with my old service revolver in my coat pocket, I left for the train station. I found Sherlock Holmes seated in a first class carriage, wearing his usual traveling garb of tweeds and ear-flapped cap. He was sprawled out in his seat staring at the tips of his steepled fingers. By the restraint in which he returned my greeting I could tell he did not wish to be disturbed, so it was in silence that we traveled to Reading. When we arrived Holmes led the way as we descended from our carriage into a cloud of locomotive steam. We were met not by Mr. Trey Giltglider or his brother, but by an alert messenger clutching a slip of paper.

"Mr. Sherlock Holmes? Dr. Watson? Your description was given to me by Mr. Giltglider. This message is for you, Mr. Holmes." The man handed the paper to my friend. He then picked up our valises and led us through the crowds.

Holmes read the note and handed it to me. I felt a thrill of horror as I perused its contents:

"BERNARD ATTACKED AT HOME LAST NIGHT. ADMITTED ROYAL READING HOSPITAL. AWAIT YOU THERE. TREY GILTGLIDER."

We dismissed the messenger, hurried into the waiting cab and set off for the hospital. Holmes and I left our bags with the porter at the door and hurried down the indicated white-tiled corridor to find our client.

Trey Giltglider met us at the door to his brother's private room. I was shocked at the change in his appearance. His face had lost its rosy pink of the day before and was pale and drawn. His halo of fair hair was flying about over tired eyes anchored by heavy bags. He wordlessly wrung both our hands on the threshold and brought us to his brother's bedside.

Mr. Bernard Giltglider laid in the bed on his back, propped up by pillows, two wrapped hands resting on the coverlet. A gauze bandage was wrapped around his brow and bruises on his cheek and left eye gave him a battered look. It was obvious by his position in bed that his ribs were sore and bandaged. My practiced eye could tell, however, that while painful, his injuries were not life-threatening. His resemblance to his brother was startling and for a moment after we were introduced I stared at the invalid in disbelief.

"I hadn't realized that you and your brother were twins, Mr. Giltglider," I stammered.

Bernard Giltglider looked up at me through his silver-rimmed spectacles and grimaced with the effort to talk. "It is worse than that, Dr. Watson," he murmured. "My two brothers and I are triplets, alike as three peas in a pod. Of course, it will be easier to tell us apart now for a while."

"I wish to Heaven that Augustus were here to prove our similarities," groaned Trey Giltglider.

"Then you have not heard from your brother?" Holmes asked. Trey and Bernard Giltglider both shook their heads. Our client drew up a couple of chairs and we sat down next to the sickbed. Trey helped his brother to a sip of water from a glass tumbler on the nearby table and then nodded to my companion.

Sherlock Holmes gently inquired as to the particulars of the attack. Bernard answered as best he could, but when he showed signs of pain or weariness, his brother endeavored to assist.

Slowly the story took shape. Mr. Bernard Giltglider had arrived in Southampton the day before and proceeded at once by rail to Reading. His brother met him at the station and they went to Bernard's flat where Trey told him everything that had happened. The brothers agreed to meet in the morning and Trey left to go home. Travel-weary, Bernard went to bed soon after.

"When I awoke, it was dark. I groped for the candle to check my watch, Mr. Holmes, but I was stopped by a hoarse whisper from the blackest corner of my room. 'Don't strike a light, Mr. Giltglider,' I heard. 'Just listen. I'm giving you the same chance I gave your brother Augustus. I have contract papers here that give me your share of Giltglider Construction. Sign them and I'll let you live. You will leave England tonight. Refuse and you'll lose everything you value, including your worthless life.'"

"I could not believe the cheek of the fellow. It had to be a joke. 'Why in the world would I do such a thing, man? You must be mad,' I replied. I swung my legs out of bed, ready to pounce on the shadow, but his next words stopped me cold. 'Don't move, Mr. Giltglider. I'm armed. If you want your brother to live, you will do as I say. I broke in here with no trouble, and I can do it again, any place, any time. Believe me, Mr. Giltglider, I'm quite serious.'"

Bernard Giltglider turned his gaze from Sherlock Holmes to me and back again. "I felt that he meant every word of his threat, gentlemen. I have never heard such a cruel, merciless voice in my life. A chill wind seemed to blow over me and without thinking I launched myself off the bed and reached out for him. I think I grabbed rough cloth lapels before I found myself taking a terrific beating. It was like being mauled by a wild animal. Whoever he was, he was much larger and stronger than I. I must have lost consciousness because the next thing I remember the room was flooded with sunlight and I was on the floor with Trey kneeling next to me, calling my name."

"I got him to hospital at once," Trey Giltglider said. "I reported the attack to the police and they met us here. Just before you arrived the local police came back and told me that they had examined Bernard's rooms and found nothing, not a broken lock or a cracked window, to explain how anyone gained entry. There were no signs of struggle. Even the bedroom furniture, which had been knocked about, had been put back in place. That must have happened after we left for the hospital. In fact, the policeman intimidated that my brother may have gotten himself involved in some brawl in a low dive and to protect his reputation told me this wild story."

Bernard Giltglider fixed his glaze on Sherlock Holmes' face. "I swear everything I have told you is the truth, Mr. Holmes," he said earnestly. The detective nodded.

"I believe you, sir. Your brother Augustus's situation confirms your own story. Obviously he was offered the same deal, but chose to handle it differently. The notes he received indicate he decided to disregard the danger."

Holmes sat in thought for several minutes as we waited silently. After a while an orderly brought in a note for Trey Giltglider. He ripped open the envelope and cast his eye over the brief message. His horrified face looked wildly around the room. "I must go to Giltglider Construction at once!" he cried. "Another warehouse is on fire!"

Holmes and I scrambled to follow the excited man out of the room. "Mr. Giltglider! Mr. Giltglider! What's in that warehouse?" shouted Holmes as our client scurried down the hospital's hallway.

His voice bounced off the tiled walls back to us. "It's lumber, sir, a whole warehouse full of the finest sticks of English walnut available!"

Holmes clutched my shoulder. "Stay here, Watson. Do not let Bernard Giltglider out of your sight. Our opponent is cunning and ruthless and never has the danger been greater than now. I shall return as soon as I can." With that he ran down the hall after Trey Giltglider.

I returned to the injured man who was now agitated and restless. I tried to calm him, but his anxiety was such that finally I had to apply to the house physician to give him a sedative. After he fell asleep I sat by the bedside, musing on the case and Holmes' last words to me.

I confess that I was baffled. Obviously this new fire was in response to Bernard Giltglider's refusal to sign that odd contract his mysterious visitor had presented to him the night before. Holmes had said that he thought that Augustus Giltglider had been presented with a similar contract but had ignored the threat. Then the first warehouse fire had broken out. What could it all mean? What had happened to

Augustus? Had he become a victim of the assailant? Did that explain his absence for the past week? Or could it be possible that he was behind these fires? Was Augustus' disappearance only a ploy to divert suspicion from his own actions? Could Bernard Giltglider have been attacked by an agent of his own brother?

I looked at Bernard Giltglider's form under the white hospital coverings. Was he vulnerable even in his hospital bed to this assailant? Holmes must think so. I took out my revolver and checked its contents. As I returned it to my coat I realized that somehow the weight of it in my pocket was a comfort. Alone in the hospital room with that quiet figure I felt that I was in the center of what now seemed a huge trap, full of whispers.

The hours passed slowly and there was no news of Sherlock Holmes or Trey Giltglider. A sympathetic nurse brought me a sandwich and a cup of coffee for my lunch. The normal sounds and movements of a large city hospital flowed past the hall door, but within the room all was quiet. I remained tense and on guard. Everyone who entered was scrutinized closely and I kept a sharp eye on their movements. More than once I was grateful that my medical training let me understand their activities for I am sure a less informed man would have burst out with suspicion at each normal action.

In the middle of the afternoon a noise at the door made me tighten my grip on the weapon in my pocket, but it was only Holmes himself, followed by Trey Giltglider and

Inspector Lestrade. I suddenly realized how relieved I was to see them and to be no longer solely responsible for Bernard Giltglider's protection.

Our greetings were muted for Bernard was just waking up. After a moment Holmes motioned Lestrade and me out into the hall and left our client with his brother.

Both the detective and the Scotland Yard inspector showed signs of having been clambering over burned timbers and trudging through ashes. The unique stench of wood smoke clung to their persons and smuts of charcoal marked their clothing.

"What have you been doing?" I asked.

"We have been investigating the numerous scenes of the crimes, Watson," Holmes replied. He nodded to Lestrade, who flipped open the pages of his official notebook with a bemused air. "We met Inspector Lestrade at the Giltglider Construction yard. He had just been summoned from London, from where he thought he had put the nonexistent Giltglider case to rest."

"Now, now, Mr. Holmes," muttered the Inspector. "A respectable businessman gone off on a spree and an accidental warehouse fire don't always add up to a case for Scotland Yard, you know."

"But the fire wasn't accidental, Lestrade. If you had read my monograph on arson fires and examined the accompanying plates, you would have recognized the unique accelerant burn pattern I found on that beam by the first warehouse's back door." Sherlock Holmes turned to me. "Of course, with the other fire still active, I couldn't examine how it started, but I have no doubt that it will be the same. Two unrelated warehouse fires at the same location within days of each other would be too great a coincidence.

"After that the good Inspector allowed me to see both Augustus's and Bernard's rooms. I found nothing at Augustus's, but the disruption had been greater at Bernard Giltglider's. Whoever had cleaned up had done a meticulous job, but I was able to obtain these hairs from the carpet." He held up a glassine envelope containing several long black hairs.

"Bernard, being an identical triplet, has blond hair like his brothers, and he keeps no pets. His valet is on leave during his trip and his grey-haired charwoman cleaned his flat thoroughly against his arrival three days ago. I believe I will just dash down to the hospital's laboratory and see what I can discover from these. At least, I can determine if they are human." Before I could say a word, Holmes was gone.

Lestrade smiled at me. "Mr. Holmes' energy is astonishing, Dr. Watson. You should have seen him, climbing over those black bits of wood and sticking his nose into dirty crevices with that everlasting magnifying glass of his at the warehouse. It was the same at the Giltgliders' flats. He crawled over every square inch of those carpets like he was evaluating them for auction and as for the knick-knacks! You would have thought he was sounding them for secret compartments!"

Before I could point out that Holmes had found the hairs, a clue which had eluded the official police search, Bernard Giltglider's doctor appeared and spent several minutes in the sickroom conferring with his brother Trey. After he left, Trey Giltglider came out into the hallway and carefully closed the door behind him.

"Bernard has awakened and is much better now," said our client. "The doctor has told us that he can leave the hospital and stay at my house until he recovers. I will make arrangements for private nursing at home. All will be ready within the hour. You gentlemen and of course Mr. Holmes are welcome to stay at my place. Unlike my brothers, I invested in a big residence years ago and I have an excellent staff of servants. Believe me, it will be no trouble at all."

We agreed to Mr. Giltglider's plan and sent word to Holmes in the laboratory as to where we were going. A message came back that he had left the hospital but was expected to return.

Trey Giltglider hailed a four-wheeler. I retrieved our valises from the porter and we carefully conducted Bernard Giltglider to his brother's house. That turned out to be a large four-storied mansion of red brick with a Mansard roof. Numerous porches and gables with dormer windows decorated every exterior wall. The roof was studded with chimney stacks. Contrasting sandstone trim outlined the windows and doors. The structure occupied a corner lot with stables and outbuildings dividing it from its neighbors. An elaborate wrought iron fence encircled the grounds. Up and down the wide street stood similar extravagant homes.

A solemn butler and two footmen emerged to assist the invalid up the impressive front steps and through a wide foyer. Broad carpeted stairs graced with a curving fumed oak balustrade led to the upper floors. Lestrade was left below as Trey Giltglider and I saw Bernard Giltglider safely to a richly-appointed guest room on the first floor, where one of Florence Nightingale's best awaited him. We left him there and returned down the stairs, where Inspector Lestrade had been ushered into a tastefully decorated sitting room.

I stood in the center of the carpet and craned my neck to admire the furnishings. "Giltglider Construction must be doing well, sir," I remarked, as Trey Giltglider gave directions to the butler.

Trey Giltglider smiled for the first time that day. "I look upon all this as an investment, Dr. Watson," he replied. "I enjoy living in a comfortable fashion, but I also make sure I get value for my money. My brothers, now, have always preferred to live in flats and spend their incomes on pleasure and speculation. We are partners, but I have always saved and carefully invested my share of the business. I founded the brickworks, after all."

Tea was soon served and the hours before dinner passed in pleasant fashion as I found Mr. Trey Giltglider to be a man of education, well-traveled and particularly well-versed in the pleasures of the table. At hourly intervals a footman would bring down progress reports from his brother's sickroom. Lestrade ate and drank and listened to us, clearly in over his head but wise enough not to admit it. At one point he received a telegram reporting that the vanquished fire was now being investigated by the Reading police.

The butler, whom Mr. Giltglider addressed as Barrowby, finally appeared at the door to announce both Sherlock Holmes and dinner.

After an excellent meal, which Holmes merely picked at, we regrouped again in the sitting room. Lamps were lit against the gathering darkness and cigars and port were offered and accepted. Sherlock Holmes silently paced back and forth across Trey Giltglider's Persian carpet for several minutes as we continued the conversation started during the meal but then motioned Lestrade out into the hall. After a quarter of an hour he returned and called to Mr. Giltglider to join him. I got up to follow, but Holmes waved me back to my chair. I began to wonder what was going on. Why would Holmes consult with others and not me? It was obvious he was laying some sort of trap for the attacker.

Soon after I finished my cigar the door opened again and Sherlock Holmes entered. To my surprise he was carrying our hats and held a stout oak stick in one hand. He spoke softly as he handed me my hat.

"I expect an attack on Mr. Trey Giltglider and his brother tonight, Watson. Our opponent has failed in his original design and I fear he will now resort to pure vengeance. We must stop him. Follow me."

I tried to ask a question, but he held his finger to his lips. We left the sitting room ablaze in lights. Quietly we entered the back regions of the mansion, walking through a baize-covered door into the offices of the staff. The area was deserted. Holmes led the way up a narrow, uncarpeted staircase past several landings to a trap door that opened onto the roof.

I climbed out onto a confusing maze of leads, asphalt and brickwork. Darkened skylights ran down the center of the leads, irregular surfaces thrust up everywhere and iron railings and wooden steps led from one section of the irregular flat roof to another. Tall chimney stacks were spotted over the surface in clumps. In the darkness I found it hard to determine just where we were.

Sherlock Holmes had no such trouble, however. Holding my elbow, he guided me over the leads as if it were broad daylight. After a few minutes he paused in the shadow of a low parapet and pointed to a thick chimney stack topped with molded pots on the edge of the roof. Beyond it I could see the leaves of a tall tree and the glow of street lights below.

"That chimney serves the sitting room we just left, Watson. I believe it will be the focus of his attack. Is your revolver loaded? Have you your whistle? Good. I have my pistol and this stick. Lestrade knows what to do. Giltglider has taken all the occupants of the house to rooms at the other end. Now we wait."

I crouched beside him and murmured, "What are we waiting for, Holmes?"

The detective's voice was low and vibrant. He could not conceal the excitement he felt at this moment of the chase. "Death."

The only sounds were night birds and the rumble of distant traffic. The moon was only a sliver and darkness picked out by the wheeling constellations filled the night. A slight breeze slipped past us and I could hear Holmes breathing beside me. I don't know how long we were huddled there in the shadows, but gradually I became conscious of a soft shuffling sound.

Advancing and pausing, advancing and then pausing again, footsteps approached our position. I strained to see in the blackness. It seemed hours until the sounds passed us and approached the chimney stack we were watching. After they stopped I could make out by the distant street lights an indistinct figure bending over something. A spark flared and then grew into a tiny flame. Something began to sputter and burn and the figure rose with it in one hand. I felt Sherlock Holmes coming to his feet and I followed.

Holmes ran ahead of me, his stick raised against the stars. I heard the crack of wood on bone and saw the sputtering package fall at my feet. The oak stick went flying and Holmes and the shapeless intruder grappled on the flat apex of the roof leads. I reached down to the sparking light and picked up what proved to be a bundle of paper-covered cylinders tied together and sporting a lit fuse less than ten inches long. In horrid fascination I watched as another inch quickly burned away.

A pistol skittered away across the leads. "Watson! Watson!" I heard Holmes yell and then his voice sank into incoherent gurgling. I didn't think to throw away the bomb. In the back of my mind I was conscious of the presence of hundreds of people in the houses around us. No place I could lob it seemed safe enough. Instead, I grasped the burning fuse in my left hand and tried to tug it free of the bundle. The sparks burned into my palm. Involuntarily, I cried out in pain and dropped the infernal device. It landed on the leads and bounced a few feet away. I leapt for it and desperately stamped out the lit fuse. When the last spark was crushed into oblivion beneath my heel I turned to look for my friend.

I saw Holmes flat on his back beneath the hulking form of his attacker. Strong fingers were clamped around his throat and his struggles were weakening.

I pulled out my revolver and crashed it on the back of the figure's head. He swung his snarling face around to look at me as if I was just an annoying fly. I cocked the weapon and placed it at his temple. "Release him now or by God I swear I will shoot!" I cried. He must have seen the determination in my eyes for he released his prey and fell back to slump on the roof at Holmes' side.

I pulled the police whistle from my waistcoat pocket with my wounded hand and blew it urgently. Scrambling footsteps pounded across the rooftop toward us and Lestrade and others ran out of the darkness to clamp handcuffs on my prisoner. A long wicked-looking knife was pulled out from inside his coat. Uniformed men took him in charge as I bent over the motionless figure of my friend.

For a moment I thought I had been too slow and my finger tightened on the trigger of the revolver that was still pointed at his attacker. Then Holmes's eyes opened and he coughed, his fingers feeling for his throat. I disarmed my weapon and thrust it back in my pocket. Wordlessly I lifted him to his feet and slowly we helped each other across the leads in the darkness toward the light coming from the hatchway in the roof.

Thirty minutes later I sat in one of Mr. Trey Giltglider's armchairs in his sitting room, my bandaged left hand throbbing in pain. The private nurse for Bernard Giltglider had tended to it, but the burns from the dynamite fuse had bitten deep into my flesh. I had accepted a painkiller by the police surgeon before he left, but now fought back its effects. I wanted to stay alert to see after Holmes, who was lying on a sitting room sofa, his face white in the lamplight, with irregular dull red blotches around his neck.

Trey Giltglider and his brother Bernard were seated on another sofa across from us. They had come down from their hiding place after our struggles on the roof. Inspector Lestrade loomed over his prisoner, who had been shoved to his knees on the floor in the middle of the room. Several husky Reading policemen stood just a few feet away. The butler Barrowby had stationed himself by the door to the hall.

Lestrade's prisoner glared at us all through a thicket of tangled black hair. He was a burly man, over six feet tall, with broad shoulders and large writhing hands, dressed in a rough coat, tattered shirt and old trousers, with heavy worn boots upon his feet. The Scotland Yard inspector had given him the official warning but the man appeared unmoved. Lestrade prodded him with Holmes' revolver and demanded, "Tell me your name!" but all he got back was a snarl through bright, sharp teeth.

Holmes raised his hand. "Watson, help me up," he whispered. I hastened to do so, propping him up with cushions, and then sat near him with my finger on his pulse.

"Try not to talk too much, Holmes," I murmured, knowing that my advice would be ignored. Sherlock Holmes looked long and hard at the man on the carpet and then addressed Inspector Lestrade.

His voice was weak and raspy, kept at a low volume by the pain in his throat. In the next few minutes, he stopped frequently for sips of water from a glass that sat at his elbow. Except for growling sounds from the man on the floor, the room was silent as we all strained to hear the detective.

"His name is Wolfgang Novak," said the detective. "He was born in Lambeth of Slavic parents, but got his education at a council school in Southwark. He began as a laborer and then learned fine carpentry. He has been employed by several Reading construction firms in the last three years. A deeper examination of his background will no doubt turn up a career of thievery and assault. He holds anarchistic views but has not yet given up his dreams of wealth. He wrote the notes Augustus Giltglider received, set both warehouse fires and, I regret to say, killed Augustus Giltglider and, given his nature, probably disposed of the body in a particularly nasty way." Holmes coughed and sipped water.

His last words caused a sensation. The two surviving Giltgliders looked at each other and tears swelled in their eyes. Lestrade stared from his prisoner to Holmes. The squad of policemen behind Lestrade muttered amongst themselves and seemed to lean even more menacingly over the prisoner. The man on the floor grimaced as Holmes' began talking, but by the time my friend had finished he was giving the detective the same amazed look I had frequently seen on clients' faces in the sitting room in Baker Street.

Wolfgang Novak stirred under Lestrade's restraining hand. "Who told you, Mr. Meddler? Who peached on me, you snoop? I'll kill him!"

Holmes took another drink of water. "You told me yourself, Novak. Your speech betrayed your origins, your handwriting showed your education and the calluses on your hands told of your occupation. Those stains upon your coat could only come from expensive varnish used in fine woodworking. The odor, though faint, is distinctive. The notes you sent Augustus Giltglider were made by the broad, flat lead of a carpenter's pencil, a marker made so it would not roll away after being put down. Search his pockets, Lestrade, and you may find it. Ah, just so.

"Armed with your physical description built up from the clues I gathered from Mr. Bernard Giltglider and those hairs I found at his flat, I visited several Reading construction firms this afternoon. I found out about all your employments, although the name was never the same twice. You used your own name, Wolfgang Novak, three years ago when you first came to Reading. After you thought of this scheme, Novak disappeared, and a man of many names but with your appearance and skills took his place. The thievery and assault were just speculation, given your personal proclivities. Your bomb is constructed on the common pattern known to the authorities of those used by anarchist groups in England. You must have been a member of such a group to be given instructions on how to build one. You chose to persecute the Giltgliders because they are among the richest men in

Reading. Yet you formed a plan to gain control of their business, showing that you still sought wealth.

"The grit on your clothing matches the dirt on the notes. The burns on your hands come from two recent fires, as can be determined by the rate of healing of each. By the way, that was really rather clumsy of you. As for Augustus Giltglider.....oh, my, he just didn't believe you were serious, did he?"

"He laughed at me," the prisoner growled. "He said my contract was worthless. I tried to make him understand I was going to kill him if he didn't sign, but he kept laughing right up to the moment I wrapped my hands around his fat throat."

Trey Giltglider leapt to his feet. "What did you with him?" he cried. He stood, quivering with emotion, before the kneeling figure on his sitting room carpet.

"One of the men I worked with before had a sister in the country with a job on a farm." Wolfgang Novak looked up at Mr. Giltglider, his eyes hard and sneering. His voice was bitter and defiant. "I got a cart and put his body in it by the light of the flames that Saturday night. I covered it with some apples and drove it out to the farm. There I dumped the whole load in the pigpen. By the time those animals were finished there was nothing left but bits of bones and apple cores. I collected up as many bones as I could find and buried them in the woods behind the farmer's house. All rich men are pigs. I figured it was a fitting end. It made me laugh, I'll tell you."

Trey Giltglider, his face a mask of horror, staggered away from Novak and sank down beside his brother, who buried his face in his bandaged hands.

"That is enough, man," said Sherlock Holmes, disgusted. "Take away your prisoner, Lestrade, and may you have joy of him."

"Not much chance of that, Mr. Holmes, but we'll have a good hanging out of him, at least." Several officers yanked the prisoner to his feet and Lestrade followed him from the room as Barrowby held the door.

I poured out more water for Holmes and at his gesture, added some brandy. Holmes looked at Trey and Bernard Giltglider and sighed. "I regret having to bring you gentlemen such bad news, but the truth cannot be changed. Wolfgang Novak was one of the most dangerous men I ever faced, and I think we can all count ourselves lucky that we escaped with our lives."

"Poor, poor Augustus," mourned Trey Giltglider. "I always told him he should be more serious, but the one time it counted he still saw nothing but a joke. My brother and I thank you both and you will see that we are most grateful. It is not yet midnight. You are both welcome to stay here until your injuries are healed."

"No, thank you, we will leave in the morning," Sherlock Holmes declared, rising to his feet. He coughed again and rubbed the bruises on his throat. "A period of convalescence is called for, and cool ocean breezes are in the prescription. Come, Watson. We shall face the new day as the poet Henley wrote, 'Bloody, but unbowed'. Good night, gentlemen."

The Case of the Wobbly Watcher

Sherlock Holmes stood on the cobblestones of the street, his head sunk upon his chest and his hands clasped behind his back. Around him bustled members of Scotland Yard, holding back the crowds and conferring with each other. Down the street several newsmen were clamoring to approach, waving their notebooks and shouting questions. The streetlamps had been lit and the glow of the nearest one threw Holmes' shadow up against the rough brick wall on his right. I stood near him, my medical bag in hand, my eyes searching for something else to look at except the broken body at our feet.

Inspector Lestrade detached himself from a nearby group and walked up to us. His sharp nose and bright eyes shone in the yellow gaslight. He ignored the detective and addressed me. "What do you think, Dr. Watson?"

I sighed. "When you called me out here, Inspector, I didn't think it was to establish time of death. What happened to your regular police surgeon?"

"Influenza. Half the force is down with it."

"I can believe you. I've been run off my feet these last two weeks with patients of my own. Well, I've examined the body. He died from crushing injuries on his left side. From the position of the body, he fell from the top of this wall and landed on the cobblestones."

"Jumped, fell or was pushed, Doctor?"

"That is the question, Inspector."

"What time do you think it happened?"

I turned and looked at the body again. "It's hard to say. What information do you have?"

Lestrade opened his official notebook. "According to witnesses Mr. Humphrey Dumfrey was in the habit of sitting on this stretch of wall observing the daily passing of the Palace Guards on their way to and from Buckingham Palace twice a day. Nothing unusual was noticed earlier this afternoon. After the parade he had tea in the little teashop on the corner. Later he was seen walking toward his flat. Little was known of his movements for several hours. Then some men coming home from the local public house found him like this just after dark."

I nodded. "He must have died just before he was found. The cobblestones are still slick. Nothing has congealed even now."

Holmes finally stirred. "Who found him, Inspector?"

Lestrade puffed up a little bit. "I'm very sure that it was kind of you to accompany Dr. Watson tonight, Mr. Holmes, but I want it understood that Scotland Yard has this case in hand. Any information given out will be addressed to the doctor in his temporary official capacity."

My friend stiffened and stepped back. "Excuse me." His voice was cold and he was clearly insulted. "Watson, I will see you back in Baker Street."

"Wait, Holmes," I pleaded. "Inspector, as the doctor on this case I may call in any consultant I need, may I not?"

Lestrade shuffled his feet. He clearly realized that he had been unnecessarily rude to Sherlock Holmes and now he grasped my inquiry as a face-saving move. "Yes, you may. Mr. Holmes, if I have said something untoward, I apologize. I have not forgotten the many times you have assisted us in the past."

I stepped closer to the still figure by the wall. "Please, Holmes. Don't leave me out here alone with only Scotland Yard."

Despite himself, Holmes chuckled. "Very well, Watson. Proceed."

Lestrade referred to his notebook again. "The three men were a butcher, a baker and a candlestick maker. They were in the habit of meeting at the "Three Blind Mice" to have a pint after work. They left there and were walking up to London Bridge when they stumbled over the victim."

"Where did Mr. Dumfrey reside?"

The Inspector turned over several pages. "He had rooms nearby. I talked to his landlady and she said he spent the time after tea in his room reading a lexicon. Humphrey Dumfrey was very fond of words and spent most of his time with dictionaries, thesauruses and other publications, making notes for a definitive work he had been compiling for years."

"Nothing strange, odd, unusual or peculiar about that," murmured Holmes.

One of the local police called Lestrade aside for a moment. The Scotland Yard man returned in the company of a little crooked man. He wore a little crooked hat and moved with the help of a little crooked stick.

Lestrade introduced him to us as Mr. L. C. Mann. He looked up at us and I could see by the lamplight that he had been crying. "'Umphrey Dumfrey were my best friend, gentlemen. Many was the times we sat in 'is rooms, arguin' about the origin of the word "glory". I still can't believe 'e's gone." Carefully Mann avoided looking at the broken body in the street.

"Did Mr. Dumfrey have any enemies?" Holmes asked.

Mr. Mann shook his head and tried to give us a little crooked smile. "There were 'at little blond-'aired girl what disagreed with 'im, but 'at were years ago. No, I'd say 'e were the most 'armless person I knew. 'Is greatest joy were sittin' on 'at wall and watchin' all the King's 'Orses an' all the King's Men ride past."

A shudder shook his little crooked body. "I shall miss 'im so!" he cried. "'E were a good egg!"

Holmes and Lestrade continued the investigation after that night but a definitive answer as to the cause of Humphrey Dumfrey's demise was never established. I once asked Holmes if he ever developed a theory of the case.

"I have a suspect, but there isn't enough evidence to go to court," he admitted.

"Well, can you tell me if he jumped, fell or was pushed?"

Sherlock Holmes solemnly filled his pipe and lit it with an ember from the fireplace. He leaned forward and fixed me with a glittering eye.

"Watson, I think he was goosed!"

The Case of the Weary Wanderer

"You must help me, Mr. Holmes, or my life is ruined!"

At the sound of that dramatic announcement, I looked up to see Mr. Ashton Fellows, just ushered in by our landlady, as he stood in the doorway of the sitting room at 221b Baker Street. I saw a young man, slim in ruddy tweeds, clean-shaven, with a thatch of fair hair and bright blue eyes shining out of a peaches and cream complexion, reddened by exposure to the cold air outside. A blue knitted muffler was wrapped around his neck. He wore a shabby grey overcoat and held a brown paper parcel in one hand and his soft cloth cap in the other. Holmes motioned him to the sofa as Mrs. Hudson closed the door against the hallway draughts.

It was during the end of the first year of my association with Sherlock Holmes. I had not begun to write of his adventures, although we had worked together in several cases. I was not yet accustomed to seeing possible clients suddenly appear at our sitting room door. I stood up awkwardly from my seat by the fire, unpleasant weather having aggravated the wound I bore as a remembrance of my participation in the fatal battle of Maiwand.

It was a stormy morning in the middle of December, with frost on the windows and snow drifts piling up on the pavement beneath our cozy rooms. The gas lights that burned in the windows of the businesses up and down Baker Street gleamed only faintly against the blizzard. For weeks the weather had been chilly and miserable. That day the leaden sky was spitting down frozen flakes of snow that drove even holiday merrymakers off the streets and into the dun-colored buildings of London.

Holmes cast his eye over our client as the young man took his seat. He scribbled something on a half-sheet of paper from his chair by the fireplace. After a minute the detective drawled, "I deduce from your flowing necktie and long paint-speckled fingers that you are an artist. From your worn shoes and frayed shirt cuffs I see that your talent has not yet been recognized by an appreciative public. Watson, stir up the fire. Our visitor has been out tramping the streets in this chilly winter weather and would appreciate some tea. Ring for Mrs. Hudson, give her this note and have her add the odd sandwich to that tea. Now, pray tell, how may I help you?"

Our visitor was sitting on the edge of the sofa and speaking earnestly to Holmes when I returned from giving the message to our landlady.

"There is this girl...let me tell you about her, Mr. Holmes. She is an angel! What a profile! Skin like the finest marble and eyes...green pools a man could drown in! And her hair...thick and glossy in a chestnut shade! When she speaks it's like singing!"

"Can you give us the lady's name?" Holmes lit his pipe and leaned back in his chair. He nodded to me and I drew out my notebook.

"Cynthia," sighed Mr. Fellows. "Isn't that a beautiful name?" He sat on the edge of the cushions, suddenly quiet, a little smile on his lips and a faraway look in his eye. I sat for a moment staring at him and then shifted my gaze to Holmes. He was looking closely at Mr. Fellows as a wisp of tobacco smoke drifting lazily upwards from his old clay pipe. Mrs. Hudson appeared with a tray of sandwiches and tea. I poured our client a cup of steaming liquid and he eagerly picked up a sandwich.

I spoke. "How did you meet?"

"She was sitting in the corner of my friend's apartment at a party a week ago. He is a sculptor and was leaving for Scotland the next day. Some of us got together and gave him a little send-off. I saw her as I came in. She was wearing a green and white dress that set off her eyes. We talked of Wordsworth. For hours, we talked of Wordsworth."

"I do not see your problem, Mr. Fellows," said the detective drily. "Surely you do not need my help in wooing this paragon."

Suddenly all the animation went out of Ashton Fellows' face and he looked forlornly at Sherlock Holmes.

"My problem is that I have lost her, Mr. Holmes."

Holmes slowly set aside his pipe and gave Fellows all his attention.

"Indeed, sir? Please explain."

"You must understand, Mr. Holmes. It was an impromptu party at an artist's loft. There were a lot of people there and I didn't know all of them. Guests came and went all evening. I never caught her last name. Our conversation was absorbing and frankly, at the time, her last name didn't seem important."

I stirred. "Who introduced you?"

Ashton Fellows smiled at me. "Clearly, Dr. Watson, you haven't spent much time with struggling artists. We live in Bohemia. The staid manners and formal conventions of society don't exist in our lives. With us everything is free and open. We sat together and talked all evening and then, in an instant, she disappeared."

"Surely she wasn't a spirit!"

Fellows shook his head. "Oh, she was flesh and blood, Doctor. Of that I am certain. But she did leave suddenly. I had turned away for only a moment and when I turned back...she was gone! I might have considered the entire evening a dream, except that she left these behind." He held out the brown paper parcel.

I took it from him and carefully folded back the paper. Within was a dainty pair of green party slippers in the current fashionable Grecian style, with long trailing tie-straps. Holmes leaned forward and drew them into his lap. He picked up his large magnifying glass and examined first one and then the other. Fellows finished the plate of sandwiches and I poured out the last of the tea. Holmes looked at our client.

"Are you saying she left the party in her stocking feet?" he inquired.

"Not in the weather we have been having!" I exclaimed.

Fellows smiled ruefully. "I saw a pair of outdoor boots tucked next to her chair while we were talking. Doubtlessly she had changed out of her boots when she first arrived, then slipped them back on before she left. There was no provision made for ladies' wraps. Her coat was folded on the back of her chair."

Mrs. Hudson knocked on our door and handed me an envelope for Holmes. He tore it open, read the contents and threw the paper into the fire.

"That party was a week ago, Mr. Fellows. What have you done in all this time to find her?' asked the detective.

Fellows shoved his weary feet with their worn shoes out in front of him on the carpet. "I searched for her, Mr. Holmes. I can't afford cabs or even always the omnibus, so I have been walking. I visited everyone I knew who had attended the party and as I talked to them I got more names of guests. Then I went to see them. No one could tell me who she was. I even visited the various public houses in the area of the party, like the "Midnight Belle" and the "Golden Coach". I tried to distract myself from thinking of her by painting but even that has failed. I can't stop remembering that night."

"What of your friend who had the flat where the party took place?"

"I telegraphed him in Edinburgh. He claimed not to know who she was either. Please find her, Mr. Holmes. I must find her or my whole life will count for nothing."

"My dear Mr. Fellows…" I began.

Our client jumped to his feet, his fists clenched. "I mean it, sir! I must find her or I…I cannot answer for what might happen!"

Sherlock Holmes rose and put a steady hand on the man's shoulder. "Calm yourself, please. I need you to do something for me while I work on your case."

"Anything, Mr. Holmes!"

"I want you to return home and get some rest. You are overwrought and exhausted. I have four different leads to follow on your young lady. Come back tomorrow morning at 10 o'clock and I should have some results for you."

"You give me hope, Mr. Holmes?"

"To go with the tea and sandwiches, Mr. Fellows."

"I will return tomorrow. Thank you!"

I watched from the window as Ashton Fellows emerged from our door and trudged down the street into the teeth of the storm. Indignantly I turned to Holmes. Emotion seized me as I thought of that young man's struggles. I shook my head at my friend.

"How could you, Holmes? That poor lad is obviously in love. You have promised him results by tomorrow and he has been searching for that girl for a week!"

"That is all the more reason for him to get some rest. I have already started inquiries."

"How?"

"With that note you gave to Mrs. Hudson. I asked Cooke, the proprietor of the art and frame shop on the corner, about Mr. Fellows. He is a respectable artist, if such a creature can exist, from a vicar's family in Setton Cross, Kent. He is twenty-five years old, poor, but greatly talented and spoken of in some circles as the next Constable."

"What other leads could you possibly have?"
Holmes picked up one of the green party shoes by one of its long straps. "Here is one. Observe, Watson. I do not claim to be a fashion expert for young ladies, but I know a hand-made shoe when I see one. Look at the stitching and the craftsmanship displayed in this dainty slipper." He handed me the footwear. "The ladies are your department, Doctor. What can you tell me of this bit of frippery?"

I borrowed his magnifying glass and examined it closely. "Well, it is obviously a party shoe. It is much too flimsy to wear to walk about in the countryside. The sole is too thin even for city streets. It speaks of hardwood floors and orchestras."

"Perfectly sound!"

I felt encouraged. I turned it over in my hand and tried to think of something more to say. "This shoe has barely been worn. The sole is only lightly scuffed."

"Well done, Watson! You progress!" responded Sherlock Holmes.

I handed the footwear back to the detective. "That is all."

"Not quite all, my dear Doctor. There are at least two more points. Look at the color. This shade of green was made very popular six months ago when the Princess of Wales wore a gown of emerald hue to a ball given by the Duchess of Marlborough. I do read more than the agony columns, you see."

"You astonish me, Holmes!"

He picked up the glass and peered inside the slipper. "Finally, if you look very closely, you can see the stamp of the maker just over the heel. 'Gottmater and Co.' Hand me down my index, if you please."

I gave him the thick volume he indicated.

"My collection of Gs has its interesting points. On this page is Geller the forger and David Gill, the explorer who found the source of the Nompuso River. Here is Preston George, who gave me such an exciting few minutes at the Monte Carlo Casino two years ago. What a talkative old reprobate he was! Ah, here is Gottmater and Co." He read silently for a moment and then snapped the book shut.

"I see I am for an Arctic expedition, Watson. I am going to brave the elements to Bond Street." He began to pull on his outer garments and slipped the shoes into his overcoat pocket. I reached for my hat. "No, Doctor. Your injury should stay out of this weather and next to the fire. I will return in time for tea."

Again I stood at the frosty window, this time watching as my friend stepped out into the storm. Thankfully I noticed that the wind had dropped and more people had ventured out upon the pavement. A couple of bundled-up figures were already sweeping away the snow drifts that had accumulated against the storefronts. I picked up a yellow-backed novel and settled down by the fire.

I took my mid-day meal tray from Mrs. Hudson's hand at one o'clock. The storm had ceased by then. A clear sparkling street greeted my eyes as I glanced out later to see Sherlock Holmes descending from a cab. He looked thoughtful.

He greeted me but said little and after drinking a cup of tea managed to occupy his time in a complicated chemical study that precluded talk until I went to bed.

The next morning I arose late to find the weather had greatly improved. Sunshine streamed though our sitting room windows and made a brave effort to melt the frost clinging to the glass panes. I had barely finished my breakfast before Mr. Ashton Fellows was shown up. Holmes had already eaten and greeted our visitor with a smile and an offer of the last eggs in the dish.

"Do you have news, Mr. Holmes?" Fellows asked between mouthfuls of food.

"Yes, I have. Finish your coffee, Mr. Fellows. If you wish, we do have an appointment in a short time with the object of your quest."

Was I imagining it, or was there a note of warning in Holmes' voice?

"You have found her? Marvelous! How?"

"I will explain as we go. Have you finished your breakfast? Very well. Doctor, your coat." Holmes hustled us out of the house and into a passing four-wheeler. He gave directions to the driver and then joined us inside. As the coach started down Baker Street toward Marylebone Road my friend turned to Mr. Fellows.

"This was an interesting yet simple problem," he began. "The first thing I did, Mr. Fellows, was establish your bona fides."

Our client frowned. "Why?"

"Please do not take offense. You admitted that the young lady was a stranger to you. I had to assure myself that you meant no harm to the object of your search. If there had been a previous history of unpleasant encounters between you and the lady, I would have informed you that I was unable to help you. I refuse to be used as a location service for harassment."

Ashton Fellows looked upset. "I assure you, Mr. Holmes, my interests are clean and pure! I want to…to…"

Holmes raised a hand. "Dr. Watson has already diagnosed your condition, sir. Once I determined that you were fairly harmless, I proceeded. An examination of the slippers you left with us disclosed the fact that the shoes were hand-made and gave the name of the maker. I questioned the cobbler. I had done him a good turn once and he was favorably disposed to me. He remembered the order and told me the name and address of the customer.

"I had already deduced that the young woman came from a prosperous family. Fashion that follows the whims of Royalty costs money to do so. I visited the household in question, returned the shoes and spoke to the young lady and her mother."

I noticed with interest that Ashton Fellows was trembling. "What did Cynthia say?"

"She easily recalled the party, you and the conversation you shared. When I explained to what great lengths you had gone to in order to find her, she agreed to see you this morning. We are nearly there now."

Our cab drew up in front of a stately mansion. I looked around as we exited the vehicle and recognized the area as a street in Mayfair. Richly appointed buildings lined both sides of a boulevard featuring a row of leafless trees running down the center.

Sherlock Holmes stopped on the pavement and looked squarely at our client, "Are you sure, Mr. Fellows, that you want to go through with this interview?"

The young man looked bewildered. "Mr. Holmes, I have thought of nothing but Cynthia for over a week. I must talk to her."

"Very well." Holmes shrugged. He led us up a broad set of steps and rang the bell. A solemn butler admitted us into a wide hallway. A moment later the three of us were ushered into a rather overly-decorated drawing room. Tall windows on two sides, draped in the finest of brocades with frilly sheer curtains peeping out from behind them, allowed in the bright winter light. Highly polished tables and bookcases loaded with volumes in rich morocco bindings filled the well-proportioned space. The floors were covered in Persian carpets. Comfortable armchairs stood next to little stands laden with tapestry cloths and china knick-knacks. Golden gaslight augmented the winter sun. Two fashionably dressed women sat side-by-side on a cut-velvet sofa facing an large fireplace wherein crackled a generous blaze.

Our client advanced before us, his eyes fixed on a young woman who sat with the light gleaming off her chestnut hair. She stood up and extended her hand. He grasped it wordlessly. The other woman, older but with a familial resemblance to her companion, rose and gave her hand first to Holmes, then to me, as Holmes murmured introductions. She frowned at the sound of Ashton Fellows' name.

"Mrs. Bock, Dr. Watson. Miss Cynthia Bock, you have already met Mr. Fellows."

Our client shook hands with Mrs. Bock. She waved us to side chairs that had been drawn up to the sofa and we all sat down. As I settled in, I detected something unusual in this meeting. Somehow it wasn't what I had expected. Flames danced in the big fireplace and sunlight shone through the tall windows but the atmosphere around the women was chilly. Cynthia Bock regarded us graciously, but there was a detachment in her attitude that I had not foreseen from the description given by Ashton Fellows. I looked at Holmes. His expression was remote and hard to read. The tense atmosphere was explained when Mrs. Bock began to speak.

She turned to Mr. Fellows and addressed him in a stern voice. "I understand from Mr. Holmes, sir, that you met my daughter at a party a week ago."

"That is correct," the young man said.

"Cynthia and I have spoken about this," Mrs. Bock said stiffly. "I must tell you, Mr. Fellows, that I did not know that my daughter had attended that party. It was not the sort of party of which my husband or I would have approved. Artistic people as a class are frequently undisciplined and often display a shocking lack of morals. Cynthia knows this. She left the house without informing us. She was not properly chaperoned. A young painter who had met her recently in regards to a possible commission had told her about the party. He escorted her, in secret, at her request. She knew that we would never have allowed her to do such a reckless thing. I am very disappointed in her and she has apologized for her actions. My major goal now is to see that her fiancé does not learn of her ill-chosen escapade."

Ashton Fellows looked stricken. "Her fiancé?"

Cynthia Bock smiled. "I am engaged to marry Viscount Sidney Jarlson, the oldest son of the Earl of Danegeld. The wedding is to take place in a few weeks."

He stared at her. "Do you love him?" he asked finally.

She looked into the fire, her profile cool and undisturbed. "He is not bad-looking, you know. He has handsome mustaches." She smiled. "Someday I shall be a countess."

"That question is unworthy of a gentleman, Mr. Fellows!" Mrs. Bock snapped. She frowned and rose to her feet. We all stood up, Ashton Fellows rather unsteadily.

At that moment a young woman stepped into the drawing room from the hall. Her long brown hair was worn in a simple fashion that framed her oval face. She was wearing a plain grey dress trimmed in small black bows in a double row down the bodice. Her eyes were brown and kind. The very air seemed warmer when she smiled.

Mrs. Bock noticed her and asked, "Miss King, has the seamstress arrived yet?"

"Yes, Mrs. Bock. I showed her up to the sewing room. I left those patterns and the new bolts of fabric you ordered for her to look over. She has some questions."

"Miss Cynthia and I will join her. These gentlemen are leaving. Please see them out and then come up yourself." With a haughty toss of her head, Mrs. Bock led her daughter out of the room. In the hall, we could hear Cynthia Bock attempting to explain the reason for her actions to her mother. "I just wanted to do something exciting and fun before I settled down with Sidney. He really is a dear but just a bit…stuffy."

"This way, if you please, gentlemen," said the newcomer. She smiled pleasantly and motioned toward the hall. Ashton Fellows followed Holmes to the door and then stopped. He looked closely at the young woman.

"Don't I know you, miss? Why, it's little Frannie! Mr. Holmes and Dr. Watson, this is Miss Frances King, the daughter of my old schoolmaster back in Setton Cross. I haven't seen you since I came down to London, Frannie. What are you doing here?"

The young lady seemed pleased to acknowledge us. Her face lit up in pleasure when she turned to our client. "Ashton, what a surprise! I work here as Mrs. Bock's paid companion. You see, Father died just over a year ago," and at that point her smile faltered and she touched one of the little black bows, "and I had to make my own way in the world. We never had much money on Father's schoolmaster salary. I was rather bewildered until I thought to write to Mrs. Bock. She was a sort of a cousin of Mother's. She brought me down from Setton Cross and I have been here nearly a year."

Fellows smiled. "It is so good to see someone from home."

Miss King opened the front door. "I would love to stay and talk, Ashton, but they are expecting me upstairs."

Our client grabbed her hand. "When can I see you again?"

She smiled. "Every Thursday afternoon I walk in Kew Gardens."

He smiled back at her. "It is very beautiful in Kew Gardens."

The door closed gently behind us.

Holmes and I found out the end of the story six months later. One morning the regular bundle of newspapers Holmes was in the habit of reading each day was carried up by Mrs. Hudson. The pile yielded up the *Daily News,* which carried an announcement of the marriage of the rising artist Mr. Ashton Fellows to Miss Frances King, only daughter of the late Mr. Wilber King, M.A., at St. Osmond's Church in Setton Cross, Kent. The happy couple was honeymooning in Paris, where Mr. Fellows' first gallery showing was being held to universal acclaim.

Also delivered was a large package. Using the jack-knife from the mantelpiece, Holmes cut the cord that secured the brown paper wrapping and opened it. A card fell to the floor. I bent to pick it up and raised my eyes to see in Holmes' hands a square of stretched canvas. He held it out for me to examine.

Signed by the artist, it was an exquisite painting of a pair of discarded green dancing slippers, their tangled tie-straps trailing into the foreground over a drift of frozen snow.

I handed him the card. On it were written only two words---'Thank you'.

The Case of the Beguiling Burglar

The effect of my experiences in service to my country in Afghanistan had sent me back to London in 1880 with my health ruined. Over time my physical state improved and I regained my strength, although bad weather and overexertion could remind me of my trials. In 1885 a particularly busy four months assisting Sherlock Holmes wore thin my resistance and I found myself in the rare position of needing a doctor for myself. A severe case of pneumonia was diagnosed and I was confined to my bed, too ill to be moved to hospital.

Sherlock Holmes and Mrs. Hudson showed me every attention. Holmes hired trained nurses and Mrs. Hudson insisted on helping to pull me through the crisis. When the worst was over Mrs. Hudson fussed over me and Holmes sent for out-of-season delicacies to tempt my appetite, played my favorite airs on the violin and found topics of interest to occupy the long and weary hours of convalescence.

One day, after I had recovered enough to lie upon the sofa in the sitting room for a few hours a day, he surprised me by bringing out his old tin trunk from his bedroom. He threw open the lid and cast a speculative eye in my direction.

"I wonder if you are strong enough for me to burden you with a story from my past, Watson. I have here the documents of a case from the first year I began my consulting detective practice."

I felt a sudden rush of excitement, the likes of which I had not experienced in over a month. "I would like nothing better, Holmes."

"Are you certain you are up to it? You have been very ill and I have strict instructions from Mrs. Hudson not to cause you fatigue."

"I shall rest afterward," I promised. Holmes arranged the pillows so I could sit up a little and I peered into the trunk at the bundles that held information about his mysterious and unknown early cases.

Apparently satisfied, my friend pulled up a chair and began to rifle through the rolls of papers bound up with tape. At last he held up a sheaf of papers and smiled.

"As I have said before, most of my early cases came from the recommendations of men I knew from college. This was among the first of those I accepted after I moved to London.

"I was sitting in my rooms on Montague Street, reading a history of Jonathan Wild, when Magnus Custennin knocked on my door. He stood at least six feet, seven inches tall, with broad shoulders, white hair, deep-set blue eyes and a permanently sad expression on his face. I deduced that he was about fifty years old, in uncertain health, and grew up on a farm near Anoeth, Wales, where he still farmed. I didn't get a chance to test my observations, however, because he immediately began to set his case before me."

I interrupted. "How did you know those things about him?"

"His age was evident. A slight tremor and the color of his skin told of the state of his health. His speech pinpointed the location where he grew up. A fragment of green vine resting in his pant cuff and the calluses on his hands told me he was a farmer.

"Amazing!"

"Elementary. I did make one mistake. He no longer lived in Wales. His farm was forty miles northwest of London, just beyond Upper Oddton. I should have seen that from the mud on his boots. I was young then."

I smothered a smile and waited for Holmes to continue his story.

"He seated himself on my sofa and told me his tale of woe. He had heard of me from a man who had been in the same botany class as I. After leaving his father's farm in Wales, he had traveled around and worked at odd jobs until he settled near Upper Oddton. There he bought and improved an old farm into a most profitable operation. He raised beans and developed a new strain of goose. The eggs were prized by dealers for their golden hue. After many years, when he had saved some money, he married a local girl and took her to his isolated farmhouse on top of a hill. She had had several suitors and he was surprised that she had chosen him.

"About a month after that, he started hearing strange noises in the night. A mysterious figure was seen in the darkness around his buildings. At first his wife was sympathetic, but when he began to sit out on his front steps each night with a loaded shotgun and refused to abandon his post until morning, she remonstrated with him. Yet every evening she would bring him a hot drink on the porch.

"Just a few mornings before he came to London to consult me, on the fifteen of October, he went to check a cache of gold coins he had secreted in the barn. It was missing. He searched all the buildings but found nothing. That evening it rained. In the morning one of his geese was gone. This time he found the mark of boots in the mud around the poultry house.

"When he declared that he was going to call in the police, his wife became hysterical. She was so upset he had to promise not to involve the authorities before she would calm down. That night he saw someone lurking around his goose yard. He chased whoever it was into the bean fields but lost him. Early the next morning he made up a reason to come to London and he sought me out."

"I had him describe his farm and his large house to me. I asked that he give me some time to think about his problem and return later that day. After he left I smoked two pipes as I considered his story. I then went out and spent some time in Tottenham Court Road. When Magnus Custennin returned I informed him that he should expect the delivery of a crate to his farm the next day. Instructions would be included and he should follow them to the letter. Most importantly, he was not to say anything about the delivery to his wife until he read the note that would come with the crate.

"He agreed to everything and left for Upper Oddton. I made my preparations. Later that night a large wooden box addressed to Magnus Custennin was loaded onto a train and delivered to Upper Oddton the next morning. From the station three men in a trap drove it up the hill to his farm. It was carried into the farmhouse and left there. He opened it and found an elaborate music box. It was so large that it stood by itself on the floor of the sitting room. He read the instructions and, doing as he was told, threw them in the fire. He told his wife it was a gift for her.

"As instructed, he waited until that evening after dinner to show his wife, Opal, how to operate the box. The results delighted her. The box played a series of arias from popular operas. After a few tunes, he went out to sit on the steps with his shotgun while she sat through the rest of the music. After that she took a walk in the light of the waning moon and retired early to bed.

"No mysterious thief stole geese that night, or the next. Every day his wife played the music box. On the third night, Magnus Custennin accepted a hot drink from his wife as he sat on the steps with his shotgun. Within half an hour he was asleep, leaning up against one of the pillars of the porch.

"The drink had been drugged. Custennin could not be awakened. A wagon came up the gravel road from the bottom of the hill and pulled up in front of the barn. A figure dressed in black went into the poultry house. After a while the person emerged and began loading crates of geese into the wagon. When the back was nearly full, the driver came out and drove it to the house. A muffled figure came out with a valise and grabbed the driver by his arm.

"I insist, Jack!" Black eyes flashed from a pale face under a mass of ebony hair.

"We have everything we planned, Opal. We have the money and the geese that lay the golden eggs. I have climbed up here through those bean fields for the last time. I love you, Opal, but if you don't come with me now, I will leave you here with him."

"Magnus Custennin's wife stamped her foot in frustration. "If you love me, Jack, you will fetch it with us. It is the only thing I want from this miserable place and you would deny it to me!" She began to cry.

"The driver hurried into the house and soon emerged, staggering under the weight of the music box. He loaded it onto the wagon, helped the woman into the front seat and with a command to the horses, drove down the road and away from the farm. As they left there was a flash of shiny metal and something dropped from the woman's hand to land with a clink on the gravel beneath the wheels.

"After a moment another figure stepped out of the front door and tapped Magnus Custennin on the shoulder. It was I. I had come down from my lookout spot in an upstairs bedroom window. I had spent the past three days investigating the case in situ. I gained entry by means of the music box on the first day, by posing as one of the men who delivered it. As you know, Watson, I require little food and what I brought with me was sufficient.

"My first action was to examine the entire place, evading both Custennin and his wife. In my investigation I included every room in the house and even the remains of the muddy footprints around the poultry house. There were several indications in the bedroom that demonstrated the wife did not love her husband. I observed Opal Custennin. Surprisingly, she never showed by word or action her true feelings to her husband. Women are such natural deceivers! I went down to the village and gathered information at the local pub, the "Beans and Bovine". Custennin and his wife had been married less than two months. He had a good name as a hard-working farmer who minded his own business, but the story was different with her. She was said to be wild and flighty, with several suitors before she married Custennin. She had been raised in the thick of the social life of the village. By the way Magnus Custennin spoke of her I could tell his love for her was genuine. I concluded that she had different feelings for him. It was unusual that a man should lose the regard of his bride in such a short time, if he ever really had it. I deduced the identity of her lover. I found them together. I overheard their plans, which dated from before the marriage.

"Custennin wasn't drugged. He had followed my later instructions carefully. He poured away the hot drink and pretended to sleep. It took a great deal of fortitude to sit quietly and watch his faithless wife drive off with her beguiling burglar and nearly half of his flock, but that was his choice. As the wagon rumbled down the hill he stepped forward and picked up the wedding ring his wife had pulled from her finger and flung to the ground. We stood on the steps together and watched them reach the main road and turn north.

"She never liked the farm," Magnus Custennin said sadly to me as the sound of the wheels died away. "It was too far away from the excitements of the village. Jack Climber was one of her suitors. She must have accepted me only because Climber had no money. He lived with his mother in a small cottage at the edge of the village. I remember he was a wild and foolish boy, full of tricks and deceptions.

"What will you do?" I asked him.

"She did not love me, I see," the tall man replied, turning the little ring over and over in his massive palm. "I did love her, but now I do not know if she could love anyone, even Jack Climber. All her love is for herself. She was so young and so beautiful! Oh, let him have her! They belong together. He has not really hurt me. Neither of them knows how to care for geese so over time the birds won't profit them much. They cannot come back to the village after this and when the money runs out both of them will have to go to work. Or he may abandon her, as she has abandoned me."

"The light from the open door gleamed upon his figure. The normal sadness Nature had etched upon my client's face was accentuated by the thoughts and emotions that now permeated his entire being. Before my eyes Magnus Custennin seemed to grow older, to loose strength, yes, even to shrink in stature as he watched with helpless yet forgiving eyes as his wife disappeared into the darkness with her lover.

"I left him there, Watson, standing on the steps of his farmhouse with the shining wedding ring in his hand. I later heard that he prospered with his geese that laid the unusual golden-hued eggs. He finally sold out and went to America, where he opened a successful chain of bakeries. Of Opal Custennin and Jack Climber I never heard another word."

I lay back against the pillows and closed my eyes, sleep already overtaking my senses. As Sherlock Holmes took up his violin and played me something soft and melodious, I dreamt of giants and beanstalks, of golden eggs and music boxes and a magic violin that soothed away the cares of anyone who listened to it.

The Case of the Silent Client

Early in my association with my friend Mr. Sherlock Holmes I discovered that he regarded physical exercise for exercise's sake as a waste of time. The very thought of lifting dumbbells in a repetitive manner, in running in circles for a predetermined length of time or distance or throwing a heavy medicine ball back and forth with others was abhorrent to his very soul. Yet he kept himself in prime physical form using a system he had developed for himself. One element was readily visible to anyone who knew him, however. Sherlock Holmes liked to take long walks.

The wound I sustained at the fatal battle of Maiwand, which was severe enough to endanger my life for months and which resulted in my being invalided out of the Army and sent back to England did not always allow me to accompany Holmes on his rambles during our first months spent together at our rooms in Baker Street. It was only during the year of this adventure that my walks with him had become a routine part of our joint existence.

The case of which I write started as a simple question, and then turned into one of the most urgent and unusual problems Holmes ever faced. It happened at a time when he had not had a new client in over two weeks. For days he had confined himself to our rooms until I was sickened by the resulting dense tobacco-laden atmosphere. I was fearful that his enforced idleness was about to bring out certain unpleasant habits that I would be forced to witness. So after an unusually early breakfast one morning I proposed a walk.

Thus it was that we found ourselves standing across the street in front of the great entrance to St. Bart's Hospital at late morning on a sunny day in June. We had walked for miles through busy London, both absorbed in our own thoughts, until we happened to pause for a moment outside the famous building. I was looking up at the statue of King Henry VIII that stood in a large niche over the entrance when my attention was attracted by a familiar figure that emerged from the archway of the old hospital.

"Watson! John Watson! Wait!" the man shouted as he neared us. I was surprised to recognize young Stamford, my former dresser, who had introduced me to Sherlock Holmes in the laboratory of St. Bart's years before.

"Stamford! How are you? Surely you remember Sherlock Holmes?" I exclaimed as we shook hands. He turned and grasped my friend's hand with delight.

"Of course I do! Hello, Holmes! What a piece of luck finding the two of you right on my doorstep like this, so to speak! A new patient has just been admitted and presents a problem for the staff. Any assistance you can offer will be greatly appreciated."

Holmes eyed the young doctor in his customary way as we walked into the old hospital. "I see congratulations are in order, Stamford. How does your wife like your flat on Montague Place?"

Our friend stopped short and stared at Holmes blankly. "What a start you have given me, Holmes! I had nearly forgotten how you work. How the devil did you know that I married and that Violet had agreed to start our life together in my old rooms?"

"It is so simple I hesitate to explain, Doctor. You wear a wedding ring on your left hand, a sure sign of marital union. The letter peeping from the pocket of your coat bears a Montague Place return address, written in a feminine hand. Your wife gave it to you this morning with directions to slip it into the post on your way to work, but you forgot. That indicates that you have been married for over a year, for no new bridegroom would neglect such a simple chore for his beloved."

Stamford shook his head ruefully. "You are right on all counts, sir. I'm glad to see your powers are as sharp as ever. But I may have a problem here that even you can't solve. Follow me, gentlemen."

Young Stamford led us through old corridors familiar to me, paved with stone and sporting dun-colored doors set in whitewashed walls, to the part of the hospital that housed the charity wards. I cannot say that it was a cheerful area, but the ceilings were high, sunlight streamed in through freshly-cleaned windows and the walls had been painted a soft green not long before. Busy nurses clad in grey uniforms and spotless starched white aprons with stiff coifs over their hair glided between single iron beds, tending to the patients under their care. In the men's ward we stopped before an bed in the far corner, by a tall window, where a figure lay quietly under white sheets. At Stamford's arrival a woman dressed in nursing garb handed him a chart from the foot of the bed and left us.

"You may look at the chart, Watson, if you wish, but I fear it won't tell you much. This man was admitted yesterday evening, brought in by two men and a constable. He had been found in a doorway on a nearby street. The men were visitors from out of town. He carried no identification. The policeman had never seen him before. I examined him and determined that he had suffered a fit of apoplexy. He must have collapsed in the street. However, it's been impossible to determine anything more about him, because he seems unable to speak."

I handed the chart to Holmes and bent over the patient, who was clad in a hospital shift. He looked to be about sixty-five years old. His worn features were creased and wrinkled, and his nose rose up from his sunken cheeks like a sharp rock in the sea. A shock of white hair spread over the pillow, and a pair of veined, knobby hands lay on the coverlet. I could see as he lay on the bed that he was above the average height and very thin. As I touched him gently in my examination he opened his eyes. They were a deep blue and gave every sign of intelligence and attention.

"My name is Doctor Watson," I told him. "What is your name? Is there anyone we can notify about your condition?"

Slowly he shook his head and his eyes closed. He was silent as I asked more questions and soon I stopped. I rose and turned to the others.

"The fit doesn't appear to have been severe. I detect a weakness on his left side. He can hear. But it appears that the stroke he suffered has affected his ability to speak."

"He's been offered broth but only takes a few sips, refusing the rest of the bowl. The nurses have kept a pan of it warm on a gas flame in their room and try to get him to take a little every hour. They don't report much success," said Stamford. "What do you think, Holmes?"

My friend peered intently into the patient's face and then carefully lifted and turned over each hand to expose the palms. He spoke quietly to the man. "My name is Sherlock Holmes. I wish to help you. Can you tell me anything about yourself?"

The man on the bed slowly opened his eyes, looked at my friend, then lowered his eyelids and shook his head. Stamford frowned and stepped forward.

"I think that is enough. We are tiring him. I'll come back later, sir. Meanwhile, try to eat." We walked far enough away to be out of his hearing.

"I find your case most interesting, Stamford," said Sherlock Holmes. "I will be glad to help identify your patient.

Please show me his clothes and any personal items he had with him when he was admitted."

As we walked through a hallway to a nearby room where such items were kept, I glanced at Holmes' face. The game was indeed afoot. I rejoiced to see again the eager eyes, the pursed lips, the determined set to the jaw that betrayed the fact that his great mind was again at work, idle days forgotten, the darker thoughts to which he was so prone set aside in the excitement of a new puzzle to solve.

From a shelf Stamford brought down a wooden box, which he set upon a great bare table in the center of the room. Holmes brought out his magnifying glass, which he always carried, and carefully examined everything it contained.

The box held no personal items but a ragged set of clothes, once of sound but rough construction, now far gone in usefulness. There was a tattered set of underclothes, a greasy cloth cap, thick hand-knitted socks bearing signs of long wear, worn brown boots and a pair of old leather gloves, marked with small punctures, scrapes and cuts. Holmes held up a threadbare collarless shirt, grey and frayed about the cuffs and seams. Next he brought out a pair of trousers, just as worn, with much wear visible on the knees and equipped with a frayed set of braces. The final item in the box was an old patched coat, made of black cloth. Holmes examined each item, paying special attention to the outer clothing. As he examined the coat he pulled a slip of buff cardboard from an inner pocket.

"Aha! What do you make of this, Watson?"

"It is a pawn ticket."

"A most useful thing to find in the pocket of an unknown man! Is there anything else in his pockets? Alas, no. Well, gentlemen, what have we here? The patient is an old man, from the working classes, poor and malnourished, but known to a woman, who put these patches on his coat. Note the fine stitches, the sign of a practiced hand, yet not quite the finished work of a professional tailor, who would not patch his coat at all. The socks are much-mended, but in a cruder manner, as though by a man who taught himself how to repair them. The boots are creased across the toes, showing that the user did much kneeling. The knees of the trousers back up that fact, and the fraying of the cloth indicates that the surface on which the knees rested was hard, such as wood or stone. The gloves are most interesting. Note the numerous cuts and scrapes. Some of these punctures penetrate right through the thick leather. The punctures come in semi-circular sets and within a small radius. They are the bites of a little animal, like a rodent. They match the marks he bears on his fingers. The grit on the clothing comes from the vicinity of Whitechapel. All the clothing is of ancient British manufacture. So here we have a man, a resident of long standing in Whitechapel making a poor living that forces him to do a lot of kneeling on hard surfaces. The scrapes and scratches on his gloves come from manipulating sharp wire catches and the punctures from handling small live rodents. In short, he is a rat catcher. Yet he carried no traps when he was brought into the hospital.

Why? Because he had pawned them earlier, hence the ticket, probably in order to buy food."

"Then why would he refuse the broth now?" asked Stamford.

Holmes turned to me. "That question may be better answered by Watson here."

I considered the problem a moment, then an idea came to me. "After such a hard life, would it not be surprising that the man has sunk into a deep melancholy and has given up? That stroke may have been the final straw. He has lost all hope and sees no reason to sustain his existence. Refusing food will only hasten the end."

Stamford shook his head. "Poor fellow. How can we help him?"

"Watson and I will take this pawn ticket and follow where it leads us. You must keep an eye on your patient and urge the nurses to continue with their feeding schedule. Speak encouraging words to him and try to make him understand that every life has worth. We will make haste."

Stamford agreed and left us to go back to the charity ward. As Holmes and I made our way out of the venerable building, my friend murmured approvingly of the young doctor.

"I am gratified to find that Stamford's early character trait of kindness has not been withered by the harsh scenes he must have witnessed as a hospital doctor. It was his willingness to help others that led him to introduce you to me, Watson. Our association these past years owes much to that young man."

"You are right, Holmes. I'm glad we can return the favor by helping him with this patient."

A quick hansom brought us to the bustling business district of Whitechapel Road, where many shops catering to the plain people of the area gave a semblance of prosperity to the well-traveled street. It was just behind these brick buildings lining the Road where the crowded lanes and ill-lit alleys of the district began, twisting between crumbling brick tenements and rotten wooden structures and where the majority of the unfortunate residents of Whitechapel lived. There were honest men among them, but life was so precarious that many found it expedient to make their living by any means possible. It was among these residents that we sought information about our silent client.

After dismissing our cab Sherlock Holmes stood on the pavement and examined the scrap of cardboard with his magnifying glass. A moment later he led the way down one of the many side streets into a maze of old lanes that finally led us to a small corner shop.

It was in a narrow alley, the entryway tiny and the window made up of many thick hand-blown squares of glass. The three balls hanging in a cluster overhead drooped on their iron stalk. When we pushed open the door and entered, a canary in a wicker cage in the back corner sang a few notes, and then lapsed into silence. The shelves displayed a typical assortment of items brought to pawn by lower-class clients, yet there was an air of neglect in the crowded room that lingered like a musty smell. The place showed its age with stained floorboards and a smoke-darken ceiling. Even the pawnshop owner, a short old woman wearing a black dress who rose from an elderly armchair to greet us, had the appearance of being sprinkled in grey bits of the past. The long counter, divided into three stations by high wooden slabs, showed little signs of recent use.

"Welcome to my shop, gentlemen! How may I help you?" The shopkeeper's squeaky voice did not match her rotund frame. Her bright beady eyes swept us up and down. Holmes brought out the buff ticket and placed it on the counter.

"Is this ticket from your establishment?"

The little woman picked it up and turned it over to examine the back. Giving Holmes a sharp glance, she reached under the counter and brought out an ancient ledger book. She opened it to a particular page and ran an arthritic finger down a list of handwritten numbers.

"Yes, this is my ticket. Where did you get it? I have never seen either of you in my life and I know you never pawned anything here."

"My name is Sherlock Holmes. This is my friend Dr. Watson. I am looking for information about a man and this ticket tells me you know him. He pawned his rat traps here. He is tall, old and thin, with white hair and blue eyes, dressed in a shabby black coat and brown boots. What can you tell me of him?"

"Seems like you know everything about him already. I've heard of you, Mr. Holmes. I've heard you play fair with people who have done no wrong. Old Willie Piper owned those rodent traps fair and square. I was surprised when he brought them in, but he was insistent and since we had known him for so long I gave him the small amount he wanted."

"'We'?"

"My husband Theodore Tillotson and I had this business here for over thirty years. There are living quarters upstairs. My Theodore died two years ago and frankly I lost interest in the shop. I kept it shuttered until only a month ago since we had no children to carry on. My husband left me well enough off so I didn't have to continue the business, but I missed the company it brought in. I decided to keep it open just a few hours a day, but not to fuss. A few old customers have returned. I'm afraid that some former clients have switched to my competitors, a mean and untrustworthy lot, who would shortchange a widow with six children. Not me. Not Adaline Tillotson. I have standards and a good name to uphold."

"I am glad to hear it, Mrs. Tillotson. What can you tell me about Willie Piper?"

"He's not in trouble, is he? A more gentle and friendly man you'll never find."

"I regret to tell you he is very ill. He is in the charity ward at St. Bart's."

The widow looked upset and twisted a bit of skirt in her fingers. "I'm sorry to hear that. I've known Willie since he first came to London. He moved here from Liverpool over twenty years ago. He told me he had a wife there but she died. He tried several jobs but he wasn't very strong. He finally settled into the job of rat catcher. He got enough work to sustain himself but never much more. I noticed over the years that his clothes were wearing thin and he barely kept himself in boots. He wouldn't take any handouts, but once I persuaded him to let me mend his old coat. Three days ago he came in with his traps. I shouldn't have let him pawn them. After they were gone how could he earn a living?"

"What did he do before he came to London?" asked Holmes.

"He told me he had been at sea in merchant ships. He had traveled the world and told such stories of adventures as I have never heard in my life. A great storyteller is Willie."

"Where was he living here in Whitechapel?"

"He moved around from place to place, as many of the people about here must. All he owned were a few clothes and his traps. When my husband was alive he stayed here once in a while, especially when the weather was bad. We were glad to have him. Oh, what stories he would tell! I told him he should write them down, for the papers but he said he never learned to read or write. Please, sirs, you say he is at St. Bart's?"

"That is correct," I replied.

"Do you think they would let me visit him?"

I smiled at her and touched her old wrinkled hand as it rested on the counter. "I think that would be the best medicine he could get. But you must be prepared. He is very ill."

"Then if you will excuse me, I will shut up the shop and go at once."

She bustled into the back. Sherlock Holmes murmured to me, "Watson, I want you to escort Mrs. Tillotson to St. Bart's and report our findings to Stamford. I think I have done all there is to do in this case. I am nearly out of tobacco. I will meet you back in Baker Street."

Mrs. Tillotson appeared, wearing a straw bonnet and a rose-colored shawl. I explained my mission and she thanked us both before taking my arm. Holmes handed her into a hansom with me and we started off for the hospital.

We went immediately to the men's charity ward, where we found Stamford standing by Willie Piper's bed. One of the nurses was feeding the old man some soup. Stamford walked up to us as we entered and I introduced Mrs. Tillotson. He asked me, "What have you discovered?"

I gave him a brief account of our findings.

"Then he does have at least one friend in Mrs. Tillotson. I'm glad to hear it. If you are quiet, ma'am, you may sit by his bed."

I arranged with Mrs. Tillotson to escort her back to her shop after a half-hour's visit. It warmed my heart to see that kind old woman seated by the rat catcher's side, speaking softly to him. I fancied I saw a little color in his pale cheeks and a bit of animation in his eyes. Stamford left to continue his rounds and I walked to the hospital's medical library to examine the latest periodicals. At the appointed time I returned and we came out into the sunshine to hail a cab for her home.

When I returned to Baker Street I bounded up the stairs to our sitting room at 221b with a cheerful heart, ready to tell Holmes about the happy reunion I had just witnessed. I was checked at the door, however, by the sounds of voices within. Holmes had a visitor. I opened the door quietly and stepped inside with a questioning air.

The first thing I saw was Sherlock Holmes standing at the window. He turned and gave me the briefest of warning glances. Then he motioned to a familiar figure sitting on our sofa.

Inspector Lestrade greeted me as I took a seat in my armchair by the screened fireplace, and then returned his attention to my friend. "As I was saying, Holmes, as a rule Scotland Yard doesn't handle many kidnappings. That is more of an American crime. It's easier to close all the ports on an island then to close all the escape routes in a country like the United States. Yet the boys have disappeared and the only explanation is kidnapping."

Holmes filled his old clay pipe from a fresh pouch of tobacco from the pocket of his purple dressing gown and lit it. Smoke rose in thin trickles from the bowl. He frowned at Lestrade.

"But you say there was no note left behind."

"It will come later. We have a man at the house waiting for it."

"Why has Scotland Yard decided that this Willie Piper is the culprit?"

Involuntarily I gave a start. Fortunately Lestrade's gaze was fixed on Holmes and he didn't notice me.

"During the past two weeks no other stranger has been admitted to the house. Mr. Rufus Sellars lives in a large five-story stucco townhouse on Sutherland Street near Eccleston Square in Pimlico with his two sons. Charlie is eleven and Stephen is nine. Their mother died when they were young and for several years they were in the charge of a series of governesses. Two years ago Mr. Sellars entrusted their care to a tutor, Mr. Lloyd Thomas. Thomas is Welsh, and told me he has spent the last five years working on a manuscript on the origins of the fertility rituals of the Pre-Roman Druids of western Wales. He seems to have a bit of a pip on the subject.

He graduated from Cambridge ten years ago and has an excellent reputation. His last post was as tutor to the son of Sir Peter Wappington, the financier. He was there for over three years.

"Mr. Sellars is a widower. He is a woolen merchant with offices in several British and Scottish cities and with connections on the Continent. He travels a great deal and depends on his household staff for the day-to-day running of his home. He was told by his butler that the house had become infested with mice. A week and a half ago he hired this Piper to remove them. The man had been spending time in the neighborhood, asking for such work. Mr. Sellars admitted that Piper looked sort of ragged, but he needed the job done as soon as possible. The staff was raising a fuss about the vermin. Rufus Sellars ran a busy import-export business and didn't want to be bothered with household matters.

"It took five days to clear the house and apparently Willie Piper spent most of his time on the job, setting out traps and waiting in the kitchen for them to spring. The cook said he told amazing stories and the boys followed him everywhere, listening to them and asking for more. She admitted that she listened to them herself and had never heard such tales in her life.

"What kind of stories?" asked Holmes.

"What does that matter?" Lestrade was annoyed at being interrupted. "She didn't say and I didn't ask. That's not important. The man was spending his time casing the house planning how he could pull off the abductions. Having to set traps in every nook and cranny of the building was a perfect cover. By the time he was done, he probably knew the place better than the men who built it.

"After five days, when he said that the mice were gone, Mr. Sellars called him into the library and told him to come back in two days for his pay. Mr. Sellars said he wanted to test the quality of the work before he handed out the fee. By the time Piper came back, a housemaid had reported an odd sound in one of the upstairs back bedrooms, and Mr. Sellars refused to give the full amount of money agreed upon. "

"What a shabby trick!" I exclaimed.

"Well, according to reports from his own butler, Mr. Rufus Sellars didn't build his business up being overly generous with his brass. Piper objected, but finally he accepted what was offered, less than half, and left. Everything went on as usual until this morning, when the tutor went into the boys' room to rouse them for breakfast and found the room in disarray and the boys gone. One thing that stuck in his memory was that the boys' moneyboxes were on the floor in the center of the room, opened and empty. He told Mr. Sellars, who hadn't left for the office yet, and the servants were dispatched to search the house. The two boys had vanished, and a window in a ground-floor box room in the back of the house was found open. Rufus Sellars called the police immediately and gave them the name of Willie Piper."

"Are there no other suspects?"

"Five men have worked on this case all day. All the servants and the neighbors on either side have been interviewed. No other name has come up. Rufus Sellars has a wide acquaintanceship due to his many business interests. He has a reputation for sharp dealing but no one can claim he has done anything to warrant the attention of the authorities. We did discover that Piper lived in Whitechapel, which is no recommendation, and hasn't been seen there since just before the crime was discovered. I've come to you, Mr. Holmes, to see if you had any ideas about the case. Will you help us?"

Sherlock Holmes slowly knocked the ashes out of his pipe. "Inspector, this problem has aspects I've never encountered before. However, right now I have several other cases that occupy my time. It seems that Scotland Yard has this one well in hand. It calls for a strong application of shoe leather, and waiting for clues to appear, and no one else does that as well than the Yard. Yet my interest is piqued. Please keep me informed as to your progress."

Lestrade looked disgusted. He stood up and jammed his hat on his head. "Of course, Mr. Holmes, I would like nothing better than to trot back and forth between the Yard and Baker Street telling you all the developments of a case you've refused to handle. If you will excuse me, I've got work to do. Somewhere out there are two frightened children depending on me to bring them home. Please, stay in your comfortable chair and smoke another pipe. No, thank you, Dr. Watson, I'll see myself out." He slammed the sitting room door behind him and we heard loud footsteps stomping down the stairs. A moment later the street door crashed shut.

I turned to Holmes. Before I could speak a word, he jumped up and shouted for Mrs. Hudson. He scribbled something on a sheet of paper and looked up at a knock at the door.

Our landlady appeared. "Mrs. Hudson, please send up some sandwiches and fruit. We are leaving in a short while and our next meal is uncertain. Also, have this telegram sent at once. Thank you. Watson, you understand what has happened. I could hand Willie Piper over to Lestrade now, but then this misguided search would be over. I believe Scotland Yard has done a much better job than usual in disregarding the clues and going off in the wrong direction. Lestrade was right about one thing, however. Two boys are missing and must be brought home as soon as possible. Do you think Piper abducted them?"

"I do not. For one thing, with his age and in his state of health he was too weak to force a pair of healthy young boys to do anything they didn't want. I do believe that since his stroke he is in no shape to be questioned by the authorities."

"Those are excellent points and I concur. Mark the abandoned moneyboxes, Watson."

"You consider them important?"

"Very much so. Five possibilities have occurred to me to explain the boys' disappearance, but Lestrade has decided upon Willie Piper. I haven't the time to convince him he is wrong right now. The only way I can clear Piper is to uncover the real circumstances."

He disappeared into his bedroom. In a few minutes the food appeared. I ate two sandwiches and an apple and drank a hasty cup of tea. Sherlock Holmes came out dressed in a shabby suit and a shirt with no collar. He put two sandwiches wrapped in sheets of my writing paper in the pocket of his coat, then added a pair of pippins.

"Now, Watson, here are your marching orders. Return to Whitechapel and hunt up Mrs. Tillotson. Ask her to help you find out where Piper has been staying. Search his room. Question his cronies as to his activities during the past two weeks. Find out as much about his past as you can. Here is some money," he said, opening a drawer in his desk. "The most effective coin with the people of that neighborhood may be liquid. Return to St. Bart's charity wards by six o'clock and wait for me there."

"What will you do, Holmes?"

"I have several questions for the servants of Mr. Rufus Sellars. Since I have no official standing, I think that a little covert work is called for. An itinerant broom seller, going from door to door with his wares, and chatting with the kitchen staff or a housemaid or two, would not be suspected of any nefarious purpose on a fine June day."

I laughed. "I suppose that Mrs. Hudson's new broom, which I noticed in the hall this morning, will accompany you on this mission?"

"Also that excellent mop she brandished at the cat from next door last night. We must not tarry. There has been no answer to my telegram. I had hoped for faster results but I will leave instructions with Mrs. Hudson if word arrives after we have left."

A moment later we had left the sunny sitting room of 221b Baker Street and I descended to the pavement. Holmes walked back to the kitchen and emerged in a moment with the aforesaid broom and mop. Our landlady made little protest at the request, having become used to his strange ways, but she followed him outside to enjoin him to bring them back unharmed. Just then a hansom cab pulled up to the kerb. A boy shot across the cobblestoned street and stopped at Holmes' side. It was Wiggins, the dirty little leader of Holmes' auxiliary force, the Baker Street Irregulars.

"Ah, I'm glad to see you, Wiggins. So you did get my message. Off you go, Watson," declared Holmes. He gave the address to the cab driver and the cab rattled away with me inside. I looked back to see my friend bending down from his great height to confer with the eager street urchin.

I found Mrs. Tillotson's establishment with little difficulty. She had just finished her lunch and was happy to help me in my quest. Within half an hour we had found his last residence and with a little monetary persuasion I was allowed to look through the simple room. The room had been swept out since Willie Piper had last spent a night there and I found nothing.

I had better luck when I sat down with Mrs. Tillotson at a table at the nearest public house, the "Drowned Rat", where Piper was known to the landlord.

Due to the money Holmes had given me earlier, I could afford to be freehanded and genial. My actions quickly drew a crowd and no one took offense at my interest in the old rat catcher. I was told by several men that Piper was a long-standing resident of the neighborhood, renowned for his travel stories, and warranted harmless by all. He drank moderately, when he had the money, was continuously looking for work with his traps, and had no romantic entanglements with any of the local women. He apparently still carried a torch for his late wife. There was more than one female in the bar who proclaimed an interest in the rat catcher, for he was more polite and courtly around them than were the other men, but he remained a loner. The late pawn shop owner Theodore Tillotson and his wife appeared to be his closest friends.

As for his activities during the past two weeks, there was little to tell. He had taken his supper at the "Drowned Rat", as was his wont, and had spoken of a big house full of vermin where he was setting traps. At the end of that week, he had entered the pub and ordered a strong whiskey, declaring that "rich men were all thieves" and bemoaning the fact he had been shortchanged on his fee for the job he had done. After a few more drinks, much more alcohol than he usually drank, he had shouted that he would "get back" at the "old miser" who had withheld his money, and make him "wish he had treated me fairly". After another drink or two the landlord ordered a couple of the men to carry Piper back to his rented room, where he could sleep it off.

No one had seen the rat catcher after that. Then he had appeared at Mrs. Tillotson's shop, pawned his traps, and spoken vaguely of returning to Liverpool. The next that was heard of him was that he had collapsed in the street and had been taken to St. Bart's.

This information left me with an uneasy feeling. Willie Piper had clearly felt cheated by Rufus Sellars' close dealings and felt he had a legitimate complaint against the merchant. Clearly a mild-natured man, he had been upset enough about the unpaid fee balance to utter public threats against his former employer. A few days later the Sellars children had disappeared. Could the injustice of the situation have caused the old man to go against a lifetime's practice and devise some sinister revenge against the man who had cheated him? Would it have driven him to harm two innocent young boys? If it were not Piper who abducted the children, then who had? Could it be a competitor, a disgruntled servant, or a stranger with evil designs? Could Holmes have been wrong? My heart sank. Could Lestrade have been right?

I pulled out my watch from my waistcoat pocket and glanced at it. It was time to return to St. Bart's. I escorted

Mrs. Tillotson back to her shop nearby and then set off to the hospital at once.

My footsteps echoed down the flag-stone corridors of the building as I made my way to the men's charity ward. Willie Piper was asleep in his small white bed in the corner, and the nurse on duty sent for Stamford at my request. Soon he appeared and joined me. There was no sign of Sherlock Holmes.

"He still suffers the effects of the stroke and can't talk, but his spirits are greatly improved since Mrs. Tillotson visited him," said Stamford. "The nurse told me he finished two bowls of broth and seemed to rest a little easier."

"I'm glad to hear it," I replied. "But a situation has arisen. Scotland Yard suspects him to be involved in the abduction of two young boys."

"What?"

"Holmes is working on the case. He doesn't believe Piper is involved, but the police…"

I was interrupted by the entrance into the ward of Inspector Lestrade and a burly constable. The Scotland Yard inspector bustled up to us and I introduced him to Stamford. Lestrade pointed at the still figure on the bed. "Dr. Stamford, is that is your patient, Willie Piper? I arrest him for the kidnapping of Charles and Stephen Sellars. Grimes, take him into custody."

The policemen made a move toward the bed, but Stamford stepped in front of him. "Wait a moment! Inspector, that is my patient and he is in very serious condition. I won't have him manhandled, not even by Scotland Yard. He is quite weak and cannot walk. There is no need to move him. In fact, it would endanger his life."

Lestrade's ferret-like face had glowed with victory when he entered but his manner turned belligerent at being thwarted in front of witnesses. "Doctor, who do you think you are? Don't hinder the police or you'll find yourself sharing a cell with Piper. Grimes, do your duty!"

"Wait a bit, Lestrade," I said. "The man is ill. He can't be moved. Why not post a guard here until a police surgeon can assess him and give his medical opinion? You want him able to answer questions, don't you? Drag him off in a carriage to prison now and he may not survive the night."

The inspector frowned at me, but finally admitted that clearly the suspect wasn't going to escape in his present condition. He did insist that Piper's wrist be handcuffed to the bed frame over Stamford's protests. Grimes was posted as a guard and Lestrade announced that he would bring a police doctor to the ward first thing the following morning.

Just as Lestrade was turning to go, another man came into the ward. He was above medium height and broad-shouldered, about forty years old and dressed in a somber suit. He carried a bowler hat in one hand and his blonde hair fell in a great thatch over his high forehead. His snapping pale blue eyes and the short blonde beard and mustache that covered most of his face didn't hide the agitation that he was feeling at the sight of our little group.

"Inspector Lestrade! Is what I hear the truth? You have found him? What did he say? Where are my boys?"

Lestrade hastily introduced him to Stamford and me, but stopped him before he could approach the bed where Grimes stood guard.

"Mr. Sellars, we have the suspect in custody. He is ill, but I will question him tomorrow. Meanwhile, you can help by answering one question. Can you identify this man as the Willie Piper that worked at your home as a rat catcher last week?"

Sellars looked earnestly at the old man's sleeping face. "Yes, that is he. I'll swear to it. The monster!"

"That is enough. Please leave, gentlemen," said Stamford. "My patient must not be disturbed." Rufus Sellars, Lestrade and I retreated through the halls of the old hospital to emerge on the street in front of the arched entrance.

We had walked just a few yards down the pavement when suddenly we were surrounded by an unruly gang of children. The tattered little rascals clutched our coats and set up a clamor. "Give a penny, sor! A penny for a bit of bread! Just a penny, please!" Dirty little fingers patted our pockets and snatched at our hands.

"Get off me, you devils!" Lestrade shouted. "I'll have you all arrested, you little beggars!" He twisted away from the ragged child who was poking at his waistcoat.

I tried to step away from the assault but found myself pressed back against the wall with no way to escape. There were at least eight children crowded around us and the air was filled with their cacophony. I had half-raised my stick when I recognized Wiggins in the center of the mob, covered with more dirt than usual, grinning at me.

"Hey!" he shouted. A moment later the urchins fell back except for two, who stood quite still and pulled off their caps. Flaxen hair gleamed in the late afternoon sun. Rufus Sellars stared at them in amazement, then cried out and threw his arms around the pair. "My boys! My boys!" He buried his face in their hair. The two hugged their father as he gathered them into his welcoming embrace.

Lestrade and I looked on in wonderment at this touching reunion. Behind us, a four-wheeler clattered up and a familiar voice called out, "Inspector Lestrade, I hope you don't mind, but I decided to interest myself in your missing children case after all."

Sherlock Holmes was leaning out of the cab window and beckoning to us. I ran up and shook his hand. "Marvelous, Holmes! A triumph! But how did you find them?"

Lestrade proffered his hand to the great detective, who accepted it. "You've found the boys, Mr. Holmes, but I found the kidnapper. Willie Piper is under guard and will go to trial for his crimes."

"I will lay you a fiver, Inspector Lestrade, that Willie Piper will never see the inside of a gaol cell or stand before a judge. You won't take it? Oh, ye of little faith! I think Mr. Sellars and his sons have had enough excitement for one day. Send them home in this cab and let us retire to some quiet pub for dinner. Ah, Wiggins! Accept these treasures of Mrs. Hudson's and take them back to her. Here's some money for you and the others and more for the omnibus." He dropped coins into the urchin's grimy little hand. "Give Mrs. Hudson my compliments. Tell her I couldn't have solved the case without her help."

The other children had stepped back in silence, but Holmes' little lieutenant was front and center. In a few moments all had been arranged. Wiggins went in one direction, the broom and mop bobbing at us over his shoulder. The other boys scattered. Lestrade introduced Holmes to Mr. Sellars. The detective spoke to Mr. Sellars as if the success of the boys' return had come from Inspector Lestrade's efforts alone.

The happy Sellars family left for home in the growler. The brothers had hesitated before entering the cab, but Holmes whispered something to them that caused them to smile at him and follow their father. Mr. Rufus Sellars had regained his composure and looked a little embarrassed at his display of emotion before us all. He offered his thanks through the window, his sons sitting on either side. Inspector Lestrade promised to visit them in the morning and explain the resolution of the case.

I walked with Holmes a few blocks to a pub I knew. I managed in a few words to tell him what I had discovered at the "Drowned Rat". Holmes' murmured, "Excellent, Watson, your information confirms my theories," just as Lestrade joined us at the door.

Holmes' garb prevented us from entering a high-class establishment, but this place had not changed from when I was a student. Back in those halcyon days the beer was good and the meat pies were memorable. We ordered both for three as Holmes, Lestrade and I took a corner table.

Lestrade dug into his meat pie and took a swallow of beer before getting to the heart of the matter. "Alright, Mr. Holmes, what's all this about Willie Piper not being guilty?"

Sherlock Holmes smiled. He neatly cut into the pie on his plate and addressed the Scotland Yard man. "You do not know that I knew where Willie Piper was when you came round to our rooms today."

"What? No, I did not!"

"I had solved an identity problem for a friend of Dr. Watson earlier in the day. The unknown man was Willie Piper. When you told me that he was wanted for abducting two young boys, I already had good evidence that he was not guilty of the charge. You were focused on Piper's guilt. I did not think you would believe me when I told you he was innocent, so I refused to help you with the case. After you left, I launched my own investigation to discover what had happened to the boys.

"I sent Watson to Whitechapel to gather what information he could about Piper. I posed as a broom seller and chatted up the cook and the scullery girl at Rufus Sellars' house. Wiggins was with me, but he stayed in the road.

"Cook told me that she liked Willie Piper and enjoyed the stories he told the boys. They led a dull, colorless life in that big house since Mrs. Sellars died, she said, and the bit of romance and adventure he brought them was welcomed. His tales were of India, the South Seas, Cuba and the Americas. The tricks of an old fakir, a struggle with a shark after falling off his ship, chasing a thief through the markets of Havana; Willie Piper had a generous fund of such stories to tell. Life in the big house was quiet and uneventful. The old rat catcher wove his own kind of spell over the residents downstairs, and made friends of them all.

"Mr. Rufus Sellars spent a lot of his time at work or traveling for his firm. The tutor was a bit of a dried-up stick who talked only of Druids. The children knew that Piper would leave when the job was finished and they were resigned to that. But after he was paid, the boys were shocked to find out that their father had complained about bad service and given him only part of what he was owed.

"All the clues indicate that they resolved to make up the difference and that is why they emptied their money boxes. They waited until early this morning to creep out of the house through the box room window and set out to find Piper. From the scullery maid I found out Piper had talked of his life in Whitechapel, glossing over the bad parts but mentioning Mr. and Mrs. Tillotson, his favorite pub and the room he rented. I figured that the boys were heading for one of those places, so I bid farewell to the charming female members of the Sellars' kitchen staff and found Wiggins.

"But why wouldn't the boys confront their father about such an injustice?" I asked.

"Ah, Watson, that speaks to the modern Victorian family dynamic. The cook was full of bits of gossip. Rufus Sellars' wife died six years ago and it turned his life upside down. To cope with his grief he threw himself into his business. It took up all his attention. The resulting neglect of his sons created an atmosphere of distance in his home. He was unable to cope with the boys emotionally. He left their care to others. In return, the children grew to see him as an all-powerful but remote figure. I deduced that the two boys would walk for miles alone through an unknown part of London in search of one old man rather than question the actions of their own father. Rather than to expect him to redress the wrong he committed, they would sacrifice their own money.

"My instructions to Wiggins were simple. He was to gather up some of the Irregulars and mount a lookout for the boys at the pawn shop and at Piper's old room. I stood watch over the "Drowned Rat" from the street. I left the broom and mop with Wiggins and turned my coat inside out. An old red scarf tied around my neck and a stiff leg completed my disguise. You didn't notice that old pensioner who lounged up and down the pavement in front of the pub asking for the price of a drink, did you, Watson? No, well, I imagine your conversations with that thirsty crowd at the "Drowned Rat" were much more interesting than the sight of an old guy hanging about outside the window.

"Charlie and Stephen showed up at the pawn shop and Wiggins struck up a conversation with them. He offered to take them to their old friend and brought them to me. It was very fortunate for those two that they met only honest people during their excursion. Whitechapel is not the neighborhood for the naive or the innocent.

"I plied them with apples and sandwiches and soon got the story out of them. I promised to take them to Willie Piper and called for a four-wheeler. Wiggins gathered up the other children and we all piled in to go to St. Bart's. Ah, that ride, Watson! It wasn't until I saw you two and Mr. Sellars on the pavement in front of the hospital that I decided on that little subterfuge that returned the missing boys to their father. I do hope, having witnessed his reaction to their re-appearance that Mr. Rufus Sellars has seen the error of his ways and the relationship between he and his sons will improve. The rest you know."

"What did you whisper to the boys when they were getting into the coach?" I asked.

"I merely told them that they could see Willie Piper tomorrow and give him his money then. You will see to that, Lestrade."

Inspector Lestrade pushed back from his empty plate and drained the last drop from his tankard. "You appear to have done it again, Mr. Holmes. I suppose I should be grateful. I will say that it's nothing the Yard couldn't have done, given the time and opportunity, of course. It seems that I now must go back to St. Bart's, speak to Dr. Stamford and send Grimes home."

"Don't forget to take that handcuff off Willie Piper while you are there, Inspector," I said.

"What? Yes, of course, yes. Good evening, gentlemen." Lestrade tipped his hat to the barmaid and walked out.

Holmes settled the bill and joined me outside. It was a lovely June evening. The summer sun hung low in the sky, reluctant to leave the lengthened day. A soft breeze floated fluffy clouds over the rooftops and moved the blossoms growing in tubs by the public house door. The mellow red brick of the façade glowed in the light. It was not yet eight o'clock and the streets were full of people and carriages out to get the most benefit from the mild weather.

"You've had a busy day, my dear Watson. Should we take a hansom back to Baker Street?"

I felt invigorated at the thought of those two little boys tucked into their own beds instead of wandering in the wilderness that is London. It made me glad to again have been of help to my friend.

"I don't feel a bit tired, Holmes. If you don't mind, I'd like to finish our walk."

We learned the rest of the story from Stamford a few days later. Charlie and Stephen Sellars had returned the next day, accompanied by their father. Willie Piper got his full fee and even spoke a few words. Mrs. Tillotson decided to take him as a lodger when he was released by the hospital. "He doesn't have to worry about any rent with me," she told Stamford. "Listening to his stories will be payment enough. I've been lonely since my Theodore died, and Willie Piper will be fine company. I may even write down one or two of his tales and see if any one would like to publish them."

She was true to her word. Months later Mrs. Tillotson sent us a marked copy of an illustrated weekly paper. Holmes read with interest and I thoroughly enjoyed an adventure story about a sailor who chased a thief through the native markets of Havana. It was advertised as the first in a series.

The Case of Whittlestick Woods

From the depths of his seat in the first-class railway carriage, Sherlock Holmes tossed me a crumpled telegram. Its message flamed from the page. "Two murders, one assault. Suspect captured, but questions remain. Rooms arranged at the "Dragon's Flagon" in Lakeworth, Bucks. Will meet all trains. Sarpent."

"I'm sorry that I hustled you out of Baker Street in such a hurry, Watson, and without an explanation, but it was necessary. As you can see, there was no time to lose. At least you had some breakfast first. Inspector Wilfred Sarpent is a good man, one of the brighter lights of the Buckinghamshire Constabulary. He solved the Poison Stones case with promising ability. I have worked with him twice. If he has questions, the case must be murky indeed."

"You know I'm always glad to be of use, Holmes."

"Well, the crime hasn't been reported in the papers yet, so we have no other information. Sufficient unto the day is the evil thereof. We'll be met at the station, so all we can do now is possess our souls in patience and admire the passing scenery."

The scenery visible out of the windows of the train was pleasing enough for anyone who had no thoughts of murder on his mind. A clear blue summer sky curved out overhead in all directions. Green fields rimmed with stone walls draped in ivy spread out as far as the eye could see. The sight was punctuated with clumps of trees and little farm buildings built of dressed stone. Shrubs tipped with white and pink blossoms bloomed in the dooryards and the growing crops of wheat and barley waved in a gentle breeze. The train was an express and we rattled past little hamlets of quaint red brick and half-timbered houses. In the far distance a blue haze indicated a distant forest. The East Midlands never appeared to better advantage. I looked at my watch. The train from St. Pancras was on time and would arrive in Lakeworth in an hour.

Inspector Sarpent greeted us on the platform. Lakeworth was a large village consisting mainly of half-timbered houses and cobblestoned streets. Flowers waved from numerous boxes that hung from every visible window up and down the street. It looked as if Queen Elizabeth I just trotted off beyond the city limits on her palfrey. Wilfred Sarpent was about forty, a man of medium height, with a military air and a bushy mustache over a thick lower lip. Eyes of bright blue shone from his round face and the brass buttons on his uniform coat gleamed in the sunlight. He smiled and shook hands as Holmes introduced me. Then he ushered us into a waiting cab, gave a word to the driver, and plunged into the details of the case.

"Mrs. Arthur Gradmutter lived in Stone Cottage deep in Whittlestick Woods outside of Lakeworth. That's where we are going. A local girl came in "to do" daily. Mrs. Gradmutter's late husband was a timber merchant and owned a big piece of the forest. He died ten years ago and left her rather well off. In fact, she sold a small piece of the woods to a local lumbering firm just a couple of days ago. After his death she retired to this little house. The family home was given over to her daughter, Mrs. Cowell, also a widow, and her granddaughter. The grandmother visited them every Thursday afternoon and little Rose Cowell was accustomed to go to her grandmother's house at least once a week.

"I must tell you that after these statements were given the young girl collapsed and she and her mother were both put under the care of a doctor. He refuses to allow further questioning. The inquest will be delayed until they recover.

"Yesterday, on Thursday, Mrs. Gradmutter's maid came by Mrs. Cowell's house. She said that the old woman was ill and confined to bed, but had insisted that Nancy, the maid, take her usual half day off. Mrs. Cowell decided to send some nourishing treats to her mother, along with a bottle of her own strawberry wine. Rose, a young lady of twelve years, had a new dress she wanted to show to her grandmother, and asked to deliver the food and drink. She'd often made the trip before and her mother had no objections.

"The path to her grandmother's house wound through Whittlestick Woods and in particular past a clearing full of wildflowers. Rose carried the food in a woven basket. She decided to pick a bouquet of flowers for her grandmother when she came to the clearing. That delayed her about fifteen minutes. When she got to the cottage, she knocked on the door and walked in.

"She said she saw her grandmother stretched out motionless on her bed, her head and the bed sheets all bloody. Rose screamed and fainted, dropping the basket and the flowers. When she regained her senses, she was lying on the flagstone walk before her grandmother's front door. Kneeling next to her was a strange man who was loosening her bodice. She screamed again and two foresters appeared. They restrained the man, one Peter Woodman, who protested that he was only trying to help Rose. One of the men searched the house, found Mrs. Gradmutter's body, and went for help. More men showed up and another gruesome discovery was made at the back door. A man named Fenris Grey was found on the porch with Woodman's axe buried in his chest. The forester was arrested and is now in a cell at the Lakeworth gaol."

"How horrible!" I exclaimed.

"What does Woodman say?" asked Holmes matter-of-factly.

"He claimed that when he went to work that morning in the forest he found his axe was missing. He said he spent several hours searching for it and saw Rose entering Mrs. Gradmutter"s cottage. Then he heard a scream. He went in and found her insensible on the floor. He carried her out at once and was loosening her clothes to help give her air. He said he knew nothing about the murders. He had no idea why his axe was used. Apparently he was a former employee of Mr. Gradmutter's and after the old man died he claimed the estate owed him money for work done. He couldn't produce proof and the case was dismissed. He left the area after that and only returned about a year ago. He got a job cutting trees for another local firm. They've had no complaints about him. That's the problem. I've known him since he returned and he's a mild-tempered, hard-working man in his mid-forties. Frankly, Mr. Holmes, he seems to be the last man in this county I would expect to suddenly rise up to do murder."

"Tell me about the other victim, Fenris Grey," Holmes said.

By this time Sarpent was consulting his official notebook. "Fenris and Lovatt Grey were summer residents, having taken rooms at the "Dragon's Flagon" about two weeks ago. They're down from London. They're both in their late twenties. Being brothers, they were similar in appearance, tall, with brown hair worn rather long, brown eyes and slender frames. Fenris wore steel pince-nez. They appeared to be pleasant, affable men, much addicted to long walks and bird-watching. This area is known for its varieties of bird life. They both joined in the village activities, according to the vicar, subscribing to the church roof, attending the Saturday afternoon concert and such like."

"Has there been any connection found between them and the grandmother?"

"None."

"Where are the bodies now?"

"They were taken to the local hospital. I've had them held there until you saw them. The local police surgeon says the cause of death is obvious, but I thought you might be able to get something more with your own examination."

"Quite so. This must be Stone Cottage."

Our hackney had passed through the village long ago and had been following a winding gravel road through the forest. We traveled past beech and oak old-growth trees, with an occasional clearing planted with neat rows of young saplings. Now we pulled up in front of a charming old home, its yellow stone walls hung with patches of green ivy and topped with a neatly thatched roof of brown water reeds. Sunlight filtered through the surrounding trees and sent patches of dappled shadow over the clearing where the cottage was situated. The trees were full of singing birds and the country air was sweet. A quaint round fieldstone well stood at the right side of the building and a curving path of irregularly shaped flat stones led up to the low porch with its carved wooden front door. Green-painted flower boxes were set before every window and the gay yellow and red flowers in them gave no hint of the horror that had happened within just the day before.

A stolid constable stood mutely by the unlocked front door. At Sarpent's gesture, he opened it and we walked in. The first thing I noticed was the smell. A nauseous coppery odor of old blood permeated the place. Instantly I was transported back to India and my unfortunate experiences during the second Afghan War. With an effort I stopped myself from pulling my handkerchief out of my sleeve and holding it to my nose. I shot a glance at Inspector Sarpent. I could tell that he was also dismayed by the sight. He contained himself admirably by keeping his eyes on Sherlock Holmes. My friend seemed unaffected. His grey eyes were darting around the room and it was clear that the excitement of the chase was upon him.

Around us all was confusion. The room was a large space that was a combination kitchen, sitting room and bedroom. A big old-fashioned fireplace on the left was hung about with pots and pans, several thrown on the floor and dented. A carved wooden work table was upset before it. A couple of comfortable chairs were overturned in a sunny corner, with a small table, a sewing box and a few books tumbled about. A Dutch bed built into the wall opposite the fireplace was strewn with bloody bedclothes thrown over a feather mattress. Beside it several dark puddles and spatters spotted the wide boards of the hardwood floor. The hand-crafted apple wood cabinets on either side had every door thrown open, the contents of clothing and personal items tossed out onto the floor. Near the front door a pathetic little overturned wicker basket of cakes and fruit and a scattering of wildflowers marked the spot where Rose Cowell fell in a faint. The bottle of strawberry wine had smashed on the floor and the puddle of red liquor added its mite to the general scene of carnage. There were flies hovering over the bed and the wine. The sounds of their buzzing and the sight of their fat black bodies crawling on the scene of violent death turned my stomach.

Sarpent and I stayed by the door as Sherlock Holmes went into action.

He pulled out his magnifying glass and began his examination of the room. Muttering and whistling to himself, he carefully went over every inch, even the plastered walls. His slender fingers touched each item, and he paid especial attention to the contents of the cabinets that had been scattered over the floor. He even went down on his hands and knees to poke into the cavities of the cupboards around the bed. At one point I heard a muttered exclamation. The detective brought out something out from within a small cabinet. He placed it carefully in an old envelope and put the envelope in his coat pocket.

The examination of the back door led him outside. Inspector Sarpent and I preferred to walk around the building to join him at the little blood-stained porch where the second body had been found. Here we watched as Holmes examined the door latch and searched every inch of the area around the door in a diameter of twenty yards. Twice I saw him pick tiny items from the vegetable garden by the porch and put them into another envelope.

"Look here, Watson, see these marks in the dirt beside the path? The place where the splashing of a pail of water brought from the well would soften the earth? These not the footsteps of a woman or a child."

"The murderer and the murdered man must have left them, Holmes."

"Two separate sets, standing side by side? What harmony!" Holmes looked around at the cottage, the well, the clearing and the ring of trees around us. He stuck the glass into his pocket and strode toward the cab. "I have finished here, Inspector."

"Is there anything you would draw to my attention, Mr. Holmes?" asked the policeman.

"Yes. Consider the well."

"The well?' Sarpent looked startled. He stared at both of us, then the round raised wall that surrounded the source of water for the cottage. "It's just an old-fashioned well. It's got a wooden roof and an attached winch with rope and bucket. It's placed conveniently close to the back door."

"Exactly, Inspector. Aren't those facts suggestive? Now it's getting late and I think it's time to return to Lakeworth."

Inspector Sarpent had a word with the stolid constable as we got back into the cab. It deposited us at the back of the local hospital. Inside an attendant led us to a basement room where two zinc tables held the covered remains of Mrs. Gradmutter and Fenris Grey. Holmes motioned me to go first and I quickly confirmed the diagnosis of severe trauma inflicted by use of an axe on both bodies.

While I did so, Holmes began with the victims' clothing and personal effects, laid out on a neighboring table. There was a muslin nightgown trimmed in lace and a matching mob cap, both saturated in rusty red. A man's suit of pale linen, underclothing and socks, a torn white shirt and a floppy blue tie, all stiff with dried blood, were stretched out next to a pair of sturdy walking shoes. On the table were the items Grey had carried in his pockets. These proved to be a pigskin wallet, a silver watch on a silver Prince Albert chain and a pince-nez on a black satin ribbon. To that Holmes gave particular attention. After holding the lenses up to his eyes he brought them over to Grey's corpse, then suddenly bent over and gave a yelp. Sarpent and I both jumped at the unexpected sound.

"What is it, Mr. Holmes?" asked the Scotland Yard man.

"Who identified this man as Fenris Grey?" asked Holmes.

"His brother Lovatt did."

"Indeed. Where is Lovatt Grey now?"

"I believe he's at the "Dragon's Flagon", waiting for the body to be released. He indicated that after the inquest he planned to take his brother back to London for burial."

"I want to see him."

"Nothing can be simpler. The "Dragon's Flagon" is just down the street."

As we walked toward the inn, a constable approached Sarpent and spoke a few words. The Inspector stopped and turned to Sherlock Holmes. "Because you mentioned the well, I had it searched. Nothing unusual was found."

"I expected that result."

"Then what is the importance of the well?"   ·

"The fact that nothing unusual was found, Inspector."

We came upon Lovatt Grey sitting at a round oak table in the private bar in the hotel, a gin and tonic before him. It was a cozy room, paneled in dark oak with narrow stained glass windows casting colored spots against the opposite wall and the floor. The panels were hung with battle shields, some scorched as if by fire, and several broken lances. I noticed a couple of ancient swords and battleaxes, stained and cracked, hanging with the shields. A dresser stood to one side, its shelves loaded with pewter plates and large flagons, each bearing a heraldic device. Overhead dark beams stretched across the plastered ceiling and under our feet clean rushes rustled softly against the stone floor with every step we made.

Grey looked a great deal like his brother, tall, slim, with light brown hair and brown eyes. He wore a summer-weight suit of light-colored linen, a white shirt and a blue cravat. He was absorbed in thought and looked up sharply as Sarpent addressed him. His eyes were bloodshot and it was obvious that the glass before him didn't hold his first drink of the day. He stood and shook hands as Sarpent introduced us.

As we pulled up rush-bottomed chairs to join him at his table, I murmured my condolences. He nodded dumbly at my words but directed his attention toward Sherlock Holmes. My friend sat at his right and I seated myself at his left. Inspector Sarpent took the chair opposite Grey and motioned to Sherlock Holmes to begin. Lovatt Grey lifted his glass and drained it, then rubbed the bridge of his nose with the tips of his fingers.

"I have heard of you, Mr. Holmes. I suppose you have questions for me about my brother."

"Yes, I have, Mr. Grey. Did you always dress alike?"

Mr. Grey looked down at his clothing. "We are…were only one year apart in age, Mr. Holmes. My mother liked to see us in matching outfits. I suppose it became usual for us to dress in similar fashion."

"Were you both actors?"

Lovatt Grey's eyes widened in surprise. "How did you know that?"

"I have been an actor myself, during my younger years. The signs are unmistakable. What was your brother doing at Mrs. Gradmutter's cottage?"

"Between engagements we devote our free time to bird-watching. Whittlestick Woods is renowned for its birds. He told me that he had heard a report of a rare tufted titmouse that was seen in that area. I suppose he was looking for it."

"Who told him about the titmouse?"

"He didn't say."

"You didn't go with him?"

"No, I had indulged too much the evening before. There was a party in the public bar. One of the regulars is getting married. This morning I had a raging headache and remained behind. I was lying down in my room when the police informed me of...what happened."

"Did either of you know Mrs. Gradmutter or her daughter or granddaughter?"

"We just heard a little local gossip. The child was a lively, active girl. We were never introduced."

"Don't you find it hard to see without your eyeglasses?"

Grey gaped at Sherlock Holmes. He made a movement to rise. I jumped up, sending my wooden chair clattering to the stone floor, and grasped his shoulders to hold him in his seat. Holmes' sudden iron grip on his wrist pinned him to the table like a beetle to a card. He looked wildly at the three of us, then fell back into his chair and cried, "How did you know?"

Holmes' voice rang like steel. "The body in the morgue does not have the dints on either side of the nose that betray the habitual wearing of the pince-nez found with it. Your nose has such dints. You are Fenris Grey. Do you have the money on your person?"

"It's in my room, hidden in the wardrobe." Suddenly the young man crumpled, covering his face with his free hand and collapsing on the tabletop. "It's been horrible, sitting here waiting for someone to come and get me, reliving yesterday over and over! Please believe me, Mr. Holmes; no one was supposed to get hurt. It was going to be a simple job, in and out, the old lady gone visiting and no one the wiser. Why did she have to stay home? Oh, God, why did she have to wake up?" He shuddered and began to moan loudly.

Sarpent stood up and motioned to the landlord, who had stuck his head through the door at the sound of the commotion.

"Mr. George, send someone to the police station for two constables. Mr. Grey is under arrest for murder. Please check to see that his room is locked and bring the key to me here." The Inspector leaned over and snapped a pair of handcuffs on Fenris Grey's wrists. I let go of him and sat down again. The landlord disappeared.

The finality of that click and the feeling of cold steel encircling his wrists seemed to bring home to the man the true circumstances in which he found himself. He stopped wailing and fixed his eyes on the fetters, breathing raggedly. Holmes released his hold. I looked from the shaking prisoner to my friend.

"Holmes! Are you sure?"

"You know I never guess, Watson. All the clues lead to one inevitable conclusion. Inspector Sarpent, when the landlord returns, order some coffee and I will explain the facts of this case. If I make any errors, I am sure Mr. Fenris Grey will be able to correct me."

The coffee and the room key arrived promptly. Sherlock Holmes took a deep swallow from his cup and then began his narrative.

"Fortunately, I came to this case with almost no previous information. Therefore I could regard each new scene with a clear and unbiased eye.

"The first thing I noticed was the isolation of Stone Cottage. The nearest habitation was nearly a mile away. An old woman living alone in the middle of a forest was the perfect victim. I also learned that she had recently sold some property and therefore there was a chance that the purchase price had not yet been deposited in the bank.

"You saw that the interior of the cottage was in a state of disruption. From blood spatters I was able to determine that Mrs. Gradmutter had been killed very early in the course of the robbery, because discarded objects on the floor were resting on top of bloodstains. Peter Woodman's axe must have been picked up out of a store of logging equipment found on the way to the cottage. Perhaps the brothers thought it might be needed to break down the door if the picklocks failed. Maybe they had other plans for it.

"It is possible that choosing that axe was not the first time such a precaution had been taken. Since the make-shift weapon was literally at hand, it was second nature when they were discovered to use it to bludgeon the old woman.

"The fact she was still in bed indicated that she had suddenly awakened and surprised the perpetrators. Otherwise the body wouldn't have been found where it was.

"You saw how minutely I examined the room. I was looking for the money. Finally, in one of the cupboards, I found this." He brought out a crumpled envelope from his pocket and dropped a shiny sovereign on the tabletop.

"My search led me out the back door, where I found marks from a picklock by the keyhole. This was the point of entry. I looked for the money in the dirt. I found more coins amongst the vegetable plants." Holmes added a few coins from another envelope. "If Peter Woodman had killed the old woman he might have taken the money and hidden it by dropping it down that oh-so-convenient well. But the two sets of footprints in the mud, along with a second body, led me to the conclusion that there had been two robbers. A confrontation occurred on that porch. Lovatt, probably because he had been the one that killed Mrs. Gradmutter, claimed all the treasure. Fenris objected and struck down his brother. As the body fell the money dropped and some of it was scattered."

Our wretched prisoner stirred. "He said that now he would hang and he needed to get away. He said he would need all the money to escape to America. He said he was tired of following me around all these years and could do much better on his own. The ungrateful dog! That's when...well, that's when it happened."

"Mr. Fenris Grey was covered in his brother's blood, but he had a bright idea. They were strangers in Lakeworth, merely tourists. He and his brother were practically identical. The only noticeable difference was that Fenris wore spectacles. He pulled off his pince-nez and dropped it by the body. He even had the presence of mind to switch his wallet with Lovatt's. He grabbed the money and hastened back to the Dragon's Flagon. He managed to sneak upstairs without being seen and changed into another suit of clothes. Fenris hid the money, the picklocks and his bloody clothes in the wardrobe. Now he could pose as Lovatt, left at the inn with a debilitating headache from the festivities of the night before. Plenty of witnesses had seen Lovatt Grey drinking heavily then. He was certain that no one had seen either of them leave the inn separately that morning. If he was wrong, well, bird-watching covered a multitude of sins.

"The news of Peter Woodman's arrest must have seemed like a gift from Heaven.

"When we walked in here, I could see at once the tell-tale dints of a pair of pince-nez on either side of Fenris Gray's nose. The corpse at the hospital had no such marks. In my files back in Baker Street I have several reports of two men who have made a career of petty burglary at summer tourist resorts. I have been on the lookout for them for several years. The rest you know."

Inspector Sarpent stood up and helped his whimpering prisoner to his feet. Two constables at the door took charge of the bound man. "I'll be around in a bit to fill out the papers," he told them. "Fenris Grey is to be charged with the murders of Mrs. Gradmutter and Mr. Lovatt Grey. Keep an eye on him. Don't leave him alone. Oh, and release Peter Woodman. He really was just trying to help Rose Cowell out of her faint."

The inspector took out the room key the landlord had handed to him and turned to Holmes and me. "I think I'd better search his wardrobe before word gets out about that money."

"Our work is finished," Holmes declared. "I will be glad to get back to London, gentlemen. Somehow, such an example of man's evil nature as this appears more terrible and dark when surrounded by bright flowers and birdsong. The capability for murder may lurk deep in the heart of every man, but the grey stones and vile alleys of the city seem a fitter canvas for it than the green grass and leafy trees of the countryside. Dr. Watson and I will have a little lunch and then return to London by the afternoon train. If you want us for the inquest you need only to send another telegram."

The Case of the Vain Vixen

It was in late October, only a couple of years after the beginning of my association with Mr. Sherlock Holmes. My friend had just solved the St. Ives Substitution Case and the newspapers were still hailing his handling of the case of Col. Pott and the Great Pease Scandal as a nine-day wonder.

We returned from Cornwall on the same night a great storm broke over London. The forceful downpour slammed down Baker Street, great sheets of water crashing against the darkened storefronts and washing over the ruddy cobblestones. The feeble gaslights gleamed through the downpour to show gutters full of black rain overflowing into the streets. Over the city jagged knives of lightening ripped heavy black clouds apart and the strong, gusty winds knit them together again. No carriages or people were abroad, all having deserted the open spaces of the city for whatever shelter could be found from the chilly tempest.

We were dull after our trip home and went to our rooms early in the evening as the storm raged.

Light gleamed through the sitting-room windows the next morning as we finished breakfast. As frequently happens after such a violent storm, the city shone around us, its dirt and grime washed away by the great volume of water. Narrow mare's tails drifted high in a soft blue sky and every bit of glass and metal below reflected the bright rays of the sun swimming overhead.

Sherlock Holmes lay stretched out on the sofa with his eyes closed. His face was pale. His long, sensitive fingers merely plucked the strings of his beloved violin. The bow had fallen forgotten to the carpet.

I watched him silently. We were both feeling the effects of the last case. Weeks of investigation, ending in a dangerous chase in the dark over high cliffs and crumbling rocks to prevent yet another murder had exhausted us both. The cunning villain had a boat waiting for him in a black cove. It was only a dangerous leap made by Holmes that prevented his escape. I hoped that there would be no cases for Holmes until he had a chance to rest and recover his strength. But I hoped in vain.

After the last dishes were carried away there was a knock on the door. Mrs. Hudson ushered in a tall, well-dressed gentleman, as distinguished and handsome as a Roman Senator. As he entered the room he took off his silk hat to display a full head of wavy prematurely white hair. He smiled at Sherlock Holmes and extended a hand in greeting.

"Welcome home, Mr. Holmes. I'm glad to see by the newspapers that your latest case was successfully completed."

Holmes rose from the sofa. "Thank you, Mr. Liddle. This is my friend and colleague, Dr. John H. Watson. Mr. Liddle is the senior partner of Liddle, Klein, Lowe, Winzig and Short, solicitors, Forestland Square, London, Watson. We are old acquaintances. He has brought me a number of cases over the years that needed extra attention before they could be handed over to Queen's Council for trial.

Mr. Liddle turned to me and bowed. "I am pleased to meet you, Doctor.

I murmured my greeting and motioned him to a seat. He accepted a place on the sofa. Sherlock Holmes dropped into his armchair by the fire and gestured for him to speak.

"Mr. Holmes, I am here on behalf of my firm to tell you of a most unusual situation in which we find ourselves."

"Please leave nothing out, Mr. Liddle. You know my methods."

"Our offices are in Forestland Square, near the Inns of Court. Our partnership is made up of old friends who have been together since we all studied law together many years ago. We have our offices in a large suite of rooms at 31 Forestland. Next door, at 29, is our boarding house, where we are taken care of by Mrs. Boddle. Her son Nip is our office boy and messenger. Our clerks, Simon Small and Bruce Weebairn, have been with us for years and also live at Mrs. Boddle's.

"At breakfast this morning we thought that last night's storm might bring in an increase of cases of property damage. Accordingly, we decided to leave for our offices earlier than usual, to be ready when clients arrive. Imagine our surprise when Mrs. Boddle opened the front door for us to find a huddled figure on the steps, dripping wet and showing effects of the storm on her person."

"Her?" I asked.

"Yes. The young woman was quite insensible and shivering with cold. Mr. Small and Nip carried her upstairs at once and Mrs. Boddle called a doctor. He arrived and saw her in Mrs. Boddle's bedroom. She had come to herself by then. He said she was suffering from exposure. He prescribed a tonic, gave Mrs. Boddle instructions about her care and diet, and promised to look in again this evening.

"Mrs. Boddle had put her to bed, warmly wrapped in flannel, but she insisted on seeing us as soon as the doctor left. We gathered around, the seven of us, along with Mrs. Boddle and Nip, as she poured out her amazing story. It was such an amazing story that we all agreed that I should fetch you at once to help us."

"You want me to establish her bona fides."

"Exactly so. We are seven middle-aged bachelors and quite unused to young ladies in non-professional situations. We cannot allow an appearance of over-familiarity to compromise either ourselves or the young woman. She says she is respectable, but is she? What if there is criminal intent in this encounter? We do have a fine collection of plate in the house. On the other hand, she says she is in danger. In that case, it is our duty to protect her and help her out of her difficulty. You understand why we have turned to you, Mr. Holmes."

"I do, Mr. Liddle. What did the young woman have to say?"

"She introduced herself as the Lady Blanche Snodonia, daughter of Alexander, the late Earl of Chillwater. You recall that he died six weeks ago, in London, after returning from three years on expedition in South America. The title and estate went to his younger brother Michael."

"Look them up in Debrett's, Watson."

I paged through the worn volume. "Here is the entry. Ah, Alexander was the fifth Earl. In his forty-fifth year he married Lady Honouria Konig, second daughter of Wilhelm Konig, the Austrian ambassador to Brazil. After two years she died giving birth to Lady Blanche. That was twenty-two years ago. He remarried three years later to Angelique, only daughter of the late Dr. François Remouleur and his wife Marie, of Rouen.

"Lord Chillwater was a noted explorer, as is his younger brother Michael."

Holmes shuffled through a pile of newspapers near his feet and drew out a <u>Times</u>. He searched through the pages until he found what he sought. He handed the paper, folded so the relevant article was uppermost, to me. I cleared my throat.

"Lord Chillwater had been at home at his townhouse for two weeks. That evening the earl and countess dined alone. Later that night he complained to his valet of stomach pains. Remedies were applied to no avail. Early in the morning Lady Chillwater called for the family physician. Sir Harvey Albern brought along a colleague. Sir Harvey diagnosed gastritis. Treatment was prescribed and the doctors left. Half an hour later, the earl's condition worsened and before Sir Harvey could return, he died. The doctors decided that under the strain of his stomach illness, his heart had given out. The certificate was signed by both men. Lord Chillwater was in his seventieth year."

"His brother Michael Snodonia, the new earl, was last seen in the mountains of northern India on expedition. A search is on to notify him of his brother's death. Officials have no way to confirm his location. It is unknown when he will return to England."

Mr. Liddle looked at both of us. "Lady Blanche claimed that yesterday, before the storm, she was shopping on Oxford Street and her stepmother, Lady Chillwater, tried to kill her."

"Indeed!" said Holmes. "How very unexpected. Do you believe her?"

"I'm not sure. She had obviously been through a physical ordeal. She asked for our help. Under the circumstances, can we turn her out? Is she whom she claims? Could her story be true? Right now she is at our boarding house, resting in Mrs.

Boddle's bed. Will you help us, Mr. Holmes? I have our carriage waiting."

"I will talk to her, Mr. Liddle. Get your hat and coat, Watson."

We set off at once in Mr. Liddle's carriage and rattled through the fresh-washed street to Forestland Square. Numbers 29 and 31 stood next to each other, identical redbrick Georgian brick buildings trimmed with sandstone quoins around the windows and at the corners. Holmes seemed energized. He grinned at me.

"Ah, here we are. Watson, pay attention. A mysterious, helpless woman, lost in a brutal storm, in danger from unknown evil forces. Just the sort of thing you live for. Take notes."

Sometimes Sherlock Holmes displayed the oddest sense of humour.

A short, middle-aged woman with grey-streaked ginger hair and dressed in black bombazine ushered us into the front parlor. There we were greeted by six men. They rose from chairs arranged around the fireplace, each dressed in a similar professional fashion, and obviously waiting for us. Mr. Liddle introduced us to his partners and clerks and then turned a questioning eye to the nearest man, a stout gentleman in a dark brown suit and figured waistcoat.

"We sent Nip over to handle the door. He will come back and tell us if any clients show up. We don't want to miss any of this, Liddle. Call it…curiosity."

"I understand, Klein," replied our client. "Now that Mr. Holmes is here, I yield the floor to him."

In his masterful fashion, Sherlock Holmes took control over his large audience. All traces of weariness were gone. It was a striking sight to see him standing in front of the fireplace, the blaze behind him, his feet apart and his hands thrust under his coattails as he surveyed the men seated in chairs in a circle before him. "I do have some questions, gentlemen. Then I will wish to interview the young lady herself. First, all of you have heard her story?"

Everyone nodded.

"Have any of you seen her before?"

There was a chorus of "no's".

"Did anyone notice her in the vicinity of your home or offices yesterday?"

He received another negative response.

"Please try to remember. Have you seen anyone lurking about in this street during the past two weeks?"

Again the collected answer was no.

"Which of you believe her?"

Six hands rose. After a pause, Mr. Liddle added his own to the tally.

Holmes pulled out his pipe, remembered where he was and returned it to his pocket. "I may have more questions later. I think I am now ready to meet the young lady."

Mr. Lowe, a slight, sandy-haired man dressed in black broadcloth, went to consult with Mrs. Boddle. He soon returned. "Her clothes have been dried in the kitchen and she is dressing. She will come down to us."

The announcement caused a stir in the room. Chairs were rearranged and a sofa with rosewood carving along the top of its back was brought forward and placed to advantage before the mantelpiece. I noticed with some amusement that more than one middle-aged solicitor straightened his tie and smoothed his hair in preparation for the lady's arrival.

As soon as the door to the hallway opened and she entered, I understood their actions. The object of our investigation was a petite young woman, just under the average height, carrying herself like a thoroughbred. The dark blue walking dress she wore fit her slender form perfectly. A thick blond braid hung down her long, graceful neck, and her soft green eyes shone with intelligence as she looked at us gathered there. Her peaches and cream complexion glowed in the natural light that lit up the parlor from the tall draped windows. A shy smile showed white teeth through full lips as she sat down daintily on the sofa. Holmes took up his position again in front of the fire. I edged my chair closer so I could better observe.

Mr. Liddle introduced Holmes. He bowed to her and ran a searching glance over her person. "I have been asked by Mr. Liddle and his partners to be of assistance to you. I understand you believe yourself in danger. Please tell me what happened, leaving out nothing. I know you have already told your story to these gentlemen, but it is important that I hear it from you. Every detail may be important."

Her voice was clear and musical. "I will do my best, Mr. Holmes. My name is Lady Blanche Snodonia. I am the daughter of the late Earl of Chillwater. He died a month ago. My uncle Michael inherited the title, but he's in India and has yet to return home."

"My mother died when I was an infant and my father remarried. He had gone to Bad Plazen to take the cure and met my stepmother there. She was fifteen years younger than he and considered very beautiful. My father was an explorer for the Royal Geographic Society. He traveled to places in South America searching for exotic plants used by the natives for medical cures. At home he would write books about his experiences. He also ran experiments on some of the materials he had collected.

"My stepmother and I spent parts of each year at the London townhouse in Castle Square, our places in Ireland and Italy and Eisig Hall, our country estate. When he was home he and my stepmother also took trips to France and Spain.

"I believe my father loved me, but my stepmother's attitude changed as I grew up. My father and I were very close, and when my stepmother convinced my father to send me to a faraway school at the age of twelve, my heart almost broke. But we wrote to each other frequently and spent time together on vacation, when my father was home. His last trip was deep into the interior of the Amazon and lasted over three years. He had only been back two weeks when he suddenly collapsed and died last month."

There was a murmur of condolences from the group in the room. Holmes motioned for her to continue. Lady Blanche touched a lace-edged handkerchief to her eyes and took a deep breath.

"My stepmother had always been cool toward me, but as I grew older she pulled away more and more. Sometimes I would find her staring at me as I sat quietly, drawing or reading a book. Then she would retreat to her bedroom. Once when I had just turned eleven years old, I followed her and found her seated before her mirror. She was touching her face and whispering to herself. She saw me and became very angry, ordering me away. She spent the next year convincing my father to send me away to boarding school. Before that I had a governess.

"I have been living in Switzerland for the last three years, studying art at my father's request. I really finished school years ago, but my father insisted I get lessons on embroidery, office skills and art at several different places while he was gone. I was taking classes in drawing and painting. I think the real purpose was to keep me away from home. I wanted to drop my lessons and come back at once when my father returned from South Africa six weeks ago, but he wrote that I should stay until he sent for me. I thought that he might be using the time with his wife to renew their marriage without distraction. After all, they had been separated for over three years. I expected a letter and ticket home every day. Instead, I got a telegram announcing his death.

"After the funeral, I stayed at Castle Square. I was very upset and the familiar surroundings of my childhood home were a comfort to me. My stepmother encouraged me to go out, to shop or to lunch, but it wasn't until yesterday that I felt up to leaving the house.

"I wanted one of the maids to accompany me, but my stepmother insisted that all of them were needed at home. The household was in a state of disruption, since several servants had retired or quit after my father's death. She told me she did not want to add more strain to the downstairs staff by seeming to favor one maid over another by giving one what appeared to be a half-day holiday trailing behind me while I shopped.

"I took a cab from Castle Square to Oxford Street and strolled along the pavement, window-shopping and watching the crowds. At one point, I decided to cross the street to a teashop on the other side. I was waiting for a break in the vehicular traffic when I felt a strong push on my back. I was propelled into the street. A heavy wagon pulled by four dray horses loomed up before me and I nearly fell before their hooves. I was terrified! It was only by the grace of God, gentlemen, that I wasn't trampled to a pulp in the street. Somehow I found myself huddled against a storefront on the other side, with an indifferent throng walking past me.

"I looked across the street to where I had been and fancied that I saw a familiar hooded figure turning away and blending into the crowds."

"Whom do you think that figure to be, Lady Blanche?"

"I believe it was my stepmother, Lady Chillwater, Mr. Holmes. I think she followed me and pushed me."

That was a serious charge, I thought. Lady Blanche was accusing her stepmother of trying to kill her. Why would she even think such a thing? I edged a little closer.

"What happened next?"

"I was in shock, I think, and could only think of getting away from that place. I began to walk away, then to run, and by the time the storm broke overhead I was lost in unfamiliar streets, far from where I began. I had lost my purse and my hat in the accident and could do nothing but walk on, afraid to ask for help because I feared she might have her agents around me.

"I turned this way and that, shuffling through the darkness, terrified by the lightening and thunder, getting more exhausted and colder and more drenched by the rain as the night wore on. Finally I could go no farther and collapsed on some steps.

I remember nothing more until I woke up in Mrs. Boddle's bed."

Sherlock Holmes paced up and down in front of the splendid old Adams fireplace a few times, and then turned to the girl. "Show me your hands," he demanded.

Surprised, she lifted up her palms. Holmes took them and examined both with a practiced eye. Then he gently folded them together and released them back to her. "I will help you, Lady Blanche," he said. "I have just a few more questions. Do you feel up to answering them now?"

At that point Mrs. Boddle entered the room, carrying a hot drink on a silver tray. She placed it on a small table one of the solicitors hastily brought forward to put by Lady Blanche's side. "It's beef broth, at Doctor Bavard's orders."

"An excellent prescription," I remarked. Quietly we waited until the cup had been drained. Mrs. Boddle carried it away and Lady Blanche looked up at Sherlock Holmes. "I am ready, Mr. Holmes."

"I have read the newspaper accounts of your father's death. Did your father show any sign of heart disease?"

"You must remember that no one in the family had seen him in three years. His letters made no mention of any illness. He wrote mostly of trips into the interior and his scientific studies. He had an amateur's interest in modern cures made from the exotic plants and creatures of primitive lands. Such work, however, was very hard. He would frequently be stranded in the jungle for months, or even years, far from civilization. If he grew ill, he would be dependent only on what was in his medical kit, plus whatever cures were offered by the native people. He was a fine-looking man, but he was just a few months shy of his seventieth birthday. South America was his last trip. He had decided to come home for good."

"Indeed. Did anyone else become ill after that last dinner?"

"No. My father and my stepmother dined alone that night. The leftover dishes were consumed by the staff."

"Please tell me about your stepmother."

"Her name is Angelique Remouleur. My father was very proud of her beauty. She was nearly fifteen years younger than he. She was the daughter of a successful doctor. He died after a lingering illness and she traveled with her mother from one fashionable spa to another, following the sun. Supposedly it was for the sake of her mother's health. It was during those wanderings that she met my father at Bad Plazen. They were married within a few months. Her mother lived with us. Grand'Mere Remouleur passed away when I was five.

"Lady Chillwater takes great care of her appearance. She has a large wardrobe and thousands of pounds worth of jewelry. I think she never felt secure in the family because she failed to give my father an heir. She lavished all her affection on a series of lap dogs, every one of which was named Chin-Chin."

"Are you familiar with the terms of your father's will?"

"We heard it read after the funeral. The lawyers were very careful to explain it to me. There were gifts made to several friends, provisions for some valued servants, and directions that his just debts should be paid. As for his family, in broad terms, my stepmother was left a life interest in the Dower House at Eisig Hall plus a generous allowance. The estate is entailed, so Uncle Michael inherited Eisig Hall, the Irish property, our summer home in Italy, the Castle Square house and most of my father's financial assets."

"What about you?"

"Father never could imagine a future in which I was not married. I was left a large sum of money. I cannot touch the principle, but a percentage of the interest will be paid to me each year. The rest will be reinvested until I marry, at which time I will receive the full amount of interest. Until I marry, that sum of money is to be managed by a board of trustees named in the will. Afterward I will gain control of it all, including the principle, which I can dispose to my heirs."

"Is Lady Chillwater on the board?"

"Yes, my father trusted her explicitly. She has an excellent record of managing his estates every time he left to explore.

The others are Uncle Michael and two old friends of my father's."

"What is your uncle like?"

Lady Blanche frowned. "Uncle Michael was restless, like my father. He did work for the Royal Geographic Society, like my father did. When I was younger he lived in London and visited us frequently. He was always kind to me and brought me presents. After I was sent off to school, I only saw him on holidays and then only when he was in England. His job had him moving around a lot. He went to India when I was seventeen. I haven't seen him since.

"He married young, but his wife developed consumption and died. He had no children."

"Did he get along with your stepmother?"

"I think she found him a bit forbidding. He looked like his brother, very handsome with the Chillwater strong chin and green eyes, but he had more of an autocratic manner than my father. No one, except my father, ever questioned Uncle Michael's actions or motives. At times, when I was a child, he protected me from my stepmother's displeasure."

"Could you depend upon him for help now?"

She looked troubled. "I…I am not sure. Of course, he is now the earl. He has control over the investments that will bring us our allowances. But I haven't seen him in five years. The last time he saw me I think he still considered me a child.

I am afraid that he might not believe me about this attack. I don't know if he would take my word over that of Lady Chillwater. He would have to be convinced with hard proofs. She can be very plausible. She has a winning way about her."

Lady Blanche raised her handkerchief to her eyes again and drooped a bit against the sofa cushions. I stood. "Have you finished, Holmes? Lady Blanche is weary."

"You are quite right, Watson. I think it is time we returned to Baker Street. Lady Blanche, thank you for your cooperation. Gentlemen, I will be in touch as soon as I have more information. Mr. Liddle, would you kindly see us out?"

In the hallway Holmes turned to the solicitor. "She is the Lady Blanche Snodonia, Mr. Liddle. I can confirm that. Have you thought about what she will do now?"

"My partners and I discussed that, Mr. Holmes. We cannot turn her away, if her life is in danger. She offered to work for us in whatever position we could offer her, even in the kitchen."

"I do not think that is necessary. She said she has taken a secretarial course, due to her stepmother's prolonged campaign to keep her away from home. She can use a typewriter."

"Then we shall find her something to do in the office. It will occupy her mind and she can feel that she is earning her keep. The room next to Mrs. Boddle's is vacant. She will fix it up for Lady Blanche."

"One more warning, sir. Guard her carefully. Her life is indeed in danger. Allow her to eat and drink nothing that Mrs. Boddle has not prepared with her own hands. If possible, have someone with her at all times. Perhaps the work you have for her to do could be done here away from the office and the public. Keep her away from windows."

Mr. Liddle nodded grimly. Holmes and I reentered the carriage and started back. I had been thinking hard about the case and had several questions. "Holmes, do you believe her story?"

"She has obviously been through a physical ordeal. That is confirmed by the condition of her shoes. Whatever else happened, she did wander the streets for hours last night, in the middle of that storm."

"Her shoes?"

"Didn't you notice their deplorable state? Even though they had been dried and cleaned, the signs were unmistakable. Always look first at the shoes, Watson. Her dress had been brushed and dried, but it was obvious the dress had been protected by an ulster or a cloak. The shoes told the tale."

"Why did you want to see her hands?"

"I needed to see their condition. She showed no calluses that would have come by heavy work. The nails were carefully manicured, as a lady would have them. The skin was smooth and pink. That ruled out her being a maid or washerwoman, masquerading in the role of a lady. The fingertips were those of a typist or a musician, but she never mentioned music. The fingers and palms were scratched and scraped, from falling on rough hard surfaces. That would confirm her story.

"She has made a serious charge against Lady Chillwater, Watson. All possibilities must be examined."

"What other possibilities could there be?" I was surprised at Holmes' hesitation to believe her. To my mind, her every word and gesture spoke of sincerity and truth.

"Doctor, try to see past her outer appearance to the inner woman. Have you considered that she may be delusional? By her own account, she has been buffeted badly by adversity during the last few weeks. She has been sheltered all her life. Such a series of shocks might unbalance anyone. She thinks that her stepmother has some sort of grudge against her and has had it for years. She mentioned at least three times that she was sent away from home by the countess's machinations. If she accidentally stumbled into traffic yesterday, what would be more natural for a delusional woman but to imagine her enemy responsible?

"Well, yes. There have been similar cases."

"Or, what if it really was just an accident? Oxford Street is famous for its shops and stores. The street is choked with pedestrians every day. It is quite possible that she was jostled by the crowd and involuntarily pushed out into traffic.

"That may have happened."

"On the other hand, we have only her story about the push. Perhaps she made the whole thing up in order to raise suspicion against her stepmother. She has admitted to a long-standing animosity, at least on her stepmother's part. This is not an easy problem, Watson, and great care must be taken to get to the real answers."

"But you told Mr. Liddle to guard her, to keep her away from windows."

"Yes. If she is truly in danger from outside forces, those precautions may save her life. However, if she is a danger to herself or others, those same precautions are just as valid. Mrs. Boddle's room is on the third floor. If Lady Blanche, in a moment of madness, flung herself out a window…"

"Oh, my God!"

My companion nodded grimly and lapsed into silence. After we returned to our sitting room at Baker Street, Holmes rang for Mrs. Hudson. He scribbled out a message on a sheet of paper and shoved it into an enveloped, which he quickly addressed. He handed it to our landlady. "Give this to the commissionaire down the street. Have it delivered at once."

"Yes, Mr. Holmes."

Holmes filled his pipe and settled himself into his old armchair. "This is quite a three-pipe problem, my friend, and I do ask that you leave me to thrash it out alone. A false step at this stage could easily precipitate a disaster."

I retreated to my bedroom and tried to read a book. After a few minutes I admitted defeat. I could not concentrate on the story before me, but kept going back in my mind to the problems of the case. The Earl of Stillwater had died six weeks before. I reviewed the medical evidence. I could see no reason why there should be a question as to his final hours. Two doctors who had seen him shortly before he died had agreed on the diagnosis and signed the death certificate.

Had Lady Blanche, understandably upset over her father's unexpected passing, imagined the attack in Oxford Street from just a chance jostling on the busy street? Did she, finding herself among many strangers and much noise after weeks of mournful solitude, panic and run away needlessly, building up in her mind dangers that did not exist?

Lady Blanche was convinced that her stepmother had tried to kill her. What motive could Lady Chillwater have to injure her stepdaughter? The girl had been hundreds of miles away when her father died. She could have no new knowledge of that evening. The earl's brother had inherited the title and estate. He had no grudge against his sister-in-law. Lady Blanche was no threat to either of them. It all seemed incomprehensible to me.

Could Lady Blanche be delusional? Could the shock and grief of her father's unexpected death have driven her mad? There had been such cases previously in medical literature. I had encountered such patients myself during my student days. I reviewed my memories of the morning. She had appeared calm and rational, but I was not an expert of the workings of the troubled human mind. Subtle signs could have eluded me.

I considered our young client. She was the most beautiful young woman I had ever seen in all my experiences of women which extended over three continents and many countries. Her face, her form, her hair, indeed her whole appearance struck me as being as lovely as a summer sunset. Could madness lurk behind those doe-like eyes? Could an unstable personality speak as clearly and as cogently through those perfect lips as she did before Sherlock Holmes and that company? Would Mr. Liddle and his entire firm of hard-headed solicitors accept her account if there was the least tinge of insanity behind it?

I could reach no firm conclusion. When I came down for dinner Holmes was thumbing through an old blackletter book. Even his pipe had failed him. No answer had come from his letter. That evening we received a note from Mr. Liddle, saying that Lady Blanche had agreed to the terms he and Holmes had discussed.

Much later, after I had retired to my room, the bell rang and I heard Mrs. Hudson's stately tread come up the stairs. I looked over the balustrade and saw her knock on Holmes' bedroom door. It open a few inches and a pale hand accepted the proffered note. The next morning when I asked about the late-night letter he ignored my query. Clearly he didn't want to speak of it. I asked no more questions. Another case did not appear for over a week, during which I monitored Holmes' rest and diet until I felt confident his health was restored.

Time passed. Other problems were accepted that occupied his amazing mind and talents. The Lady Blanche Snodonia and her accusations against her stepmother had faded back into memory until a Tuesday afternoon in mid-December. We had already had several snowfalls, the drifts piling up in building corners and dirtying the streets with slush and ice. Cold winds exposed every crack around our sitting room windows and the sea-coal fire was welcoming to Sherlock Holmes and me as we returned from lunch at Romano's.

I was reaching for a magazine when the bell rang at the street door. I went half-way down the stairs to see who it could be. Mrs. Hudson admitted a young man of twenty-five, with a shock of red hair and a freckled face. He announced that he was Nip, from Liddle, Klein, Lowe, Winzig and Short and had a note for Sherlock Holmes.

I left him standing in the foyer and taking the stairs two at a time, carried the note up to Holmes. He ripped it open and after reading the contents, thrust it into my hands.

"Please come at once and bring Dr. Watson. Lady Blanche has collapsed and does not respond. Liddle."

Nip had already sprung to the driver's seat of the solicitors' carriage as Holmes and I, with my medical bag, climbed in. We rushed back to Forestland Square.

Bruce Weebairn, the short, bald clerk, opened the door. Mr. Liddle was waiting for us in the hall. "She was changing her dress and cried out. We found her on the floor and sent for help."

It took only a minute to reach Lady Blanche's room at the top of the house. There we found Lady Blanche lying on a feather mattress in a polished brass bed. A black-coated man with a wispy head of brown hair was leaning over her. He turned at our entrance and said, "I've tried everything I know. She has sunk into a coma."

"Dr. Watson, Dr. Bavard. He saw her that first day," gasped Mr. Liddle.

"Sir." We shook hands. He stepped aside. I examined Lady Blanche. Having collapsed during dressing she was wearing only a chemise. A thin sheet covered her body. Her breath was shallow and slow, her skin pale and damp. The pulse at her neck was weak and her eyes had rolled up in her head. Lady Blanche was in great distress and sinking.

As I bent over my patient, Holmes wandered around the room. He stopped at a small opened trunk. On top was draped a green dress and a grey evening shawl. "Whose things are these?" he demanded. Mr. Liddle answered.

"They belong to Lady Blanche. With the money she has been earning, she has been buying needed items for her wardrobe. Shoes, a few dresses and the accessories a woman likes."

"Did she go shopping this morning?"

"Yes. Mrs. Boddle went with her."

"Call up Mrs. Boddle."

The landlady appeared at the door. "Mrs. Boddle, tell me everything that happened while Lady Blanche and you were shopping today."

Her honest Scottish face looked anxiously toward the bed. "We always go t' Homestead's, sir. It's not what she's used t', but its good quality an' no one knows her as Lady Blanche there. She was lookin' for some laces for her stays, sir. We found some an' came out t' the carriage. Nothin' happened."

Holmes was relentless. "Something must have happened. Think."

"Well, there was that old peddler."

"Tell me."

"He was standin' outside the store entrance, carryin' a tray of rings an' combs. She was attracted to his goods an' looked the things over. I had gotten int' the carriage an' couldn't hear what was said, but she came back with two little packages."

Holmes poked around in the trunk. He found a tiny crystal casket, the kind that would hold a ring. It was empty. "The little fool!" He groaned. "Watson, check her fingers!"

I drew her arm out from under the sheet. On one finger was a gold ring with a large green stone. "Holmes, see here!"

He sprang to her bedside and gently pulled at the ornament. I saw a single drop of blood below her knuckle as it came off. Holmes fumbled with the gem for a moment. There was a faint click and he held forth his palm, the ring in the center showing a hinged jewel. Clear liquid dripped over his fingers, spilled from the cavity within the stone.

"A Borgia ring! See the sharp hollow needle that delivered the drug, activated when it was pulled tight to the finger joint. Watson, she has been poisoned!"

"Dr. Bavard, please assist me." Together the other physician and I worked over the unfortunate girl. Mr. Liddle and Holmes stood back. Our restoratives were not pleasant but they did prove effective. After fifteen minutes her vital signs improved and in half an hour I wearily stepped back and began gathering up my medicines and instruments.

"She will recover," I said. "She is still affected, but it's a normal sleep now. If the drugging had continued, she would have gradually sunk deeper and deeper until death was inevitable. I'll stay here tonight to monitor her condition."

Sherlock Holmes clapped his hand on my shoulder. "Good man," he muttered. "I think we can surmise where that ring came from."

He turned to the other two men and raised his voice. "Could Lady Chillwater know where to find Lady Blanche?"

Dr. Bavard spoke up. "I recognized Lady Blanche from a newspaper account of her father's funeral after I returned home from seeing her that morning. I notified Lady Chillwater as to the location of her daughter."

"I think we have no more need for your services, Dr. Bavard," said Mr. Liddle stiffly. "I imagine that we can expect no more communications between you and the Countess of Chillwater. I am sure you would not want to be known as a physician who babbles to outsiders of his clients' affairs and breaks confidentiality between himself and his patient." He pulled a few gold coins out of his pocket and led the physician to the door. "Our carriage will convey you back to your surgery."

Holmes followed the two men out. I summoned Mrs. Boddle to help me clean up the sickroom. After she carried away the dirty pans and towels he returned and began to examine the contents of the trunk.

Almost at once he gave a cry of triumph and held up a package wrapped in plain paper. He unfolded it to display a pair of silver combs. They were simple but elegant, bearing a graceful chased design. As he held them out to me, I could see that the tines were marked with faint grey stains.

"Don't touch them, Watson!" Holmes warned. "The tips have been sharpened to a razor's edge. An analysis of these stains will bring up unpleasant results, I wager. I have no doubt that if Lady Blanche had tried wearing these combs she would have been risking her life just as surely as she did with the Borgia ring. Lady Chillwater leaves little to chance." He wrapped the combs in a thick cloth and carefully put them aside. The rest of his search yielded nothing of interest.

Holmes took the ring in its crystal casket and the silver combs back to Baker Street for analysis. I remained with my patient.

Lady Blanche gradually improved through the night. When she awoke in the morning I explained what had happened and prescribed a day of rest. Sherlock Holmes returned and gently questioned her to confirm Mrs. Boddle's story about the peddler. We reported her condition and the results of Holmes' researches to the concerned solicitors downstairs.

"The ring contained a highly concentrated solution of a sedative based on an Amazonian plant which had been delivered to the Royal Geographic Society several years ago. I woke up their director, Sir Jasper Oldfellow, who told me it had been discovered by Lord Chillwater. He had brought back samples from a previous expedition.

"The stains on the comb were distilled from the venom of a rare lizard found on the same trip. Introduced into the bloodstream through bites or scratches, its results were invariably fatal."

Holmes enjoined the solicitors to heighten the guard on their charge. We returned to Baker Street after stopping at a telegraph office on the way. Holmes jumped out and dashed inside, reappearing a few minutes later. "Events progress, Watson," was all he would tell me.

"I think we can rule out any remaining thoughts of delusion, Watson," my friend said back in our sitting room. "The threat has proven to be quite real. But Lady Chillwater has tipped her hand by sending that peddler with those deadly accessories. I must consider our next move." He reached for his pipe. I went upstairs.

Feeling the effects of my disturbed night I fell asleep. I slept restlessly, and at one point dreamed that a visitor had walked up the stairs and entered the sitting room to confer with Sherlock Holmes. I fancied he had a booming voice and when I awoke it took a moment to convince myself it was a dream. It was noon. I found Holmes by the fire alone.

"Watson, come in. Mrs. Hudson is bringing up an early lunch. I am going out later and may not return for some time. It is best to start such a venture fortified."

I wanted to ask what venture he was referring to, but as he turned to poke up the fire the look on his face forestalled any questions.

Sherlock Holmes did not return by the time I retired to bed that night. In the morning I waited in vain for some word. Another storm built up, not a snowstorm this time but rather a freezing squall that went on and on. The steady drizzle of the sleet that coated and dripped down the window panes mirrored my mood. I stayed by the fire all day, save for one brief trip to Forestland Square through the icy streets to check on Lady Blanche. I heard nothing from my friend and again that evening I mounted the stairs to my room none the wiser of whatever plan Sherlock Holmes had devised. .

Three days passed in this aimless fashion.

It was still overcast at breakfast on the fourth day and frankly I had little appetite. I thought about Holmes' actions. I knew that he had at least five small refuges scattered around London. Each was stocked with various materials and clothing he used for disguises he needed in his work. Using those places, Holmes could sustain different identities for weeks at a time. I had no fear that he was stranded somewhere, cold and hungry and wet, unless he thought it necessary to the job. Yet I worried.

The day passed slowly. I perused the morning and afternoon papers, searching for news. I resisted going to Scotland Yard with a missing person report. Holmes had made it clear to me when we first met that that was truly the action of last resort. But I could scan the papers, looking for accounts of unidentified bodies dragged from the Thames or found dead in back alleys. Thankfully, no descriptions matched that of Holmes.

Then the bell rang. In a moment I heard strangely familiar footsteps on the stairs. The door opened to reveal a tall, lean man dressed in a Savile Row suit. His dapper attire did not match his salt and pepper mop of hair or his nose and cheeks, ruddy and weatherworn, burnt by tropical suns and coarsened by high altitude winds. His strong chin was covered with a full, unruly grizzled beard and bushy mustaches.

He fixed a pair of green eyes on me and held out a rough, red hand. In a voice geared to call across deep valleys, he said, "Good afternoon. You must be Dr. Watson."

I accepted his greeting, bemused. I had a good eye for faces and I was sure that I had never met this man before. Yet he clearly knew my name. He saw my confusion and let out a booming laugh.

"Let me introduce myself. I am Michael Snodonia, or rather Lord Chillwater. I'm still not use to my new title. Mr. Holmes sent me a message to meet him here."

My heart leapt. I offered him a chair and a drink, both which he accepted. While we waited for Holmes to appear, we traded impressions of India and Afghanistan.

Footfalls were heard on the stairs and Sherlock Holmes appeared, an evening paper folded under his arm. He greeted Lord Chillwater with a hearty handshake. Soon he was standing before the fire, packing tobacco from the Persian slipper into his favorite pipe. He had an air of satisfaction he could not conceal.

"Alright, Holmes," I said. "What's going on?"

"It was to Mycroft at the Diogenes Club that I sent that note when we returned from first meeting Lady Blanche, Watson. I alerted my brother to the case and its dangerous possibilities. The personalities involved are placed high in circles close to the Throne. We met a few days later. I asked that he intercept the new earl upon his arrival in France and to keep that news out of the papers and away from the countess. Lord Chillwater was notified in the wilds of the Himalayas and it took weeks for him to return. He arrived several days ago. Brother Mycroft's men met him at the dock at Marseilles, per my request, and spirited him to England and into hiding. Lord Chillwater had previously done a little work for the Foreign Office…"

"Nothing more need be said, Mr. Holmes," said our visitor, raising a hand.

"Exactly so. The next day was the day of the poisoning of Lady Blanche. I notified

Mycroft by telegram. Lord Chillwater was escorted here. I explained the situation to him. I showed him my proofs and he agreed to the plan Mycroft and I had devised.

"After the meeting that afternoon I left in order to apply for a place as footman in the house of the Countess of Chillwater. I knew there were positions open. Lady Blanche had said that the household was disrupted by the death of her father. The countess was hard to please and many servants loyal to the old Earl had left her. I was hired to begin at once."

"Why become a footman?" I asked.

"I needed a front-of-the-house position. I could do little good stuck in the kitchen or the stables. I need to be near Lady Chillwater in order to protect Lady Blanche."

"You would have little chance at disguise, Holmes. You are tall enough and have a decent appearance but footmen are not allowed to have facial hair. All you would really have is the Chillwater livery."

"That would be enough to render me invisible. I would be able to watch Lady Chillwater's every action and keep tabs on all visitors with impunity."

"How so?"

"No one notices the servants, Watson. They hold their master's secrets, yet he knows nothing of theirs. If you seek anonymity, become a servant in a great house."

Holmes unfolded the edition of the newspaper he carried. "This is today's early edition of the <u>Evening Standard</u>. I think you may be interested in the Society column, Watson."

I read, "An engagement has been announced between Lady Blanche Snodonia, only daughter of the late Earl of Chillwater, and John Murray, M.D., of Edinburgh."

I looked at Holmes. "Who is John Murray?"

"You are, my friend. That is, you are if you agree to act in this ruse. In order to bring this matter to a head, we need to bring Lady Blanche and Lady Chillwater together in the same room. We can't allow a chance meeting. It would be too dangerous for Lady Blanche. This *faux* engagement is the perfect cover. Lord Chillwater will return home to the townhouse in Castle Square tonight. He will arrange for the countess to invite Lady Blanche and her fiancé there in order to arrange for the increase of the interest payment from Lady Blanche's inheritance on the occasion of her marriage. Remember, Lady Chillwater is on the board of trustees.

"Lady Blanche will accept the invitation only if she can be represented by counsel. She has retained the firm of Liddle, Klein, Lowe, Winzig and Short to represent her. Mr. Liddle will be present. The countess doesn't know that she is suspected in the attacks on her stepdaughter. She will believe herself to be the spider, waiting for the fly."

Lord Chillwater said earnestly, "I hope you will help us, Dr. Watson. Mr. Holmes suggested your name. He told me there was not a more trustworthy and stauncher defender of womanhood to be found in the British Empire than John H. Watson, M. D."

His words struck me dumb. I could say nothing after such an accolade, but I managed to nod and smile. I vowed to myself to play my part as well as Holmes had ever played any of his during his career.

Holmes continued. "I hope my choice of alias is satisfactory, Watson. Due to your published reports of some of my cases, I think that it would be better that the name of Dr. Watson, the friend and biographer of Sherlock Holmes, not appear in this case."

I saw the wisdom of his words. All our efforts would come to naught if Lady Chillwater, after her attempts on Lady Blanche's life, thought she was being ensnared in a trap. Yet the name needed to be familiar enough that I would remember it. The faithful orderly Murray had saved my life at the fatal battle of Maiwand. That was one name I could never forget.

Lord Chillwater got ready to leave. "That paper will be out on the streets by now. I think it is time for the prodigal brother-in-law to return home. Coming, Escott?"

Holmes laughed. "I fear my alias is an old one, but one that has served me well in the past. Mr. Liddle will be in touch with you in a few days, Watson. He will have all the arrangements completed by then. Hold yourself in readiness."

I was left with my thoughts. We were up against a cruel and cunning antagonist. One slip in the roles of either of us could cost the Lady Blanche Snodonia her life. Even Holmes, living in the servants' quarters of the Castle Square townhouse, was in danger if he was discovered by the countess. It was obvious that Holmes and Lord Chillwater hoped to trick Lady Chillwater into some action that would expose her plot against Lady Blanche. Would she feel secure enough in her own house to do something in front of witnesses like myself, Mr. Liddle and even her brother-in-law?

In a few days the arrangements were made. At the appointed time the Earl of Chillwater sent his equipage to collect Mr. Liddle, Lady Blanche and myself. Lady Blanche looked lovely in the restored dark blue dress she had originally worn when she last left Castle Square. Over it she wore a velvet cloak. Her shiny blonde braid was coiled around her head and on it perched a tiny hat of feathers and flowers.

"I am grateful for all the attentions you gentlemen have given me," she said simply. "I never knew one could have such kind friends. Dr. Watson, you have been especially thoughtful. I thank you not only for your efforts in saving my life, for which I shall be forever grateful, but for your acceptance of your present role. Mr. Liddle, you and your partners have shown me nothing but kindness. Mrs. Boddle has become my true friend. I want to say this now, before I see my stepmother again, in case something goes wrong."

Both of us hurried to assuage her fears, but it was obvious that the closer we came to her old home, the more nervous she became. I tried to divert her attention by declaring that now our engagement was published in the public press, she had to call me John and I would exercise the right to call her Blanche.

That made her smile and she agreed. She and I spent several minutes repeating each others' names in different ways. By the time we reached our destination, she appeared more relaxed and ready for her ordeal.

Castle Square was situated in a fashionable part of Mayfair. Our carriages stopped before the four-story marble façade of a Palladium townhouse. An elaborate stone porch topped with a carved helmet and shield that bore the Chillwater coat of arms faced the street. Mindful of possible suspicious eyes peering at our arrival from the floors above, I carefully handed Lady Blanche out of the carriage. The light from the streetlamp lit our way across the pavement. I tucked her arm into mine to walk up the steps to the carved front doors. They stood at least twelve feet high. Mr. Liddle's finger at the electric bell brought a portly butler in somber black, who directed two tall footmen wearing Chillwater livery to take our hats and coats as we entered.

I looked at them both but neither was Holmes. Had something gone wrong? Had his impersonation been discovered and were we stepping into the countess' trap? I gently removed Lady Blanche's cloak and handed it off to one of the footmen. As I tucked her arm into mine again, she looked up at me and smiled. Never had I been more conscious of the importance of our mission.

In a few minutes we were ushered into what appeared to be the library. It was a large room lined with bookshelves to the height of the coffered ceiling, at least ten feet above our heads. A library ladder hung on rails on one side. Old volumes bound in soft calf and red morocco stood grouped between Inca bowls and bits of ancient Italian statuary. A long mahogany table with matching chairs took up space on our right, while green leather armchairs and small marble-topped tables were placed on the left near tall windows overlooking the street. The floor was covered with Persian rugs. On the black marble mantelpiece opposite the windows was a gold Italian clock of Baroque design that showed exactly five o'clock. Soft pink electric lights gleamed from the overhead chandelier and threw a glow on the shiny surface of the polished table.

We stood about the room, looking at the books and the objects d'art. The butler, who introduced himself as Merroare, directed the footmen as they wheeled in an elaborate tea service, along with trays of plates filled with tiny sandwiches and little cakes. In their wake appeared the Countess of Chillwater on the arm of her brother-in-law.

In her day she must have been a beauty. She was tall for a woman. The high cheekbones were still there. Under the pink lights her skin retained a translucent glow. Her hair, piled high on her head, appeared as glossy as oiled ebony. Her figure was lush. She wore a flowing burgundy-colored gown which carried no signs of mourning. Rings covered her fingers, silver bracelets set with precious stones hung from her wrists and a matching necklace was clasped around her neck. Earrings dripped from her ears. She was dazzling. Yet I couldn't help but notice, despite the lighting, that tiny lines surrounded her full lips. Her eyes were marked with faint circles underneath and around her eyes radiated creases that the most skillfully applied make-up could not mask.

"Dear Blanche," Lady Chillwater gushed, hurrying up to us. In her arms was a golden bit of fluff that was barely recognizable as a dog. She briefly embraced Lady Blanche, who was obviously taken by surprise, and stood back to take her in. "Now where have you been? You just walked out of the house months ago and disappeared! Chin-Chin missed you so, didn't you, my dear. We were so worried!"

Lady Blanche went a little pale, but following instruction she must have gotten from Holmes she said, "Father's death was such a shock. I have been staying with friends. I thought I sent you word long ago."

Lady Chillwater turned her attention to me. Her sharp black eyes swept over my best suit and fixed on my face. "How do you do? You must be my dear Blanche's fiancé." She spoke in honeyed tones but I sensed that under this sweet exterior was a woman who seldom heard the word no.

"Mother, this is Dr. John Murray. He is retired from the British Army and has a practice in Edinburgh. We met in Switzerland last year."

"Such a handsome man, dear Blanche! What a distinguished mustache! Dr. Murray? You will allow me to call you John. After all, you shall soon be a member of our family."

I smiled and kissed her hand. Sherlock Holmes would not find a flaw in the performance of my role.

"I insist, Lady Chillwater. I can think of no greater joy."

I swear the woman simpered. She introduced Lord Chillwater, who greeted his niece with a hug and then shook my hand as if he had never seen me before.

The countess drew me aside. Her little dog bared its tiny sharp teeth, its beady little eyes staring at me.

"When you marry dear Blanche, you shall live in Edinburgh but you must spend time here with us in London. This is all so exciting! It was so negligent of her never to mention you in her letters! But you see she frequently forgets to tell me things. I am ever so vexed with her and so is Chin-Chin. Chin-Chin is quite upset, aren't you, my darling? But now that we have met, you must join us in a cup of tea. Indeed, everyone must have some refreshments. This meeting is merely to gather information for the other members of the trust, Sir Joshua Noble and Lord St. Mauvaise, to consider later. There is no better way to really learn about people than to break bread with them."

I murmured agreement and led Lady Chillwater to the table, where the footmen had spread a white tablecloth and laid out the tea things. Lady Blanche followed with her uncle and performed the introductions. The earl seated her at the countess's left hand and I was given the chair on the countess's right. Mr. Liddle sat next to me and the earl sat next to his niece.

I noticed with dismay that Lady Blanche's attitude had changed. Now in the presence of the woman who had unpleasantly influenced her childhood and repeatedly attempted her life, she seemed to retreat emotionally to her earlier years. Her eyes followed the countess's every move as would a doomed mouse watching a cobra.

Lady Chillwater took command of the table. Chin-Chin sat in the countess's lap. Merroare and the footmen melted back into the corners, invisible to us but ready to step forward if anyone dropped a serviette or needed a new cup.

"Shall I be Mother?" Lady Chillwater trilled as she began to pour. For a few minutes the only sounds were the clicking of china and the metallic ring of silver spoons. She gestured toward the plates of sandwiches and cakes on the table. "Everyone, please help yourselves. Dear Blanche, I have a special treat for you."

She picked up a plate set among the others and extended it to Lady Blanche. "See, here is the applesauce cake I used to make when you were young. I hope I haven't forgotten the recipe. I haven't made it in years."

My "fiancée" glanced at me and then peered at the confections. "I used to love your applesauce cake, Mother. But you must have a slice too, after all your hard work."

Her stepmother smiled. "Of course, my dear. I will serve." The rings on her fingers sparkled as she reached for a stack of small plates. She put a slice of applesauce cake on the first plate and put it before me. The second slice went to Lady Blanche. Mr. Liddle and the earl got the next two and Lady Chillwater gave herself the last piece. "Mr. Liddle, I hope you enjoy my treat. I baked this cake with my own hands."

Mr. Liddle said something suitably gallant and looked at Lord Chillwater. Neither man moved. The Countess picked up a morsel of the confection with a fork and smiled brightly at us all.

"Dear Blanche and dear John, you have no idea how happy it makes me to have you both here enjoying my hospitality. I hope that this is but the first of many meals you enjoy at my table. Blanche, you haven't tasted your cake."

Lady Blanche looked at me. She was clearly frightened. We both suspected that there had just been some clever bit of sleight of hand with the cake, but I couldn't see how the slice before Lady Blanche could be considered more dangerous than any of the others. I looked at the other men. No one wanted any of that cake. Mr. Liddle poked at his serving with his fork and shrugged. He knew something was wrong but couldn't figure out quite what. I decided to act, just in case.

"My dear, I am very hungry and you have a larger piece. May I trade with you?" I smoothly switched her plate of applesauce cake for mine.

Lady Chillwater popped the morsel into her mouth. Her smile grew broader. "I love to see a man with a healthy appetite. Do tell me if you like it, dear John. Blanche, have I remembered the recipe correctly? I am anxious to know if it tastes the same as when you were a child."

"Mother, I..."

"Everyone is watching you, Blanche. Don't cause a scene. Eat your treat." There was an undercurrent of steel in her voice.

Lady Blanche picked up her fork. I realized that something had to be wrong with that cake. I looked from Lady Blanche to the countess. She was watching her stepdaughter with an indulgent smile. I tried to think of a way to stop what seemed to be so dangerous and so inevitable. I looked around for Holmes. Neither footman resembled him in the least. The girl put her fork into the cake. Just as she lifted the bite to her lips a well-remembered voice rang out. "Stop, Lady Blanche! Don't move!"

The man I thought was Lord Chillwater grabbed her wrist and she dropped the fork. He snatched up her plate holding the applesauce cake. Lady Chillwater made a move to stand up. I heard, "Watch out, Watson!" as her hand swept toward me.

Before she could smash my plate on the floor, I grabbed her arms, pushing her away from the table. She turned a shocked face to me as Holmes retrieved my plate and stood up, holding them both. "Dr. Murray! Take your hands off me!" she cried. She turned from me to my friend and snapped, "Michael! What are you doing?"

Merroare started to say something, but the supposed Lord Chillwater ignored him as he carefully placed the plates on a high step of the library ladder. When the butler balled his fists and took a step forward, Mr. Liddle threw his tea cup at the man's head.

One of the footmen yelled, "Now, Nigel!" The two footmen grabbed Merroare. After the butler had been forced into a chair, one man secured him with a serviette and guarded him as the other left the room.

The Countess screamed and knelt down. Chin-Chin, thrown from her lap in the confusion, was eating the piece of cake that had fallen from Lady Blanche's fork to the floor.

"No! No! Spit it out! Spit it out!"

A moment later Lady Chillwater stood up, a limp body in her arms. I checked the dog's breathing and heartbeat. It was dead.

I guided the stricken woman to an armchair. She sat with the poor mite in her lap, stroking it and sobbing. The door opened and the real Earl of Chillwater walked in. He went straight to Lady Blanche and enfolded her in his arms. He glared at Lady Chillwater and thundered, "I want an explanation, Angelique! Why have you been persecuting this girl?"

Lady Chillwater stopped mourning over her pet and glared at us all. Her voice was icy and controlled. "Michael, I want you to call the police and have these men arrested. They entered this house under false pretenses and disrupted a private party. That man assaulted me…this is intolerable! And you sir, who are you?"

Holmes stripped off the last of his false beard and mustache and rubbed a handkerchief over his face to remove the ruddy make-up that had deceived me.

"My name is Sherlock Holmes. Your two footmen are colleagues of my brother, placed in your employ weeks ago as a precaution. I have been investigating the assaults against Lady Blanche since you pushed her in front of that wagon on Oxford Street. The evidence is now in the hands of Lord Chillwater."

The Earl of Chillwater pulled out a sheaf of papers from inside his coat. "These are the results of analysis of the ring and the combs your agent gave to Lady Blanche. Either of them would have killed her."

The countess sneered. "You can't prove any connection between me and some peddler."

"No one said anything about a peddler," said Holmes quietly. Lady Chillwater gasped.

"The applesauce cake," cried Lady Blanche, trembling in her uncle's arms, "the applesauce cake was poisoned! She made it with her own hands!"

"Nonsense, the girl has gone mad," said the countess. "Cook made that cake. I never went near the kitchen. I just told you that story to amuse you."

"Lady Chillwater is telling the truth," said Holmes. "She didn't make the cake. Every slice was perfectly safe to eat…except for the two that were placed on the plates on the top of the stack she had previously coated with an absorbent toxin in the butler's pantry. I retrieved the brush she threw away after she finished. Those two slices of cake soaked up the poison and became deadly. They were the ones served to Lady Blanche and Dr. Watson."

"Why try to kill the doctor?" asked Lord Chillwater.

"I think that became part of her plan as soon as she heard of the engagement. If Lady Blanche escaped her trap, her fiancé might not. His death was sure to plunge Lady Blanche into an emotional nightmare. Her life would be ruined. If she could not kill Lady Blanche, by the death of Dr. Murray Lady Chillwater planned to cripple her happiness forever, thereby making her as miserable as possible."

The earl handed the papers to Mr. Liddle. He turned to Sherlock Holmes. "Could she have done all this alone, without help?"

"She had help. The butler, Merroare, is a failed chemist. He knows his way around a laboratory."

The sullen butler spoke up. "There you are wrong, Mr. Busy-body Holmes! I never did a thing. The lady used to assist her husband with his researches. I never helped in any of this!"

Lord Chillwater stared at his sister-in-law. "Why, Angelique? I always knew you weren't fond of Blanche, but I never understood why."

Lady Chillwater burst into tears, all defenses breached. "You don't understand! No man can understand! My husband and that man," she gestured to Mr. Liddle, "are fine examples. Men can become more handsome as they age. Their attractiveness only increases. But women, as they grow older, become victims of time. I was beautiful! Everyone told me so! I could see it myself. But my father kept me at home, a nurse to him, never seeing people, never going to parties, never having beaus. I was thirty when he died. As soon as I could I went out into the world, met people, and had fun! Those two years touring the spas were the best ones of my life. After I married Alexander, there were parties, travel, and admiration from many famous and important men. I had tea with the Queen. I dined with three Prime Ministers!

"I could tell as soon as I met her that Blanche would grow up to be a beauty. But as she grew and blossomed, my charms began to fade. I tried every cream, every potion, and every treatment I could find. Age is a relentless predator. Every day she bloomed, I found another line on my face. That was why I convinced her father to send her away. I couldn't bear to look at her.

"After her father died, and before you say anything, Michael, his was a natural death, she came home. She was more lovely and graceful than ever. Her presence became unbearable. Every mirror in this house became an abomination to me. Your brother brought back things from his travels, roots and tinctures. I am the daughter of a doctor. I won't apologize, Michael. She has been a millstone around my neck for years. I hate the sight of her. I want never to see her again!"

It may have been my imagination, but every harsh admission from Lady Chillwater's mouth seemed to coarsen her appearance. Her hair dulled, her skin became splotchy, her body twisted and her face became a mask of hatred.

"Then you shall have your wish, Angelique," said Lord Chillwater. "You will agree to the plan I have drawn up. You

247

will give up your life interest in the Dower House. You will resign from the board of trustees overseeing Blanche's inheritance. Your allowance will be paid to a bank in Paris. Travel the world, spend the rest of your life going to spas and resorts but never return to these shores or come within a hundred miles of any of my properties abroad. If you breach this agreement, these papers remain available at my bank, to serve as evidence at any time. If they will not get you convicted in a court of law, they will certainly kill you in Society."

Lady Chillwater stared at her brother-in-law in horror, astonished into silence. Then, with a toss of her head, she swept from the room. Merroare was released and silently followed her, carrying the body of Chin-Chin.

I turned to Lady Blanche. "I suppose this means our engagement is ended. As your former fiancé, I entrust you to the care of your uncle. As your doctor I recommend carriage rides, fresh air, parties and pleasant company that will have you back to yourself shortly."

"I will follow your prescription, John. Thank you very much. Thank you, Mr. Holmes. Thank you, Mr. Liddle. Oh, I feel so free!" Lady Blanche hugged each of us in turn, even Holmes, and kissed her grinning uncle.

"What a remarkable woman," I said later. We had returned to Baker Street and were standing in the hallway at the bottom of the stairs that led to my room. Sherlock Holmes leaned against the door to his bedroom. I could sense the lassitude that frequently crept over him at the conclusion of a case.

"The wife or the daughter?" drawled Holmes.

"You cannot admire the countess!" I said, amazed. "I admit there was no proof she was involved in her husband's death, but you must admit her actions toward her stepdaughter were reprehensible."

"Lady Chillwater had her faults, vanity being not the least of them," said Holmes. "You know my opinions about women, Watson. They have not changed. But I will say that she did understand the realities of her world. Men hold the power and women must do what they can to survive. It is regrettable that it is so but thus civilization has evolved. Some day that may change but not yet.

"Lady Chillwater's greatest failing was that her emotions became stronger than her natural weapons. Youth and beauty failed her and she didn't have enough faith in herself to rely on her real strength, her intelligence, to sustain her in a man's world. Otherwise it might well have been said of her that 'though she had the body but of a weak and feeble woman, she did have the heart and stomach of a king.'"

Holmes yawned and bid me good-night, turned away and closed the bedroom door behind him.

The Case of the Starving Swine

I came down one pleasant July morning to find my friend, Mr. Sherlock Holmes, sitting over the remains of his breakfast and going through the post. I sat down to a plate of Mrs. Hudson's eggs and ham and poured myself a cup of coffee. Holmes opened another envelope and silently read the note inside. As I ate I looked at the pile of letters by his plate and remarked, "Surely there must be something of interest in your correspondence. You haven't had a case in over a week."

"I haven't had a case in over a week because there is no imagination within the criminal element of London anymore. Bleat, Watson, nothing but bleat! A man named John Hamilton Potter, visiting Lady Wickham at her country house, underwent great trials at the hands of a man named Clifford Gandle. He wants to prosecute, but refuses to appear in the same courtroom as Gandle. He thinks I can do something. Under those circumstances, what could I do? People are unreasonable."

Suddenly there was a battery of knocks at our door. I got up and opened it. To my astonishment I found four telegram couriers of various ages jockeying for position on our threshold.

"Telegram for Mr. Sherlock Holmes!" they chorused.

Holmes accepted the little yellow envelopes and, after suitably rewarding each outstretched palm, returned to his chair and laid down the stack.

He tore open the first telegram and read the contents. He reached for another and repeated his actions, then another and then stacked the three yellow sheets together. The final telegram in the pile made him whistle and he gathered up the four missives and handed them to me.

"Now these four prove my theory, Watson. Read them aloud."

Each of the telegrams had been sent from Market Blandings, Shropshire.

"A dreadful thing has happened. Angela has broken off her engagement to Lord Heacham. She means to marry a wastrel. Come at once. Lady Constance Keeble."

The next one was just as mysterious.

"I'm going to marry Jimmy if we both have to starve in the gutter, any gutter. Aunt Constance says Uncle Clarence will not give me my money. He is a pig. Come at once. Angela."

I read the next one with a furrowed brow.

"I cannot understand why my engagement to Lady Keeble's niece has been cancelled. I rode over to see if there was anything I could do about this dreadful business. All Lord

Emsworth could talk about was linseed meal as a food for pigs. I am not interested in pigs. I don't want to discuss pigs. Come at once. Lord Heacham."

I looked up in amazement at Holmes, who by now had abandoned his breakfast and had lit his first pipe of the day. I wrinkled my nose against the stench of the plugs and dottles of yesterday's tobacco he had used to fill it and read the last telegram.

"Empress of Blandings is refusing her food, and Smithers says he can't do anything about it. He calls himself a vet! The man is an ass! And the Agricultural Show is next Wednesday week! We've tried acorns. We've tried skim milk and we've tried potato-peel. But she won't touch them. Come at once. Lord Emsworth."

I tossed the last telegram back on the pile. "Holmes, what can all this mean?"

"I admit the messages in these telegrams are enigmatic, Watson. You will notice that in a strange, round-robin sort of way, each one seems to be connected to the others. But what unity can be made of mention of a wastrel, starving in a gutter, any gutter, a broken engagement and untouched potato-peels presently elude me."

"Then these people are unreasonable."

Holmes began removing his purple dressing gown. "Even unreasonable people have problems that might be solved. I think we shall go to Market Blandings. This will be the first case I have ever had with four separate clients. And four separate fees."

Holmes and I easily made the train from Paddington that morning. It was due to turn around at Market Blandings at two o'clock. In the meantime, research at Doctor's Commons had yielded the information that Uncle Clarence was the ninth Earl of Emsworth, living at Blandings Castle in Shropshire with his sister Lady Constance Keeble and a revolving roster of relatives and friends of relatives. He controlled the inheritance of his niece Angela and was particularly interested in all aspects of farming, including flowers and livestock. Lord Heacham was an upstanding young man with no history of criminal behavior. But in all the information that Doctor's Common yielded Holmes there was nothing about wastrels or linseed meal. The Empress of Blandings was not mentioned anywhere, not in Debrett's or even the Almanach de Gotha. I was as baffled as ever when we stepped onto the train just before it puffed out of the station.

The trip up to Shropshire was quiet and uneventful. As Holmes and I stood on the Market Blandings platform just before two o'clock, looking about us for the cab stand, we were passed by an amiable old gentleman wearing country tweeds and a deplorable old slouch hat. He was mumbling to himself and I heard him clearly.

"Don't see why she shouldn't marry the fellow. Seems fond of him and all that. I remember him now. A pleasant lad,

I recall, with a healthy fondness for the rural life. Well, I'll see him at the Senior Conservative Club tomorrow and give him the bad news. Bother! Just when I need to be here, with the Agricultural Show coming up!"

With that, he popped into a carriage and the train pulled out toward London. Meanwhile Holmes had engaged a cab and motioned to me. "Take us to the Goat and Feathers, driver. Hurry, Watson, and bring the bags. I have reserved rooms at that establishment. From there we shall hasten to Blandings Castle."

"I knew there was money in this case, Watson," murmured Sherlock Holmes, as our cab approached The Earl of Emsworth's vast estate. The sunshine descended like an amber shower-bath on rolling parks, green lawns and wide terraces. Crenellated turrets stood at each corner of the ancient keep, and the Castle's ivied walls stood as they had since the first Earl of Emsworth accepted the entrance key from the vassal who had overseen its construction, back when Henry the Seventh was a pup.

A dignified butler with a large, bald head opened the front door for us.

"I am sorry to tell you gentlemen that Lord Emsworth has just left for London and is not expected back until tomorrow. However, Lady Constance is in the library. Please follow me."

He announced us to the lady who was waiting for us in the library. Lady Constance Keebler, a masterful woman, displayed the spirited handsome features that carried her through life as the daughter of the eighth Earl of Emsworth and which sustained her through the ordeal she bore as the sister of the ninth Earl. She held out her hand.

"I am very glad to meet you, Mr. Holmes, and you, Dr. Watson. Beach, bring us some tea. Gentlemen, please be seated. Mr. Holmes, I have heard of you from Lady Ickenham. You must understand that under ordinary circumstances I would have no use for a private detective. I always thought of them as furtive, weasel-faced little men, sneaking about prying into good peoples' private affairs, but dear Jane spoke so highly of how you got Lord Ickenham out of that...misunderstanding...in Mitching Hill, I thought you might be useful during this emergency. She also mentioned how discreet you were."

Holmes was spared having to respond to this extraordinary speech by the appearance of Beach, who solemnly bore an enormous silver tray filled with tea things into the room as if he carried St. John the Baptist's head ready for Salome's approval. He set it before Lady Constance, who smiled brightly at us and asked, "Shall I be Mother?"

Holmes and I had just accepted our cups when the library door opened and a young woman stamped her way across the carpet. She was a pretty girl, with fair hair and blue eyes which in their softer moments probably reminded all sorts of people of twin lagoons slumbering beneath a southern sky. This, however, was not one of those moments. She put her hands on her hips, her eyes flashed blue sparks at us all, and her lip curled in a startling manner I hadn't seen since Holmes confronted Hugh Boone to solve the disappearance of Neville St. Claire in the tale I chose to entitle "The Man with the Twisted Lip."

"Stuffing your face, Aunt Constance? Refreshing yourself after spending the afternoon dancing on the bits of my broken heart?"

"Mr. Sherlock Holmes and Dr. Watson, allow me introduce my niece Angela, who is obviously not at her best today."

"Not at my best, you say? I should think you could say I'm not at my best today. Dr. Watson, have you ever been thwarted in love?"

"Well, not exactly thwarted, my dear…"

"Well, you should try it sometime. It's like being kicked in the stomach by an avalanche and then thrown by a gorilla through a bramble bush and over a cliff. A high, rocky cliff. My own aunt tells me I won't get my money because I want to marry Jimmy Belford!"

"Jimmy Belford?"

"James Bartholomew Bedford, the only man I shall ever marry."

Lady Constance Keeble thrust a plate of scones at Angela as if she was striking a harpoon deep into the belly of a particularly troublesome whale. "Please sit down and have something to eat, Angela. These gentlemen did not come all the way from London to hear you prattle of that wastrel."

"I don't want any scones. The food would choke me. I can't eat." Her attitude suddenly changed from anger at her aunt to interest in my friend. "Are you Sherlock Holmes from London?"

"Yes."

"I want to talk to you."

"Mr. Holmes is here because I sent for him, Angela. If you must, you may speak to him after this meeting. Go away now. I invited Lord Heacham here to express my sympathy over what your foolishness has done to him. He is due in half an hour."

"Ewww." Angela disappeared like cold dishwater down a kitchen sink.

"You now understand, Mr. Holmes, why I sent for you. Angela is being totally unreasonable about the engagement between her and Lord Heacham. They have known each other for ages. The engagement has been set for months. He is a highly respectable young man and Angela seemed content with the arrangement. I had just picked out their crystal pattern when she dropped this bombshell."

"James Bartholomew Belford?"

"Yes, Mr. Holmes. He had been sent away to America two years ago because he…well, it is distasteful for me to talk about it. Suffice it to say, he would not make a suitable match for the niece of the Earl of Emsworth."

"If he has been in America for the last two years, how did he and Angela manage to get engaged?"

"He came back and they ran across each other in London a couple of weeks ago. Angela and he used to play together when they were children. His father is our vicar."

"What do you expect of me, Lady Constance?"

She threw up her hands and seemed to be addressing the chandelier.

"I am so tired of no one listening to me. I give the best advice possible and no one follows it. You cannot imagine how frustrating that is. Angela doesn't listen. My brother Clarence doesn't listen. I know what is best and what is best is for Angela to marry Lord Heacham and forget all about James Belford."

"I will look into your problem, Lady Constance. My first step will be a stroll about the grounds. Come, Watson. Such a fine afternoon is better spent outdoors."

"Lord Emsworth returns late tomorrow afternoon, Mr. Holmes. I would like this entire problem to be resolved as soon as possible."

We bowed ourselves out of her presence but our journey to the terraces was interrupted by Angela, who waylaid us in the hall.

"This way! This way!" She beckoned to us and led us to the left along a palatial corridor to what appeared to be a game room. A heavily carved billiard table with a surface of green baize, its surface set up for a game of snooker, took pride of place in the center of the parquet floor. A row of French doors framed pretty sights of the terraces and landscaping outside, leading down to the water meadows where a lone cow grazed contently. The surrounding walls were hung with numerous large animal heads, each of which fixed its glassy eyes on us as if it pondered holding us personally responsible for its present state.

"How may I help you?" asked Sherlock Holmes.

"I brought you here because Aunt Constance never comes in this room unless she needs to speak to Uncle Clarence and he's not here. In his woolen-headed way I think Uncle Clarence has always been fond of me. But Aunt Constance is the original Tartar and keeps a sharp eye on us all, especially Uncle Clarence. She told him that he can't give me my inheritance if I don't marry Lord Heacham. She had her heart set on that match. I admit he's good looking and wealthy and he's pretty harmless. I thought by saying yes Aunt Constance would get off my case. But then Jimmy came back from America and we bumped into each other in London and all the London church bells of the old nursery rhyme rang out at once."

Her face was transformed. Gone were the blazing eyes and the snarl from her pretty lips. She clasped her hands together and addressed Holmes with fluttering lashes.

"Now it is Jimmy and I forever and he has quite enough money to marry me on, but he wants some capital to buy a partnership in a---."

"Angela! Angela! Beach, go fetch Miss Angela. Tell her Lord Heacham is here." Lady Constance's voice echoed down the halls of Blanding Castle like the crack of doom, if the voice of the crack of doom sounded like that of a determined middle-aged frustrated daughter of the British aristocracy presently on the warpath. Angela gave us a startled glance and headed for the French doors. "Get Uncle Clarence to give me my money, Mr. Holmes!" With that final hissed instruction she vanished into the greenery and was gone.

Holmes and I turned toward the door. To my surprise, instead of the butler, we perceived a solemn young man dressed in pinks and riding breeches.

"I say," said the young man. "I say, I've just ridden over at Lady Constance's request to see if there is anything I could do about this fearful business."

Holmes introduced himself and me to the young nobleman. "I fear things look very black."

"It's an absolute mystery to me. I mean, she was all right last week. Seemed quite cheery and chirpy and all that. And then this happens---out of a blue sky, as you might say."

"Miss Angela doesn't want to go through with the marriage, Lord Heacham," said Sherlock Holmes gently.

"It's all so dashed unexpected."

Holmes spoke a little louder.

"She has broken off the engagement. She just spoke to us and that was distinctly stated."

"I mean, she was all right last week."

Holmes took a deep breath and tried again.

"Angela has decided to marry someone else, sir. My name is Sherlock Holmes. Your telegram to me mentioned linseed meal as a food for pigs. What did you mean by that?"

"When I came to Lord Emsworth to speak to him about Angela and the engagement, all he could talk about was his pig, Empress of Blandings. I found him by her sty and when I tried to talk to him, he meandered on and on about her diet. What do I care about her diet? Curse all pigs! All I care about is Angela! Uh, what was that you said about her?"

"She wants to marry someone else. There is no way to change her mind."

Lord Heacham stared at Holmes. From his furrowed brow and the slight quivering of his nose it was clearly apparent he was trying to think. Several minutes passed in silence. I fancied I could almost hear breathing from the animal heads on the wall. Suddenly the information hit him and he staggered, clutching the table in an effort to remain upright. Billiard balls rolled in every direction.

"She wants to marry someone else. There is no way to change her mind. Oh, my. Oh, dear me. How unexpected." He stood in thought for another minute. "Good afternoon, gentlemen. I see Angela is lost to me. I must go home and check the railway timetable. I seem to recollect there is a French Foreign Legion recruiting station next door to the Casino at Monte Carlo."

With that Lord Heacham stepped out another French window and disappeared into another clump of shrubbery.

Holmes was thoughtful. "At least we have uncovered the meaning of the mysterious words 'Empress of Blandings'. Follow me, Watson." Instead of trekking through the labyrinth of corridors that made up Blandings Castle in search of an exit, we bowed to local custom and stepped through the French doors and into the green shrubbery.

Holmes' keen sense of smell soon brought us to a tidy little porcine residence far from the main buildings. We draped ourselves over the rails and peered at the vast expanse of pig within.

Empress of Blandings may not have been wolfing down any potato-peels lately, but her appearance was still astonishing. She was a black Berkshire, and resembled a captive balloon with ears and a tail, and was nearly as circular as a pig could be without bursting. In a corner was a long, low trough, only too plainly full to the brim with succulent mash and acorns.

"Note the thin layer of dust on the contents of her trough, Watson. I think we have found the origin of Lord Emsworth's concern." Holmes pulled his magnifying glass from his pocket and, climbing over the rails, proceeded to give the sty, the trough and Empress of Blandings a thorough examination.

My nose was not as sensitive as Holmes', but by the time he rejoined me I was positive he had done one of the most complete investigations of his career. I stepped upwind of the detective as he paced up and down the lawn edging Empress of Blanding's bijou home. His head was bent on his chest and his hands were clasped behind his back. For several minutes there was no sound except the buzz of insects and the squelching of Holmes' shoes on the grass, leaving a thin brown trail.

"There is nothing more to be learned here, Watson. Our best course is to retire to the Goat and Feathers, eat some dinner and tackle Lord Emsworth when he returns from London tomorrow afternoon."

A quick wash-up and a change out of our traveling clothes filled the time until dinner was called. I was careful to place Holmes' odiferous shoes outside his room door to be cleaned just before we went down to eat.

The attractions of Market Blandings were such that after dinner, Holmes and I found ourselves sitting at a corner table of the tap-room of the Goat and Feathers. A previous brisk walk around the town had shown us the wisdom of that choice. I was engaged in lining up our empty bottles of Bass in a perfectly straight line when Holmes drew my attention to certain items of furniture scattered about the room.

"Observe, Watson. That table over there clearly shows a thin line of fresh wood in two legs, indicating the legs were broken quite recently. Those three chairs at the next table display new cracks in their seats and chair backs. The smell of fresh glue is distinctive. Each of the tables in this room is supplied with four chairs, but that mended table has only three. Obviously one chair was broken too badly to be mended."

"What can it mean, Holmes?"

"There has been a fight in this tap-room within the past two days, Watson."

"The past two days?"

"Yes, presuming the table and chairs underwent repair as soon as possible. Otherwise the smell of glue would have dissipated by now. It must have been quite a fight to have left behind such a large amount of damage."

Sherlock Holmes stood up and went to the bar, where he engaged the landlord in conversation. In a few minutes he returned, bringing two more bottles of Bass, and smiled at me.

"Landlords and public houses, my dear Watson, are the finest sources of local gossip one could ask for. Mein host over there told me a most entertaining story of George Cyril Wellbeloved, who while celebrating his birthday the evening of the eighteen of this month, managed to get himself arrested by Police-Constable Evans for being drunk and disorderly in this very room. By the damage done to the furniture, I should say very disorderly. He was very properly jugged by the magistrate the next morning for a term of fourteen days without the option of a fine."

"But what does that have to do with this case, Holmes?"

"It is elementary, my dear Watson. George Cyril Wellbeloved is employed as the pig-man for Lord Emsworth. He has not been at his post for two days. Empress of Blandings has stopped eating. Obviously she misses him."

"Holmes!"

"She probably misses his afternoon call."

"His call?"

"He must have had some special call that he used when he wanted her to come to dinner. Behold the advantage of country squire ancestors, Watson. Life in the country, if experienced only during the school holidays, can teach a young boy a wealth of curious and useful information.

"One of the first things you learn on a farm is hog-calling. Pigs are temperamental. Omit to call them, and they'll starve rather than put on the nosebag. Call them right, and they will follow you to the ends of the earth with their mouths watering."

"God bless my soul! Fancy that."

"A fact, I assure you. Calls can even vary by region. A well-bred Yorkshire hog would never respond to the same call as that which brings a future Smithfield ham to their mutual trough."

I placed a hand to my throbbing forehead.

"But if there is a wide variety, we have no means of knowing which call Wellbeloved…"

"Ah," said Sherlock Holmes, "But wait. I haven't told you all. There is a master-word."

"A what?"

"Most people don't know it. It is to the pig world what the Masonic grip is to the human. Sufficient to the day is the pig-calling thereof, Watson. Let's make an early night of it, and go over to the Castle after dinner tomorrow night. The Earl will have returned by then and an interview with him should prove very profitable."

Having no plans for the next morning, and having discovered already the cultural wasteland that is Market Blandings, we both slept late the next morning. A long luncheon at the Goat and Feathers and a leisurely stroll down the High Street filled our time until dinner. We lingered over the port as long as we could but as the moon appeared over the Shropshire hills I found a cab and we set forth through the dusk to Blandings Castle.

As we pulled up to the courtyard before that picturesque pile, we saw two figures near the parts adjacent to the rear of the castle. I could identify Angela as one and the other as the same amiable old gentleman wearing the same deplorable old slouch hat I had spied on the train platform when we arrived at Market Blandings the day before.

Holmes dismissed the cab and we walked around the building to join them. It was quite a distance and we overheard part of their conversation as we approached.

The old gentleman spoke first.

"I wish you would go in, my dear. The night air might give you a chill."

"I won't go in, Uncle Clarence. I came out here to look at the moon and think of Jimmy. What are you doing out here, if it comes to that?"

"I met young Belford in London today and he says Empress of Blandings will not eat until she hears the proper call or cry. He learned that while working on a pig farm in Nebraska for an applejack-voiced patriarch with strong views on work and a good vocabulary. He learned the call from Fred Patzel, the hog-calling champion of the Western States. It has been known to bring pork chops leaping from their plates. Belford very kindly taught it to me, but unfortunately I have forgotten it."

"I wonder that you had the nerve to ask Jimmy to teach you pig-calls, considering the way you are treating him."

"But---"

"Like a leper, or something. And all I can say is that, if you remember this call of his, and it makes the Empress eat, you ought to be ashamed of yourself if you still refuse to let me marry him."

"My dear," said Lord Emsworth earnestly, "if through young Belford's instrumentality Empress of Blandings is induced to take nourishment once more, there is nothing I will refuse him---nothing."

"Honour bright?"

"I give you my solemn word. It began with the word 'pig-
--"

We stepped up to the old gentleman and his niece. Holmes
nodded to Angela and addressed the Earl.

"Lord Emsworth, my name is Sherlock Holmes and this is
my friend Dr. Watson. I believe I can help you with your
current problem."

The Earl of Emsworth shook our hands in an absent-
minded manner, his brain clearly working on something else.
"Yes, I can distinctly remember as much as that. Pig—Pig—
"

"Excuse me, Lord Emsworth, could the word you are
searching for be "PIG--HOO-o-o-ey?"

Lord Emsworth leaped into the air. It was as if an electric
shock had been applied to his person. The peace of the
summer night was shattered by a triumphant shout.

"PIG—HOO-o-o-o-ey!"

A window opened. A large, bald head appeared. A
dignified voice spoke.

"Who is there? Who is making that noise?"

"Beach!" cried Lord Emsworth. "Come out here at once."

And presently the beautiful night was made still more
lovely by the added attraction of the butler's presence.

"Beach, listen to this. PIG--HOO-o-o-o-ey! Now you do it."

"What do you want Beach to do it for?" asked Angela.

"Two heads are better than one. If we both learn this pig-call, it will not matter should I forget it again."

"By Jove, yes! Come on, Beach. Push it over the thorax," urged the girl eagerly.

The butler had appeared obdurate at the request, but Angela's pleadings seemed to soften his attitude.

"Very good, your lordship," he said in a low voice. "I would merely advance the suggestion, your lordship, that we move a few steps farther away from the vicinity of the servants' hall. If I were to be overheard by any of the lower domestics, it would weaken my position as a disciplinary force."

Holmes spoke up. "I would suggest, Lord Emsworth, "that the place to do it is outside the Empress' sty."

The sty stood some considerable distance from the castle walls, so Lord Emsworth had ample opportunity to rehearse his little company during the journey. By the time we had arranged ourselves against the rails, Angela, Beach, Sherlock Holmes, the Earl of Emsworth and I were letter-perfect.

"Now," said his lordship.

"PIG—HOO-o-o-o-ey!" we all sang.

Birds shot off their perches in the trees above like rockets. We paused to listen. Inside the Empress' boudoir there sounded the movement of a heavy body. There was an inquiring grunt. The next moment the sacking that covered the doorway was pushed aside, and the noble animal emerged.

"Now!" said Lord Emsworth again.

"PIG--HOO-o-o-o-ey!"

Empress of Blandings stood motionless, her nose elevated, her ears hanging down, her eyes everywhere but on the trough where, by rights, she should now have been digging in and getting hers. A chill disappointment crept over Lord Emsworth, to be succeeded by a gust of petulant anger.

"I might have known it," he said bitterly. "Mr. Holmes, you are a scoundrel. You have been playing a trick on me."

"He wasn't," I said indignantly. "Were you, Holmes?"

"It is possible that the passage of years have dulled my pig-calling skills, Watson. Lord Emsworth, let us try it one more time. I may not have had it quite right. The first syllable should be short and staccato, the second long and rising into a falsetto, high but true."

"Pig—HOO-o-o-o-ey!" we all caroled.

The echoes died away. And as they did a voice spoke.

"Community singing?"

"Jimmy!" cried Angela, whisking around.

"Hullo, Angela. Hullo, Lord Emsworth. Hullo, everybody. I'm spending a few days at the Vicarage with my father. I got down by the five-five from Paddington."

James Bartholomew Belford had the unmistakable air of one who had spent considerable time in the American Middle West, and in those energetic and forceful surrounding had learned to Talk Quick and Do It Now. Angela performed hasty introductions.

Lord Emsworth cut peevishly in upon these civilities.

"Young man," he said, "what do you mean by telling me at the Senior Conservative Club that my pig would respond to that cry? It does nothing of the kind."

"You can't have done it right."

"I did it precisely as you instructed me. I remembered everything you said. Mr. Holmes merely jogged my memory. I have had, moreover, the assistance of Dr. Watson, Mr. Holmes, and Beach here and my niece Angela…I would have had Lady Constance in the front row if I thought it would do any good."

"Let's hear a sample."

"PIG--HOO-o-o-o-ey!" We all stretched our vocal chords.

James Belford shook his head.

"Nothing like it," he said. "You want to begin the "Hoo" in a low minor of two quarter notes in four-four time. From this build gradually to a higher note, until at last the voice is soaring in full crescendo, reaching F sharp on the natural scale and dwelling for two retarded half-notes, then breaking into a shower of accidental grace-notes."

"Of course," said Sherlock Holmes.

"God bless my soul!" said Lord Emsworth, appalled. "I shall never be able to do it."

"Jimmy will do it for you," said Angela. "Now that he is engaged to me, he'll be one of the family and always popping about over here. He can do it every day until the show is over."

James Belford nodded.

"I think that would be the best plan. Like this!"

Resting his hands on the rails before him, James Belford swelled before our eyes like a young balloon. The muscles on his cheekbones stood out, his forehead became corrugated, and his ears seemed to shimmer. Then, at the very heights of the tension, he let it go like, as the poet beautifully puts it, the sound of a great Amen.

"PIG—HOOOOO-OOO-OOO-O-O-ey!"

We looked at him, awed. Slowly, fading off across hill and dale, the vast bellow faded away. And suddenly, as it died, another, softer sound succeeded it. A short of gulpy, gurgly, ploppy, squishy, wofflesome sound like a thousand eager men drinking soup in a foreign restaurant. And, as he heard it, Lord Emsworth uttered a cry of rapture.

The Empress was feeding.

The next day, as Holmes and I traveled back to London on the two o'clock train, I ventured to ask the one question that had burned in my mind since Holmes had returned empty-handed from Blandings Castle that morning.

"Holmes, no one would pay your fee. How can that be justified?"

Holmes rattled his Market Blandings World-Guardian newspaper and coughed.

"Lady Constance put it to me most succinctly, my dear Watson. I did not solve her problem, which was the broken engagement between Angela and Lord Heacham, because Angela is still engaged to James Belford. I did not solve Lord Heacham's problem, which was the same. Besides, he left yesterday for Monte Carlo and is unavailable to countermand her decision. I did not solve Angela's problem, since Lord Emsworth promised to give her the inheritance if James Belford was instrumental in getting Empress of Blandings to eat and he said that just before we met him. I did not solve Lord Emsworth's problem, because I did not teach him the pig-call correctly. It is doubtful if an amateur could ever produce real results. You need a voice that has been trained on the open prairie and that has gathered richness and strength from competing with tornadoes. You need a manly, sunburned, wind-scorched voice with a suggestion in it of the crackling of corn husks and the whisper of evening breezes in the fodder. George Cyril Wellbeloved spent four years on an apprenticeship in Wisconsin before he came to Lord Emsworth."

"Well, this case does prove your theory, Holmes."

"My theory?"

"People are unreasonable."

"A touch, Watson, a distinct touch! I never get your limits. Yes, I must admit that the most reasonable actor in this little comedy has not been a person at all. I must tip my hat to the Empress of Blandings. She knew exactly what she wanted and would accept no substitutes. It is a lesson for us all, Watson."

With that, Sherlock Holmes retreated behind his newspaper.

The Case of the Pilfered Painting

In one of the accounts I have been privileged to set before you, my readers, I wrote that Holmes' ideas about art were of the crudest. I must clarify that statement.

Sherlock Holmes was the grandson of a sister of Vernet, the French artist. From childhood he had been instructed in the finer points of oil paintings, watercolors, charcoals and art history. He was thoroughly schooled in the Classics and the Romantics. I agreed with many of his opinions. But he and I disagreed widely on the new school known as "Impressionism".

He saw genius in the works of Paul Cezanne, Claude Monet and Edgar Degas. Even the American friend of Monet's, Theodore Robinson, drew Holmes' praise for his depictions of the French and Dutch countryside.

I saw nothing but dabs and spatters of paint spoiling perfectly fine canvas. My favorite artists were Constable and Landseer. After many an animated talk, we agreed to disagree on the subject and each held to his own thoughts when we found ourselves strolling through various London art galleries.

Thus the matter stood one spring day when Holmes and I evaded a sudden shower by ducking into The Sheppard Gallery just off Bond Street.

The gallery was one large narrow room. A series of six backless benches ran down the center of the space from the front to the back. Under a skylight that filled the ceiling except for a row of oak panels running around its edge hung a single line of Romantic paintings in oil along white plaster walls. Another set of oak panels served as wainscoting under the paintings. As we strolled around the room I noticed one other person. He was short and tended toward *embonpoint*, dressed in a dark suit and sporting a carefully waxed mustache. His bald head gleamed in the overhead light and he blinked through bright hazel eyes. He stood silently in front of a framed canvas. As we grew nearer I could see that the painting he was looking at differed greatly from all the others.

It was an "Impressionism" work. I could make out a blurry mound of blobby greens beneath a splotched bluish background. Along the lower third of the canvas were dabbed irregular spots of white and grey. He was gazing at it with a great deal of satisfaction.

The man turned and noticed us. "Mr. Holmes! Welcome to my little shop."

"Mr. Sheppard, I am glad to see you. Watson, this is Mr. Noel Sheppard, the noted art dealer from Brighton. You remember, I told you about that little affair of the counterfeit Napoleonic snuffboxes last year. Mr. Sheppard was very helpful in exposing the fraud and capturing old Felker, wanted in seven countries for misuse of his remarkable talents."

"Pah! I merely locked the door and signaled the police. The entire honor goes to Mr. Holmes. I am glad to meet you, Dr. Watson. How do you like my latest acquisition?"

I stared at the painting and tried to think of something diplomatic to say. "It is different from the others here."

"Yes, I am trying something new. My client base is interested in the Romantics, but there is a revolution coming out of the Continent with these "Impressionist School" artists. Since I have expanded to this place in London, I thought I would try to test the new market, especially with American clients. This is the first one on display. It is called "Beau Peak with Sheep" and is by an artist named Vincent Bergstrom."

"Have you many of his works?"

"Unfortunately, no. He was a poor young man who only painted for four years before dying of consumption in Saint-Remy-de-Provence. Most of his canvases were burned as trash by his landlord when it was discovered he had no money with which to settle his debts. My agent managed to rescue this one from the Philistine's torch and sent it here last week. I currently have a call out to all my agents in France to be on the lookout for any others he may have left behind in other locales."

Outside the shower had stopped. Holmes and Sheppard talked for a few more minutes as I toured the rest of the gallery. When we stepped out into the street again, I asked Holmes what he thought of Mr. Sheppard's new discovery.

"I know your reaction, Watson, and I think you did an excellent job of hiding it. I am intrigued. If more of the young man's work can be located, he might become one of the most famous artists of the new school. Right now, with only one canvas available, he must rate as only a novelty."

There the matter rested and I thought no more about the little man or his unique canvas. Then, a few days later, at mid-morning, as Holmes and I were walking past the same door, Mr. Sheppard waved at us urgently through its glass. When we entered we found the little art dealer in an agitated state. He locked the front door behind us and greeted my friend with a shower of words.

"Mr. Holmes! Mr. Holmes! How fortunate to see you now! You must help me! I cannot go to the police! The scandal! The rumours! The press! It would ruin me!" The man held onto Holmes' hand as if it were a lifeline.

"Is there someplace we can go to talk?" Holmes asked.

"My office is the door on the right, back there." He waved a hand to the rear of the gallery, where two doors stood side by side against the back wall. We helped him to the office, where he sank into a chair by a cluttered desk. I found a bottle of brandy on a shelf and poured him a glass. He sipped at it and thanked me.

"Now tell me your trouble, sir." said Holmes, "although I have a good idea what it is already."

"How could you know? I only just found it missing myself. I could not believe my eyes and then I saw you passing and called you in. Oh, this is a nightmare! My good name! What about my good name?"

"What is he talking about, Holmes? What is missing?"

"Didn't you see the blank white space in the procession of paintings you admired here only last week, Watson? The Vincent Bergstrom is missing. And from Mr. Sheppard's actions, I deduce it wasn't by sale. "Beau Peak with Sheep" has been stolen."

The art dealer fixed his eyes on Holmes. "It's true. I opened the doors not ten minutes ago and saw it was gone. It was here last night. I had locked all the doors myself at nine o'clock. Oh, what will Mrs. Muchthaler say? She is due here today at two o'clock to pick it up."

"Is that the wife of Montgomery Muchthaler, the American cattle baron? I read he was in London as part of a Grand Tour," said I.

"Yes. I had a small reception for the painting four nights ago, a select showing. She was insistent that her husband buy it. She kept talking about "getting one in the eye on that snooty Mrs. Potter Palmer in Chicago". It sounded like the two ladies might be in some sort of rivalry about art."

Holmes was thoughtful. "Who else was at the reception?"

"Really, it was arranged just for Mr. and Mrs. Muchthaler. I invited Oscar Reinhardt, an artist I have managed for years and Arthur Wilson, another artist, not as well known as Oscar, who came with his wife. All my other artists live too far away to come here for an impromptu gathering. Mr. Muchthaler is not interested in art. He is interested in money and beef futures. It is his wife that likes the Impressionist artists."

"Has there been any other interest shown in "Beau Peak with Sheep"?"

"None. Dozens have toured this gallery in the past week since I hung that painting and no one seemed to like it. That was why I was so delighted when Mrs. Muchthaler showed interest. She even said that if I could find some more of Bergstrom's work, she would buy it sight unseen."

"Tell me about Oscar Reinhardt and Arthur Wilson."

"Well, Oscar is one of my oldest artists. He had sold very well in my gallery in Brighton and naturally I brought down a good supply of his paintings with me when I decided to open a second gallery in London. He is a member of the Royal Academy and lives here in town. Sales of his paintings have fallen off quite a bit during the past few years, but I thought that was because the Brighton market was becoming saturated. It was one reason I determined to expand. I also wanted to open up opportunities for the works of Arthur Wilson."

"Arthur Wilson is married, you said."

"Yes, Ida Wilson is her husband's greatest fan. I think that woman would do anything to advance Arthur's career. I have carried him in my gallery for two years. He is very intense about his art and his wife supports them both with a small inheritance."

"His wife supports him? Don't his paintings sell?"

"Since I started representing him, his name has become better known but sales of his works have not kept pace with his publicity. I am sorry to say that even in London his works have been ignored. It was the drop in revenue here since the opening that decided me about trying my hand on selling Impressionism works. Bergstrom is my first discovery."

"Would you ask both artists and Mrs. Wilson to come here in two hours? I need to interview them. Meanwhile, that will give me time to examine the scene of the crime. Perhaps it will not be necessary to call in the police after all."

Mr. Sheppard wrote out two short notes and had them dispatched by messenger.

Sherlock Holmes examined all the door and window locks. None were disturbed. The skylight windows were locked, as was demonstrated by Mr. Sheppard with the use of a long staff tipped with a hook made for the purpose of opening and closing them.

Holmes motioned me to follow him. He entered the room next to the office, which proved to be a combination storeroom and frame shop. One side held wrapped and crated works of art, protected by tarps. Quickly but methodically he searched each item, untying packages and bundles, leaving the repacking to me. After he finished with that side, he switched over to the piles of molding and framing and cleaning supplies that were arranged behind a thin partition. I had just finished resealing the last crate when he returned, a frown on his face.

"One thing this case has already disproved, Watson, is the old adage about hiding a leaf in a forest. It would be the simplest thing in the world to remove "Beau Peak with Sheep" from its place on the wall and tuck it in this storeroom, wrapped in canvas, until it could be carried out unnoticed at a later date. But our opponent is cleverer than that. Would he have the audacity to hide it right under the gallery owner's nose? Let's check the office."

The art dealer and I waited in the gallery while the detective turned out the office, finally admitting that the painting wasn't there either.

Sherlock Holmes stood in the center of the gallery and ran his eye over the row of paintings. Starting with the painting to the right of the gap made by the missing picture, he carefully took down each one and examined it, including the painting's back and the plaster wall behind it. He even ran his magnifying glass over the oak panel wainscoting that ran around the room under the pictures. Finally he dropped to his knees and brought his glass to bear on the carpeted surface before each painting.

He saved the bare spot on the wall and the carpet before it for last. He gave no sign of discovery when he examined the wall, but seemed to find something very interesting on the carpet. He spent several minutes measuring invisible points on several places before the gap, and only ceased when Mr. Sheppard unlocked the front door to admit two men and a woman.

Oscar Reinhardt was an elderly man with a grenadier's bearing, dressed in a grey velvet suit and a flowing red tie. His eyes were dark grey and rather bloodshot, as if he hadn't been getting enough sleep. His hair was cut short and was suspiciously black. He walked with a cane and his fingers were gnarled and knobby, as if they had developed arthritis.

Arthur Wilson was a man of about thirty years. He was clad in a russet set of tweeds and carried a soft Homburg in his hand. His eyes were brown, as was his hair, which he wore long in a theatrical style. There was a certain softness to his jaw line that hinted at rich food and long naps in the afternoons. His wife was dressed in similar tweeds and on her piled up blonde hair there perched a wide-brimmed black straw hat dressed in pink ostrich feathers. Somehow she made me think of a Leghorn hen.

Mr. Sheppard relocked the door and performed the introductions. When he blurted out the news of his loss, both men began snarling at each other.

"Mr. Holmes, if you're looking for a man who had reason to steal "Beau Peak and Sheep", here he is. Oscar Reinhardt hates Impressionism with a passion. He's so stuck in the past that he still remembers George IV as Beau Brummell's friend."

"At least I have memories, Wilson. You don't know anything. Here is a man, Mr. Holmes, who painted "The Charge of the Light Brigade" with the cavalry not only wearing the wrong uniforms but obeying the Duke of Wellington.""

"I hear you use paints so cheap that they have started to flake right off the canvas after a few months."

"You wouldn't make one sale a year if your wife didn't hold your hand while you painted."

By this time both men were livid with rage. Wilson took a foot forward and raised his fist. "You don't have the right to even look at my wife, old man. Mention her again in any context and I'll knock you down, damn your grey hairs."

"Grey hairs!"

At this point Sherlock Holmes stepped between the artists. He gripped both men by the arm and drew their attentions to himself.

"I will not allow such disruption, gentlemen! Mr. Reinhardt, sit on this bench. Mr. and Mrs. Wilson, please take a seat on the bench over there. Watson, watch Reinhardt. Mr. Sheppard, keep an eye on Mr. Wilson. I have a few more things to do before I wrap up this case."

I wanted to ask Holmes what he had discovered about the theft, but of course I could not. He went back to examining the marks on the floor that only he could see. Oscar Reinhardt sat upright on the wooden bench, his gnarled hands gripping his cane and his bloodshot eyes staring at the couple across the room. Mr. and Mrs. Wilson huddled together, whispering to each other, periodically darting murderous glances at Reinhardt.

These two men were behaving like unruly children, I thought. I had heard of the artistic temperament but I had never seen such a manifestation of it like this in my life. Were all artists this jealous of each other? Was the art world of London such a cutthroat place? It was a wonder, I mused silently, that there was only a painting missing in this gallery. In my opinion there could have so easily been spilled blood and a mangled body to greet Mr. Sheppard that morning when he arrived to open up his shop.

Sherlock Holmes finished his examination of the carpet and stood up. He slid his gaze over the skylight and turned to me.

"Watson, I noticed in the storeroom a tall ladder in the far corner. Please bring it here."

I fetched the old wooden ladder. Holmes opened it up and carefully aligned its legs with certain spots he had marked on the carpet with a bit of chalk he brought out of his pocket. Reinhardt and Wilson had stopped glaring at each other and now watched in fascination as he began to mount it.

Suddenly the ladder wobbled and he almost fell. I grabbed the wooden legs and steadied it. Without acknowledging my rescue he proceeded to climb to within reach of the ceiling.

Suddenly all three of our suspects stood. "This is ridiculous," said Oscar Reinhardt. "Mr. Sheppard, you can't keep me here. I demand that you unlock that door."

The Wilsons edged toward the front. "For once the old man is right," said Arthur Wilson. "Open the door, Sheppard. If you don't I'll take my work elsewhere."

"As will I," said Reinhardt.

"Keep them here, Mr. Sheppard, if you do not want to hand this investigation over to Scotland Yard," said Holmes. At the mention of the police, all three people froze. Their eyes fixed on Sherlock Holmes.

He took a little jackknife out of his coat pocket and poked at the molding around the recessed oak panels within his reach between the plaster wall and the steel and glass skylight. After another examination of the area using his magnifying glass, Holmes suddenly dug a blade into the edge of one of the panels and dragged it along in a straight line toward the wall. He sliced again along the wall edge and a flap of material hung down over his head.

There was a commotion at the front door. I turned my head to see the three suspects nervously grouped together. Oscar Reinhardt fumbled in his pocket. Suddenly he produced a key, which he thrust into the lock. The door opened and instantly he fled into the street, closely followed by Mr. and Mrs. Wilson. The door banged shut behind them.

Stunned, Mr. Noel Sheppard stood alone in the center of the gallery. He turned to look at Holmes, still standing on the ladder and busy with the ceiling. I gripped the ladder securely, knowing that if I let go Holmes would fall.

"What just happened?" Sheppard asked. He staggered to a bench and sat.

"I shall explain everything when I have finished here," replied Sherlock Holmes. He disengaged the square of material from the surrounding wood and dropped it to the floor. A blur of blue and green was revealed, pressed against the ceiling. Gleams of gold around it showed that the missing painting was still in its frame. Carefully Holmes pried it free and finally stood triumphant, holding "Beau Peak with Sheep" in his hands. He lowered it down to Mr. Sheppard and carefully descended to the floor. I released my grip on the ladder and picked up the piece of material from the carpet.

"Why, it is a painting!" I exclaimed.

I held in my hands a large square of unframed canvas, jagged around the edges where Holmes had cut it free from the glued edge which had held it to the ceiling molding. The inner side was blank, but on the side which had faced the room was painted a finely detailed pattern of oak grain matching those of the surrounding ceiling panels.

"A fine example of *trompe l'oeil*," said Sherlock Holmes. "Could this be Arthur Wilson's hand?"

Mr. Sheppard looked it over with a critical eye. "No," he replied. "It is too exact to be Wilson's work. It looks like Oscar Reinhardt's style. Then they must have been in this theft together! But I do not understand why."

"I suggest that we sit down with some more of that excellent brandy you keep in your office and I will explain everything."

In a few minutes we were established in Mr. Sheppard's office, Holmes seated behind the desk and the art dealer and I opposite him in chairs. The painting "Beau Peak with Sheep" was propped up against the desk under Mr. Sheppard's eye and the flap of canvas from the ceiling rested on top of a pile of papers in front of Holmes. The detective set down his glass and addressed us both in that familiar didactic way of his.

"When Mr. Sheppard motioned us to enter in such obvious distress, my first thought was he was ill and it was Dr. Watson he needed. But as soon as I noticed the blank spot on the wall, I knew we were faced with a theft. My first question was why didn't the thieves leave the frame? To break the picture out of its frame would be only the work of a moment and the canvas could be rolled into a smaller bulk that could easily be smuggled out of the building under a man's coat.

"The absence of the frame indicated that the painting was still on the premises. I decided to leave the question of why for a later time and concentrate on locating the missing item.

"I considered that the painting may have been wrapped in canvas or put into a wooden crate and placed among the other works of art in the storeroom. Hiding a leaf in the forest, Watson, as I told you. The plan could have called for the removal of the artwork before the storeroom could be thoroughly searched.

"After that theory was disproved, I fell back on the idea that the thief may be more bold than I first thought and hidden the painting in Mr. Sheppard's office, a poke in the eye to the art dealer and a place unsuspected in the normal course of events. It is a cluttered room, sir, and a painting the size of "Beau Peak with Sheep" could have been tucked into a corner and hidden behind other things. However, that theory also fell before reality.

"The gallery itself became the next place to search. The vast swaths of carpeting precluded any trap doors or hidden cavities in the floor. I proceeded to remove each painting in a methodical manner. I examined the back of each, in case the thief had used one as a hiding place for the Bergstrom. I also checked the plaster wall to ensure that there were no niches or holes that might have served to conceal the painting. I found nothing.

"I also examined the carpet before each painting for footmarks or other clues. Perhaps the thief smoked and left traces of tobacco ash. Maybe he had left traces of dirt or mud from his shoes. At the very least there might be outlines of the shoes themselves, particularly in front of the missing Bergstrom. Here I did find something, but not shoe prints. The carpet was too thin to retain them.

"In front of the blank gap I discovered four rectangular marks sunk into the nap of the carpet. They formed a rectangle of their own, four feet long and two feet wide. At this point my two hours to search expired and Oscar Reinhardt and Mr. and Mrs. Wilson arrived.

"As soon as they learned of the theft, the two artists began to snarl at each other. They nearly came to blows. I wondered at such a show of artistic temperament. Such men may be protective of their own styles and theories, but they seldom show such animosity to a fellow artist. There is a freedom of thought and *bonhomie* among such people that was not in evidence between these two men. Mr. Sheppard had not mentioned any hard feelings between them before. Indeed, it was only four nights before that they had attended the same party and there had been no mention of bickering then.

"I decided the squabble was an act. That immediately made these two men and possibly Mrs. Wilson suspects in the disappearance of "Beau Peak with Sheep".

"I asked Watson to bring out the old ladder I had noticed before in the storeroom. I placed it in the marks I had found before the blank gap and noticed the legs fit them perfectly. As I climbed up the rungs, the ladder lurched and might have thrown me off, if not for Watson's quick response. Obviously, this ladder could not be used unless a second person steadied the legs.

"Since I did not believe the painting had been removed from the gallery, and I had searched everywhere else, the only place left was the ceiling. With my glass I began to examine the oak panels within reach. It was then that all became clear.

"I do not need to explain to you that *trompe l'oeil* is a painting technique also known as illusionary painting. The artist creates such a detailed painting that the total effect fools the eye of the beholder into believing the items depicted are real. In this case, the painting was of the pattern of the oak grain of the ceiling panel. The painting "Beau Peak with Sheep", including the frame, just fit into the recess. With the canvas replicating the wood grain of the ceiling glued in place, the painting was hidden from sight.

"When I began to cut away the concealing canvas, Arthur Wilson and Oscar Reinhardt realized their plot was discovered and fled. In their flight they demonstrated the existence of a second front door key. Mr. Sheppard, did you know of this key?"

"I knew the renting agents had a second key. It might have been stolen from their offices. Since this place was rented months ago, its absence now would not be readily noticed."

"But, Holmes," I protested, "why would those men hide the Bergstrom? Why not destroy it or at least take it out of the gallery?"

"I surmise that their own falling sales had warned Reinhardt and Wilson that the future of art did not lie with their style of painting. That fact was driven home the night of the Muchthaler reception, when Mrs. Muchthaler's enthusiasm for Vincent Bergstrom's Impressionistic painting proved their suspicions. When they found that their own art dealer, Mr. Sheppard, was seriously considering carrying more Impressionistic paintings, thereby changing the direction of the gallery and squeezing out their own works, the two men became vengeful. They plotted to discredit and embarrass Mr. Sheppard by preventing the "Beau Peaks with Sheep" sale, thus giving the impression to others in the art world that Mr. Sheppard was unreliable and possibly even crooked."

"Oh, the devils! They would have ruined my business, after I have worked on their behalf for years!" Mr. Sheppard poured out another drink with shaking hands.

"Why not destroy the painting, or take it out of the gallery, away from all detection?" I asked.

Sherlock Holmes smiled. "Unwillingly, both men recognized the worth of the Bergstrom. It was valuable and might be sold privately at a later date. They did not trust each other. Neither man could be allowed to hold the treasure for fear the other might be cut out of any future profit. To leave it in a neutral but accessible place was the best solution.

"Reinhardt painted the covering and held the door key. Mr. and Mrs. Wilson might manage the ladder together, but they couldn't enter the gallery without Reinhardt's help. It was a stand-off."

Mr. Sheppard stood up. "I will not turn them in to the police because the scandal would ruin me. But I will return all their paintings at once and never handle them again. From now on I will concentrate on these new artists, these Impressionists like Bergstrom, Monet and Robinson. With a connection like Mrs. Muchthaler in America, I think I can tap into an entire new clientele. That reminds me, Mr. and Mrs. Muchthaler are due here at two. I must rehang "Beau Peak with Sheep" before they arrive."

Sherlock Holmes smiled. "I suggest that you tell them the entire story but omit Reinhardt and Wilson's names. Americans love things like this. The story Mrs. Muchthaler will tell at dinner parties will bring you a flood of future sales."

"I'll do as you suggest, Mr. Holmes. Thank you for everything you have done today. Please tell me how I can repay you."

Holmes glanced at me. "I could ask for a small example by one of your new discoveries, Mr. Sheppard, but hanging it in the sitting room at Baker Street might affect Dr. Watson's digestion. I ask instead that you add my name to your guest list for future exhibitions. As for Dr. Watson, might I suggest that you make him a gift of the *trompe l'oeil* after it has been framed. It is much to his taste. I doubt the artist will be asking for it back."

"It really is a fine example of *trompe l'oeil*," Mr. Sheppard responded. "I think it might be Oscar's masterpiece. I will be glad to give it to Dr. Watson. If Oscar Reinhardt puts up a fuss, I'll offer to send it to Scotland Yard instead."

Also from MX Publishing

MX Publishing is the world's largest specialist Sherlock Holmes publisher, with over a hundred titles and fifty authors creating the latest in Sherlock Holmes fiction and non-fiction.

From traditional short stories and novels to travel guides and quiz books, MX Publishing cater for all Holmes fans.

The collection includes leading titles such as _Benedict Cumberbatch In Transition_ and _The Norwood Author_ which won the 2011 Howlett Award (Sherlock Holmes Book of the Year).

MX Publishing also has one of the largest communities of Holmes fans on Facebook with regular contributions from dozens of authors.

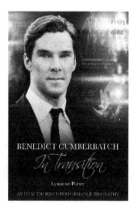

www.mxpublishing.com

Also from MX Publishing

  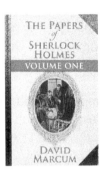

Our bestselling books are our short story collections;

'Lost Stories of Sherlock Holmes' , 'The Outstanding Mysteries of Sherlock Holmes', The Papers of Sherlock Holmes Volume 1 and 2, 'Untold Adventures of Sherlock Holmes' (and the sequel 'Studies in Legacy) and 'Sherlock Holmes in Pursuit', 'The Cotswold Werewolf and Other Stories of Sherlock Holmes' – and many more......

  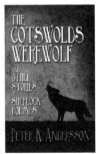

www.mxpublishing.com

Also from MX Publishing

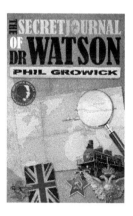

"Phil Growick's, 'The Secret Journal of Dr Watson', is an adventure which takes place in the latter part of Holmes and Watson's lives. They are entrusted by HM Government (although not officially) and the King no less to undertake a rescue mission to save the Romanovs, Russia's Royal family from a grisly end at the hand of the Bolsheviks. There is a wealth of detail in the story but not so much as would detract us from the enjoyment of the story. Espionage, counter-espionage, the ace of spies himself, double-agents, double-crossers...all these flit across the pages in a realistic and exciting way. All the characters are extremely well-drawn and Mr Growick, most importantly, does not falter with a very good ear for Holmesian dialogue indeed. Highly recommended. A five-star effort."
The Baker Street Society

www.mxpublishing.com

UK Ltd.

'9
'909/P